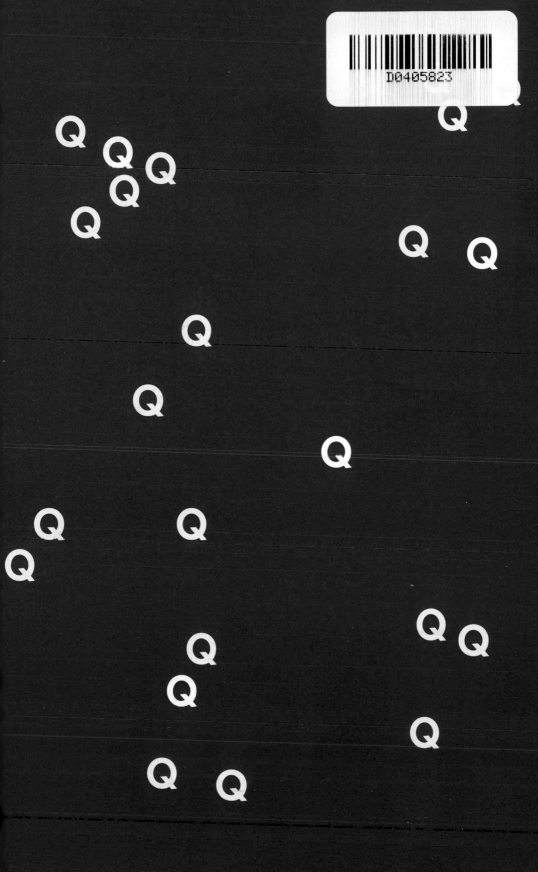

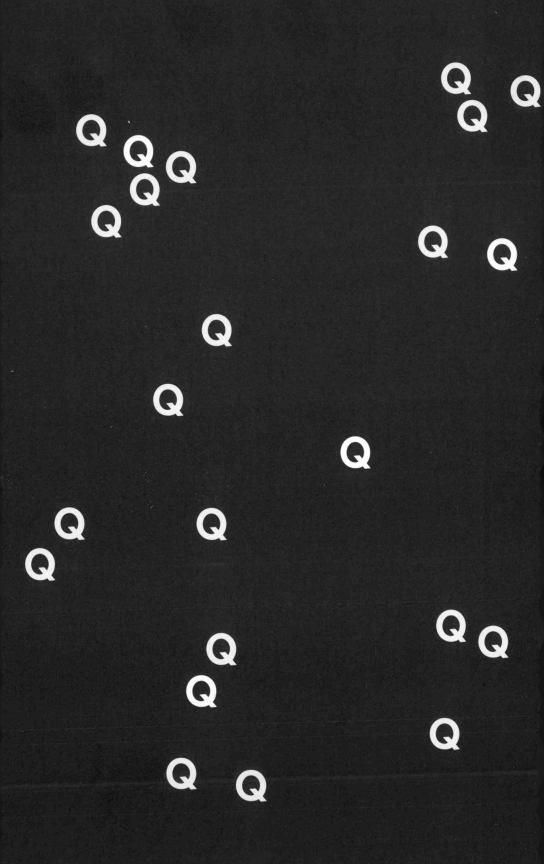

Praise for
Christina Dalcher

'The book of the moment!'
MARIE CLAIRE

'Intelligent, suspenseful, provocative, and intensely disturbing'
LEE CHILD

'A truly compulsive novel'
STYLIST

'A novel ripe for the era of #MeToo'
VANITY FAIR

'A fast-paced, twisting thriller that left me speechless'
DAILY MAIL

'Thrilling and provocative, you'll be flipping through the pages at
breakneck speed'
OK!

'Set to dominate dinner party chats'
COSMOPOLITAN

'This book will blow your mind'
PRIMA

'Petrifying'
ELLE

'A dazzling debut'
GOOD HOUSEKEEPING

'Terrifying'
RED

'Frighteningly relatable'
WOMAN

Christina Dalcher is the *Sunday Times* bestselling author of *VOX*. She earned her doctorate in theoretical linguistics from Georgetown University, specializing in the phonetics of sound change in Italian and British dialects. *Q* is her second novel.

Also by Christina Dalcher

VOX
Q

CHRISTINA DALCHER

ONE PLACE. MANY STORIES

HQ
An imprint of HarperCollins*Publishers* Ltd
1 London Bridge Street
London SE1 9GF

This edition 2020

1

First published in Great Britain by
HQ, an imprint of HarperCollins*Publishers* Ltd 2020

ISBN HB: 978-0-00-830334-1
ISBN Hardback (Waterstones): 978-0-00-840960-9
TPB: 978-0-00-830335-8

MIX
Paper from
responsible sources
FSC™ C007454

This book is produced from independently certified FSC™ paper
to ensure responsible forest management.

For more information visit: www.harpercollins.co.uk/green

Printed and bound in Great Britain by
CPI Group (UK) Ltd, Croydon, CR0 4YY

In memory of
Carrie Elizabeth Buck, 1906-1983
and to the children she and so many others were denied

They done me wrong. They done us all wrong.
—CARRIE BUCK

ONE

It's impossible to know what you would do to escape a shitty marriage and give your daughters a fair shot at success. Would you pay money? Trade the comfort of house and home? Lie, cheat, or steal? I've asked myself these questions; I suppose many mothers do. One question I haven't asked, mostly because I don't like the answer. Not a bit. I have too strong a survival instinct. Always have.

Last night, I spoke to Malcolm again after the girls had gone to bed. I tried to put a light spin on things, to not turn him from phlegmatic to angry with my words.

"I've had enough of this, Malc," I said. "Freddie's had enough of it."

He looked up from his paperwork long enough to meet my eyes. "Had enough of what?"

"Of the numbers. Of the pressure. Of all of it."

"Noted," he said and buried himself again in pages of reports and memos. I think I heard a relieved sigh when I left to go to bed.

Things haven't been good here for a long time.

I almost can't remember how it felt before we all started carrying the Q numbers around with us, like an extra and unnatural print on the tips of our fingers, a badge of honor for some, a mark of shame for others. I suppose, after more than a decade, you can get used to anything. Like cell phones. Remember not having the entire universe in your back pocket? Remember sitting on the floor, talking to your best friend about nothing, unwinding a curly cord only to watch it kink up again? Remember all that? I do and I don't. Blockbuster two-day video rentals and bookstores the size of an airplane hangar are distant memories, faded impressions of life before streaming and same-day delivery.

It's the same way with the Q numbers, although we've carried numeric strings with us in one form or another for most of our lives: our social security numbers for tax returns; our home telephone numbers in case an emergency call to Mom became necessary; our grade point averages that would fill boxes in dozens of college application forms. Men, in a clothing store, became thirty-four long or sixteen-and-a-half, thirty-three. Women became dress sizes: six, eight, fourteen. In the more upscale shops, we were our measurements. In doctors' offices, we were our height and weight, watching one number creep down while the other number crept up.

We've always been our numbers. DOB. GPA. SSN. BP (systolic and diastolic). BMI. SAT and GRE and GMAT and LSAT; 35-22-35 (Marilyn, damn her); 3 (the Babe). PINs and CSCs and expiration dates. Jenny's phone number from that old song. And, for the extreme among us, the entire sixteen-digit sequence on our Visa cards. Our ages. Our net worths. Our IQs.

I think about this in the grocery store, while I stand in one of the priority lines with close to a hundred bags and cans and boxes in my cart, enough to get my family of four through a few days. Yesterday, at Safeway, five other women glared at me from three lines over. One of them, I remembered from high school. I think she was a cheerleader. Pretty, thin, not too bright. What the hell was her name? Paulette? Paulina? Patty? Patty. That's it. She was fifth in line at the only open nonpriority checkout, holding a carton of skim milk.

Patty's one item compared to my one hundred. I nearly let her cut in before me, but the cashier shrugged and shook his head in a hopeless no.

"Her card won't work in this line," the kid said. "You know."

He scanned my card, my magic card with its magic number encoded on it. Nine-point-something. It's the first digit that matters.

Patty didn't say a word. She would have, once. She, or one of the other women, would have rolled her cart over and refused to move. I saw a fistfight break out at a gas station once between a short man in a suit and that guy who worked at the hardware store down on Main. No competition there. The suit checked over Mr. Ex–High School Football once, got back into his Lexus, and drove off. When his card wouldn't work, Mr. Ex-Football punched the gas pump display until his fists were bloody and the police showed up. I don't know what his Q number was, but it sure as shit had to be below nine.

Now we're all used to the lines and the tiers and the different strokes for different folks.

I guess, if enough time passes, people can get used to anything.

TWO

There are nine alarms in my house now. One next to my bed set for five o'clock, one that chirps an hour before Anne's school bus arrives, three more to mark the final thirty minutes, fifteen minutes, and seven minutes. Same for Freddie's bus, which shows up slightly later. Nine pings and pops and chimes, five days a week. I feel like I'm on a goddamned game show.

All so my daughters don't miss their ride to school.

When I was a girl, my mother would call up the stairs. Her voice walked the fine line between gentle and firm as she spoke my name, spurring me on to get up, get dressed, get ready. I still failed to reach the bus stop on some days, only arriving just in time to watch it turn the corner, see the red taillights disappear in the morning fog. Everyone missed a bus now and then. No big deal.

There weren't incentives to make sure you got on the bus—the right bus. Not back then.

Malcolm's already out the door, ensconced in a bright office with some junior aide bringing him coffee and whole-grain bagels glazed with nonfat cream cheese. He never sees his daughters, two contestants in the daily *Who Won't Make It to School on Time?* show, on weekday mornings. It's too bad, really. The prizes aren't anything to get worked up about, but the penalties bestowed on the losers make for solid motivation.

"Freddie!" I call from the kitchen, sounding less like my mother and more like a desperate lioness with a pack of hyenas circling my cubs. "Anne!"

Her thirty-minute warning pings while I'm spooning yogurt from a quart-sized tub and teetering on one leg to hitch the ankle strap on my left heel. Anne pokes her head around the corner and gives it a quick, silent shake.

Freddie's not ready, not even close.

Shit.

On the second testing day of the school year, I'm running late, my daughter hasn't shown up for breakfast, and all I can think about is the yellow bus idling up the street with the Child Catcher sitting behind the wheel.

When I was young, I had dreams of the Child Catcher from that old musical, the one with the flying car and Dick Van Dyke stumbling through a bad British accent. He lurked outside my house in predawn shadows, grease-slicked black hair and Pinocchio nose. Waiting.

The Child Catcher wasn't immediately scary, not when his wagon tinkled with bells and lights, or when he danced around in a Technicolor coat, or when he promised all good things and sweets to children. After all, what child shies away from bells and colors and sweet things? And you didn't know the first time around that the wagon was really a cell with iron bars, or that the Child Catcher wore black underneath his robes, or that he would take his prey to a dark cave.

But you knew the second time you watched the movie. And the third. And all the times after that.

You knew exactly what he was waiting for.

In my early forties, I learned there's still such a thing as the Child Catcher.

He's old, and his hair is a blurred froth of white through the windshield of his bus, the one with *Federal Schools* printed in black along the sides. Instead of colored robes, he wears a plain gray uniform with the Department of Education logo embroidered on twin shoulder patches, a peace-symbol design in three colors—silver, green, and yellow. Around it are the words *Intelligentia, Perfectum, Sapientiae*. Intelligence, Perfection, Wisdom. I'd know two out of three even if I didn't speak Latin. The yellow paint on the bus—Chrome Yellow, they used to call it when it still contained lead, but it's been National School Bus Glossy Yellow for a while now—is chipped and peeling around the fenders and the accordion door. I guess no one gives much of a shit about what the yellow buses look like. It's not essential, given where they're headed, or what their cargo is.

The green ones and the silver ones are always in good condition, polished to a high sheen, not a dent or scratch or mark on them. When the doors open, they slide silently and smoothly, unlike the creaking doors on the yellow bus that rumbles along our street this morning. Drivers of the green and silver buses smile as children climb aboard, dressed in uniforms advertised as Harvard Crimson and Yale Blue, even for the five-year-olds.

There's something else about the yellow buses. You don't see them every day, picking up their cargo in the early fog of morning, dropping off in that time that could only be called the after-school show-and-snack hour, that limbo when the kids are no longer temporary wards of the state but once again home and settled with their families.

The yellow buses come only once every month, always the Monday after testing day. And they don't return in the afternoons.

They never return. Not with passengers, anyway. Also, they don't roll into neighborhoods like ours.

If I'd kept newspaper headlines from the past ten years, they would tell the story better than I could.

IMMIGRATION RATES CLIMB—PROJECTIONS FOR 2050 DIRE

**SCHOOL OVERCROWDING, TEACHER SHORTAGES:
LAWMAKERS IN STANDSTILL OVER SOLUTION**

**GENICS INSTITUTE PARTNERS WITH DEPARTMENT OF
EDUCATION, OFFERS EXPANDED Q SOFTWARE**

FITTER FAMILY CAMPAIGN RELEASES GUIDELINES

NO CHILD LEFT BEHIND MEANS ALL CHILDREN SUFFER!

INITIAL DIRECTIVES TO BE ROLLED OUT IN COMING MONTHS

It started with fear, and it ended with laws.

I pour a third cup of coffee and check the clock. "Freddie! Please." I'm careful to keep my voice low and steady, mom-like. Anything I can do to keep her calm.

The yellow bus is idling across the street, two houses up, at the end of the Campbells' driveway, which is strange, since Moira Campbell doesn't have children anymore, not at home anyway, and since today is testing day. Still, across and up the street is better than in front of my own house, whether or not the bus is on schedule. The thought makes me shiver, despite the heat wave from a late Indian summer. When did something as banal as a yellow school bus become such a threat? It's like taking a smiley face and giving it fangs. That's so fucking wrong.

"Freddie!" I call again. "For chrissake!"

Here's the thing about nine-year-olds: As bad as the pain in the delivery room was, as hair-raisingly chaotic as night feedings and croup and terrible twos were, as much as you now dread that first *I've got a boyfriend, Mom!* from a kid who seemed to be waddling around in diapers just yesterday, there is nothing worse than the pretween girl. Mainly where morning bathroom routines are concerned. I know I shouldn't get my temper up, not with Freddie and the way she is.

Note to self: Change tone. Take it down two octaves and a million decibels.

"Hurry up, hon! Test today!" I say, this time with more sugar in my voice, wondering if I'm going to make it to my own job on time. I try leveraging the big sister, making her the bad cop. "Anne! Get your sister out here in two minutes. Matching barrettes or not."

This seems to work. Anne, when she isn't nose-to-screen on her iPad, scouring the Q rankings of every boy in town for a homecoming dance date, is the responsible one. Always ready, always on time, always coming home after testing day with that insouciant little smile on her face and beaming when the app on her phone or tablet pings its pass alert later that night. It's Freddie who stays in the bathroom, worrying over her bangs, washing her hands five more times than necessary. Once, I found her slouched over on the toilet, head between her knees, shaking, refusing to leave.

"You have to, honey," I said. "Everyone has to take the tests."

"Why?"

Why? I tried to think of an answer that would calm her. "So they know where to put people." And then, "You've always done fine."

What I never said was, "You've squeaked by each time. You'll squeak by again." That wouldn't do a bit of good.

Anne emerges from the hall, still glued to her iPad, swiping and pinching and expanding, reciting numbers. "Nine-point-one. *Quel dud,*" she says. "Oof. Eight-point-eight. Major dud." And "Oh, Mom, you should see this one from that school in Arlington. He's down to eight-point-two-six and doesn't look like he could pass a blood test. Gag."

"Eight-point-three used to count as a B," I remind her.

"Not anymore, Mom."

She's just like her father, I think, but I don't say it out loud. As far as Anne is concerned, the sun rises and sets on—and probably revolves around—Malcolm. There is that, at least.

"Where's your sister?" I ask, buttoning my raincoat. Anne tells me she's on her way.

Anne's silver bus, the one that goes to the top-tier school with the rest of the nine-point-somethings, has turned the corner and starts to slow, its stop-sign wings unfolding as it approaches the pickup point. There's a trail of cars behind it, students clutching shiny identification cards in the backseats, waiting to be let out. A steel gray Lexus SUV, the first in line, pulls to the curb, and the rear door swings open. I've seen the girl before, at one of those parent-teacher days they hold at Anne's school every fall. Today her hair hangs in thick, uncombed ringlets around her face, but enough of her eyes show that I can see the whites of them, the look of a frightened dog, when she catches sight of the yellow bus up the street.

Anne joins me at the front window, backpack slung over one shoulder, silver passcard clutched in one hand, stretching the lanyard tight around the back of her neck. It looks something like a noose.

"That girl," I say, "she looks nervous."

"She shouldn't be," Anne says. "Sabrina's Q is fine. Then, in a confidential whisper: "Not like Jules Winston. Jules barely passed last week's advanced calculus test." She takes a bite of apple, swipes again at her iPad.

I turn away from the rain-sheeted window. "I thought results were supposed to be confidential." But, of course, I know how kids are. I was in high school once.

Anne shrugs. "They are. But the rankings aren't. You know that."

Yeah. I know.

"Anyway, Jules now has the lowest Q in the whole junior class, thanks to the calc test," Anne says. "*And* she's had three sick days this term. *And* she didn't make the bus last Wednesday. *And* her mom got laid off, so the family income's down. It all adds up." Another bite of apple. Another swipe of her tablet. "If she doesn't score some serious points, she'll be on the green bus next week. Maybe that one by December." Anne knocks her chin toward the yellow bus waiting in the rain. "A couple years in a yellow school and then it'll be burger-flipping time for Jules."

"Anne. Honestly."

Another shrug. My older daughter is the queen of all things shrug these days. "Someone has to do it. At least until they finish automating all that shit. Looks like they're picking up this morning. On our street. Weird."

Her tone is bland, journalistic. So much like Malcolm's when he delivers his daily report on how many new state schools will be opening next month, or on the average Qs by state and city and school district. It's something he does every night at dinner, as if we're all interested. Anne usually sits next to him, never taking her eyes off her father, rapt by the numbers.

Freddie's a completely different story.

THREE

Anne's out the door, iPad in one hand, silver card dangling from the lanyard around her neck. She's five feet, five inches of confidence as she strides down the driveway toward the waiting bus. She passes the other girl—what was her name? Sabrina?—without so much as a greeting and joins a pack of neatly turned-out sixteen-year-olds who, like Anne, see failure as contagious.

Sabrina doesn't look fine to me, high Q rankings or not. She's well turned out, hair glistening in the way only teenage hair can, uniform pressed to within an inch of its life. By the look of Sabrina's ride, the girl's got everything. But there are all kinds of handicaps, and even a bottomless pit of money doesn't cure most of them.

I don't know what Sabrina's brand of problem is, but I want to run out in the rain to where she's standing under her umbrella. Give her a banana, an oatmeal bar, hot chocolate, a hug. I want to tell her failing a test doesn't make her a failure.

But it does. In this age, it does.

One by one, the kids approach the silver bus, hold their cards up to be scanned. There's a ping, shrill and piercing enough to be audible from across the street and through my living room window, whenever a new card grants access to the bus. Doors swing open, the student climbs aboard, and the doors close, waiting for the next one in line. You wouldn't think high schoolers would be so organized, but there are rules to be followed. And there are laws to enforce those rules. They're the real Child Catchers, I think, the men and women who write the laws.

I should know. My husband is one of them.

Sabrina is last, and her lips form a weak smile at the ping and the doors and the rain-free sanctuary of the bus. She looks backward once before boarding, takes in the full length of the street, all the way up to the Greens' house, and the smile fades. Today she's got a silver card. Next week, who knows?

I don't see Anne's best friend, though, which is strange, since Judith Green is almost always the first to the bus, silver card ready to scan. It's as if she lives and breathes for school, homework, book reports.

Davenport Silver School students, this is your final call. Davenport Silver School bus is ready to depart. Final call for Davenport Silver School.

"Call" isn't the right word. The monotone, accentless fembot voice booming through the neighborhood should say it like it is. It should say "warning."

When the doors slide closed, there's still no Judith Green.

As the silver bus pulls away, a green one moves toward the empty space. Another line of cars waits in the rain, and a few of the neighborhood middle-graders tread through puddles. One jumps into a shallow pothole, spraying water everywhere, muddying up three of the kids closest to him. They only laugh—as children do.

"Freddie!" I call. "Last warning, I swear." The second I say the word I want to take it back.

She finally comes into the living room, backpack weighing down her right shoulder, making her look more like the crippled Quasimodo than a healthy nine-year-old. Her face is old-womanly. Tired. She's not swiping through tweets and snaps, not crunching an apple, not doing anything but staring past me, out the window, out at the waiting green bus.

"What's the matter, hon?" I say, pulling her to me, even though I know damned well what the matter is.

"Can I be sick today?" The words come out in a shudder, staccato, a space of air between each sound. Before I can answer, Freddie's entire body is shaking in my arms. The backpack slides to the floor with a dull thump.

"No, baby. Not today," I tell her. "Tomorrow, maybe." It's a lie, of course. Illness requires verification, and even if I did manage to fake and report an elevated temperature by the six o'clock deadline tomorrow morning, a secondary check by Freddie's school nurse wouldn't show anything other than normal. And then Freddie would lose even more of the Q points she can't afford to lose—the usual for the sick day, plus something extra for the failure to verify. Still, the best I can do is lie today and take it all back tomorrow. Anything to make sure she gets on the bus. "Come on, sweetie. Time to go."

Freddie turns in the time it takes me to catch my breath. One foot kicks the backpack across the room, and it lands on Malcolm's peace lily, the one he's been cultivating since before we were married. She goes from sobbing to hysterical in a split second. Malcolm will not be happy when he gets home.

"I can't go!" she says. "I can't go. I can't, I can't, I can't—"

Holy shit.

All of a sudden, we're both on the floor, Freddie pulling at her hair, me trying to stop her before she does more damage. Wisps of blond are in her fingers, floating onto the carpet. I know it's bad when she stops as abruptly as she started, when she begins rocking slowly back and forth like one of those animals on a spring they put in playgrounds. Her eyes are just as sightless and unfocused.

I can't touch her when she's like this, no matter how much I want to.

There should be a word for what Freddie is, I suppose, but I don't know what that word would look or sound like. In my mind, she's just Freddie. Frederica Fairchild, nine years old, sweet as sugar, no problems or hang-ups aside from the problems and hang-ups of any girl her age. She spikes a mean volleyball, gives Malcolm a run for his money at chess, loves everything except Brussels sprouts. But here she is, terrified because it's testing day.

Again.

"Freddie," I say softly, checking the line of students standing by the green bus. Only two of them are left, waiting to scan their cards and board. "Time to go."

Sanger Green School students, this is your final call. Sanger Green School bus is ready to depart. Final call for Sanger Green School.

I could kill the fucking fembot.

While Freddie collects herself, I gather up the kicked backpack, snatch a handful of Kleenex tissues from the box in the kitchen, and put the green ID card into Freddie's hand. "You'll do fine. I know it."

All I get is a silent nod. And not much of one. Christ, I hate the first Friday of the month.

She's out the door by the time the next-to-last kid boards the bus. Again, I tell her not to worry, but I don't think she hears me. My coffee's gone cold, and Malcolm's stupid peace lily looks like a meteor hit it. I turn the planter so the really ugly part faces the wall and decide what lie I'll tell my husband tonight. Not that it matters. Most of what I've told Malcolm for the past few years has been a lie, starting with the daily "I love yous," and ending with whispered words on the rare occasions we have sex, always with a condom from the stash he keeps in his bedside table, always with a slathering of spermicidal jelly to ensure we won't be making any more little ones.

I haven't lied to Freddie, though. I know she'll do fine. After all, it's supposed to be in her genes. The prenatal Q report I showed Malcolm confirmed that nine years ago.

But that was another lie.

I never went in for the test.

FOUR

I go into the kitchen to microwave my stale coffee. I can't think about genetics anymore without remembering a conversation with my grandmother, not long after finding out I was pregnant with Freddie.

It's not a happy memory.

"I don't like this Q." Oma poured herself a petite glass of schnapps, examined the level, and poured out another half inch. I unscrewed the cap on a water from the fridge before sitting down in the den with a belly that felt like a small tuna had decided to start growing in it. "I don't like to say 'hate,' because a little bit of hate someday turns into a great amount of hate, but I hate this Q."

A month before, even a whiff of alcohol had sent me on a bathroom run. Now, it looked tempting.

"Sure you don't want a drop?" she asked. "It won't kill you. Or the baby." One hand reached out and gave me three quick taps on my sweater, which had already begun to stretch—a constant reminder that time was running out. "She'll be fine. Like your father was, and like you were."

I hated when she patted my stomach like that. Besides, Oma was drowning out Petra Peller's voice on the television.

What's your Q? Petra asked. She seemed to be looking straight at me.

The bottle beckoned. Malcolm wouldn't know—I could always use Oma as the scapegoat when he asked about the level of dark liquid. But someone would know. Someone in a sterile white room stuffed with urine samples from my doctor's office. Someone with a yellow school education who got paid to sift through the effluvia of pregnant women and tick boxes. Someone who hated her job so much she wanted to take out that hate on another someone, especially the wife of the man who'd invented the tier system and the Q rankings and pushed the importance of both at every opportunity.

And more important, what's your baby's Q? Petra continued.

"What a lot of silliness," Oma said. "A baby's a baby. Who cares about its Q?"

I wanted to say Malcolm gave a shit. Two or three, maybe.

"Do we even know what this Q is?"

I try to answer her as best I can, cobbling together pieces I've heard from Malcolm and the news. The algorithms have become so much more complicated than the initial grade-point-average equivalents they used to be. "It's a quantifier, Oma. A quotient."

"Explain to me what is being quantified," she says.

"Oh—grades, of course. Attendance records and participation. The same things we've always calculated."

"And that is all?" There's doubt in her voice.

I continue ticking off the components I remember. "Parents' education and income. Siblings' performance. All the other Qs in the nuclear family."

"You also have this Q?"

"Everyone of school or working age does. And each month it's recalculated." The fact is, I don't even keep track anymore. My numbers have been in the high nine-point-somethings since the Q rankings rolled out a few years back. This is partly thanks to my own degrees, partly because I keep acing my teacher assessments. But I'm stupid to think the numbers are all my own—Malcolm's position undoubtedly adds a few tenths of a point, maybe more. As deputy secretary in the Department of Education, he's only one degree of separation removed from the president, for chrissake.

Oma fiddled with her earpiece and then turned up Petra's television pitch. Phrases came out from the screen like sharp little darts, piercing.

. . . especially for those of us over thirty-five . . .

. . . earlier is better . . .

. . . a prenatal quotient gives women the information they need to make that all-important decision . . .

. . . before it's too late . . .

A number flashed in red on the bottom of the screen, along with a website address of the Genics Institute, while Petra advised all mothers-to-be to sign up for a free consultation with one of the institute's experts.

"Here is something true," Oma said, turning away from the television and facing me, "you really can't tell what they are going to be. So you take a test, and the test tells you your baby will be 'average.' What does that mean? There is only one measure?" She tipped her glass with a gnarled hand and went on. "When I taught art—oh, too many years ago—I had a student who could not make the change from a dollar. But she had different talents. Do you know where that girl is today?"

I knew where the girl was. Fabiana Roman was in every gallery from coast to coast, or at least her paintings were. Malcolm once looked at the splattered canvases that were half–Jackson Pollock and half–Edvard Munch, with a sprinkling of Kandinsky thrown on top for good measure. He called them "degenerate."

"Maybe I should go in and have the test. Just to see," I said, scribbling the number and URL on one of the parenting magazines from the coffee table.

Oma reached over and snatched it from me.

"What?"

"Elena, tell me you are not seriously considering this," she said. "The amniocentesis I understand." She pronounced "amniocentesis" carefully, the unfamiliar concatenation of sounds tripping up her tongue. "But a prenatal intelligence test? Was this maybe Malcolm's idea?"

"No," I lied.

Of course we'd discussed the testing—several times. Each argument ended with Malcolm telling me it was my decision, whatever I thought best was fine, no pressure. I knew better, though. I knew exactly what Malcolm thought was best. I took a stab at justifying the Q business.

"You know how it is, Oma," I said. "Schools aren't like they used to be."

She poured herself another glass of schnapps. "What do you Americans like to say? 'Say me about it'?"

I corrected her German-to-English translation. "'Tell me about it.' That's how you say it."

"Say. Tell."

"I mean, would you want your kid in a third-tier school?" I said.

Oma went on, talking about tiers and classes. I tuned her out and listened to Petra's television interview. She'd been joined by another woman who I recognized immediately as Malcolm's boss at the Department of Education.

Madeleine Sinclair is hard to miss. Tall, with blond—so blond it's nearly white—hair swept up into a classic French twist, she seems to wear nothing but electric blue suits, fitted to her curves in the way only custom-made clothing does. On her right lapel, there's always that same pin, the yellow emblem of the Fitter Family Campaign. Today was no different, but her features seemed sharper, more hawkish than ever.

"It was going to happen sooner or later," Petra said to the reporter. "We reached a point where the public school system couldn't handle the disparity anymore, couldn't supply an across-the-board education. When the Department of Ed started the voucher program, I guess I saw it as an opportunity. When they needed hard science to strengthen the Q algorithm, I knew the Genics Institute would be the first of its kind."

Oma stopped talking and froze with the schnapps glass halfway to her lips.

The on-screen reporter nodded and spoke to the other woman. "Dr. Sinclair, there's been some backlash about your policies. Can you tell us about that?"

Madeleine Sinclair turned her blue eyes toward the camera, as if she were addressing not the interviewer but someone on the other side. Perhaps she was speaking to me; perhaps to the old woman at my side. When she spoke, her voice was patient, an experienced teacher talking to a confused child, straightening things out. "There's always going to be backlash," she said. "It's natural. Most of the criticism comes from"—she smiled, and in the smile there was a mix of sweetness and condescension—"certain factions. Certain factions who desperately want to believe we're all the same."

Oma drew in a shallow breath.

"What is it?" I asked.

"Nothing. Let me listen."

"The thing of it is," Madeleine continued, "the crux of the matter, and the point people need to understand, is that we are not all the same." She paused, and when the reporter opened his mouth to interrupt, Madeleine put up a hand. "I'll repeat that. We are not all the same." Once again, she looked out from the screen. "Tell me, parents, do you want your child in a classroom with students who are two standard deviations out? With children who don't have the capacity to understand the kinds of struggles and challenges your five-year-old faces? With teachers whose time is pulled in so many directions that everyone—everyone—ends up falling through the cracks?"

"I don't think she is telling the truth," Oma said. "What she is asking is if you want your baby Einstein in a room with twenty normal children. They might hold your little genius back, or they might interrupt his progress." She stabbed at the remote control, missing the buttons, only increasing the volume as Petra and Madeleine nodded and provided each other with verbal reinforcements. "These women are evil, *Liebchen*. Ah, here is my taxi. At least I can still hear."

A second blast of a horn announced Oma's ride back to my parents' house, and I went to the door with her. Our parting hug felt different—her hand on my back, ordinarily firm and warm, was light, and even in the hug there was empty space between us. A half-drunk glass sat on the coffee table, forgotten. I ignored its siren call and dumped the schnapps into the kitchen sink, then returned to the television.

Petra was talking again, telling us how she owed her success to the Fitter Family Campaign. "What started as a grassroots movement snowballed," she said.

Avalanched was more like it. Somewhere in the middle of the country, in that expanse of former dust bowls and farmland that no one pays attention to, it started. Somewhere in the champagne-communism salons of Boston and San Francisco, it started. Somewhere in suburban living rooms where upper-middle-class mothers gather to share stories of sore nipples and sleepless nights, it started. And spread. And mutated like a virus, weaving into itself, reduplicating. A few voices turned into a chorus of voices, all calling for education reform. What we needed, they claimed, wasn't more special programs in the schools; we needed more buckling down, more effort, more recognition that throwing money at a problem wasn't going to solve it.

We needed to move on from the one-size-fits-all mentality.

"But," Petra said, "change in a system doesn't happen without change in the people who make up that system. That's where the Genics Institute comes in."

She was right. By the time the Fitter Family Campaign turned ten years old, they were holding Best Baby Contests in every single state. The motives were different, but each of them united together in a sickening solidarity. Middle America was tired of what they called underprivileged overbreeders; the Boston Brahmins wanted schools that focused resources on their own child prodigies (although even the champagne communists voiced their concerns about overpopulation—they just voiced them in their penthouse salons); the baby brigade worried over allergies, autism, a growing list of syndromes. Everyone wanted something new, some solution, a reason to feel safe about their little wedge of the human race pie in a country that would see skyrocketing population numbers in another generation.

It didn't take long for people to "climb aboard the commonsense train," as my husband is fond of saying. Of course, in exchange for major changes in the education sphere, the public had to make a few concessions: Administrators, not parents, knew best. And the federal government had the last say when it came to testing students and placing them in an appropriate school. As long as the moms- and dads-to-be took prenatal precautions, everything would run smoothly.

If they didn't, there was the tiered school system: best, better, and somewhere around mediocre.

Madeleine came back on the screen, as if I'd just asked her a question and she decided to answer me personally. ". . . As I was saying, the state schools are there for the young people in this country who need—and deserve—extra attention. Please don't think of us as taking your children away. Think of us as giving them the chance to blossom." She did one of her classic nods, to the audience. "You want flowers in the spring? Give them the best soil money can buy. That's what the state schools are about."

I turned the television off, thinking about Oma, her reaction, her quick departure, the empty hug. Maybe she was right. Maybe these people were evil.

Evil or not, they won. They yelled and voted and screamed for stricter anti-immigration policies. They voted down No Child Left Behind and the Individuals with Disabilities Education Act. Not that people didn't want to give a leg up to the disadvantaged or the differently abled. They did. They just didn't want them in the same classrooms with their own kids.

What they didn't know then, but I know now, is that you can get rid of the old fish at the barrel's bottom, but that just means there's a fresh layer of rottenness waiting to be dug up and tossed out. By the time the Sarah Greens of the world figured out what was happening, tier systems and Q rankings were the laws of the land.

Back at the window, I watch Freddie's green bus pull away through a veil of rain and wonder if I would have done things differently ten years ago if I knew then what I know now.

FIVE

THEN:

I was somewhere between four and five months pregnant with Freddie, only just beginning to feel that uncomfortable pinch whenever I buttoned my jeans, but happily well past the morning sickness that made me unable to eat anything other than dry toast without running to the hall bathroom. Even so, the husband-wife talk that had been sitting between Malcolm and me like unwanted leftovers was about to happen. Again.

"You know what we discussed, El," Malcolm said when I came back from tucking Anne into bed. We were alone now, free to talk as married couples and life partners do, even though I hadn't felt like a partner for some time. "El?"

"I heard you," I said.

"So? When are you going to do it?"

It.

This single word covers all kinds of sins, from backseat gropes after a high school dance, to putting the dog down when he's too old and too needy, to taking a fetus from a woman's belly. Sex, euthanasia, abortion. All conveniently collected under the umbrella of *It.*

Our conversation took turns, doubling back on itself, coming full circle. An hour later, Malcolm hadn't budged from his original position, or really said anything other than reminding me of what we discussed, of how utterly selfish it would be to bring a baby into the world only to watch her struggle and suffer while she tried to claw her way to a level she couldn't possibly attain. He showed me pictures of the future, reminding me of Q scores and college admissions boards, of how no one would want a girl with a lower-than-average quotient.

"She'll end up with nothing," Malcolm said. "Or she'll get someone like that kid who used to follow you around in school. Jack something."

"Joe," I corrected. "He was a nice guy, you know."

"Nice doesn't cut it anymore, El. Q matters. You know that."

I did, and I didn't want to. I didn't want to think about Joe, or what happened afterward. I didn't want to think about more tests and more Q numbers and the possibility of ever doing that again.

Malcolm rose from the table, taking the rest of the plates into the kitchen. Our conversation was over, and I sat alone reading through a long list of pregnancy management services on the back of the Q testing literature while Malcolm, who was supposed to be my partner in all things, presterilized dinner dishes with his back to me.

And there were no more postdinner talks. The next morning, I drove into town for my appointment at one of the Genics Institute's prenatal clinics. It was well before they rolled out WomanHealth, before Petra Peller took things to a new level. Behind a dozen or so women, walls of green and yellow, verdant and sunshiny colors, set off posters of perfect families—perfect hair, perfect bleached teeth, perfect skin. Nowhere in the room were photographs of babies, only of grown children, and the usual stacks of pamphlets advertising formula or offering free samples of diapers were noticeably absent.

Everything from the decor to the reading material was targeted at women who would never see the inside of a delivery room.

And then there was the chatter:

"If they tell me its Q is one-hundredth of a point lower than nine-point-five, I'm getting rid of it," said a pale woman behind her mask of painstakingly applied cosmetics. "Just like I did the last time."

"Thank God it's so quick now," said the twenty-something next to her. "Wouldn't it be great if manicures were that fast?" They both laughed.

As they traded phone numbers and emails, insisting their five-year-old whiz kids really *must* get together for a playdate one of these days, the door behind the receptionist's cubicle swung open. A woman walked out, clutching an envelope close to her rather ample mid-pregnancy bosom. She had wisps of gray curling around her temples and faint feather lines at the edges of her lips. Easily forty, I thought. Maybe older. Ms. Perfect Makeup and Ms. Manicure looked her up and down, following the woman as she crossed the waiting room and exited hurriedly through the street door.

"What was she thinking?" Ms. Makeup said. "At her age."

"I wouldn't even try it after thirty-five," the other one came back. "No way."

"They're saying now that even thirty is too late. I was reading this article the other day, and—"

"Saw it. Way too much science for me."

I'd read the article, too, because Malcolm had left the magazine open on my pillow one night. A subtle hint and convenient timing, given we'd had yet another postdinner talk about the geometric decline of a baby's Q score as the mother's age increased.

The women stopped their conversation long enough to look across the room at me. Glances were exchanged; lips pursed. I could practically hear their thoughts: *Bad luck for her. Wonder if she'll keep it. Has to be pushing the envelope on the big three-five. And there could be other problems. No need to mention the D word.*

Not many issues outranked a low Q score, but trisomies were on the top of the list of lousy outcomes. Down syndrome, in particular.

When the receptionist called my name, a thing happened. My baby, my little-person-to-be who I had already named and loved, already sung to sleep with old lullabies my grandmother had taught me, stirred somewhere deep inside my swollen body. I thought: *Screw nature. Nurture counts more.* And I knew I had a hell of a lot to give in the nurturing camp.

So I walked out the way I'd come in, eighteen weeks full of baby-to-be, no envelope with a magic number inside it, no fodder for a decision that would end up being more Malcolm's than my own. I spent two hours that afternoon looking up Google images of prenatal Q reports and forging the one I'd later show my husband. It would say, I decided, 9.3 in large, silver-toned ink. A good number. A fine number. And it was the first time I made the right kind of choice after a series of poor ones.

SIX

I'm halfway down my driveway, fiddling with the Acura's windshield wiper controls and cursing the defogger that's been on the fritz for months now, when the yellow bus honks. It's a different sound than the light but piercing ping of the silver and green buses. This is a sound that shakes you, like when you're rolling steadily down a highway, humming along to top forty or classic vinyl, and out of nowhere a tractor-trailer driver yanks hard on his cord, blasting its horn at you. Most of the time, I think they do it for no reason at all.

The yellow bus, though, seems to have a reason.

It's moved one house farther along and isn't parked in front of the Campbells' house anymore but in front of the blue and white colonial where Judith Green lives. It honks again.

I'm already late, so I tap in the school secretary's number and hit send.

"Davenport Silver School," the secretary chirps. "This is Rita. How can I help you?"

I tell Rita a lie about my car's battery and ask if she'll send a substitute to my morning biology class. "They can work on their chromosome mutation essays," I say, thinking that first-year high school students in my day were still memorizing phases of the Krebs cycle, not working out advanced genetic theory. "I'll be there as soon as I can get the car jumped."

"No problem, Dr. Fairchild. Your freshman class is performing way above the benchmarks this semester." A tapping of keys as she checks numbers; a pause as she seems to be considering the kindest way to remind me of the cost of tardiness. "And your Teacher Q can handle a few tenths of a point. Nasty weather to have car trouble in, though."

"Yeah," I say. Then I end the call and wipe fog from the driver-side window with my sleeve as the front door of the Greens' house inches open. Judith's mother comes out first, arms wrapped around her body so tightly her hands almost meet at the back of her waist. She's got a terry-cloth robe on—not nearly enough protection from the rain— and her face moves in small, chipmunk-like motions, like she's chattering from the cold.

Except it isn't cold today. Only pissing rain.

Now Judith steps out. She's dressed in jeans and a windbreaker, not her usual Harvard Crimson uniform with the knife-pleated skirt and vest, ivory blouse freshly pressed. Her mother hands her a flat yellow card, then steps back inside for a few seconds. When she returns to the porch, she's carrying a single suitcase, which she sets down so she can fold Judith in her arms. The terry-cloth robe sags open and slips off a little, but Sarah Green doesn't seem to notice.

Then the bus honks again.

I want to put the Acura in gear and race toward it, scream at the driver. *Give them five more fucking minutes, will you? Just five minutes!* It wouldn't do any good, just like it wouldn't do any good to go running after the Child Catcher, begging for more time. So I sit here with a drenched raincoat sleeve from wiping down the condensation on my window. Helpless.

Judith breaks the hug first, picks up her suitcase, and walks down the brick path, the same brick path she's walked down since she and Anne started school, the same brick path Sarah Green lines with begonias in the summer and chrysanthemums in the fall. She presses her yellow card up to the bus door, and it folds open. A few blurred shapes through the front windows tell me Judith isn't the only pickup this morning—I can't make any details out through the rain. But I don't imagine there are many smiles in that bus today.

As the bus pulls away, I throw the car into reverse, back out onto the street, and pause. Even after the time change, darkness lies over our neighborhood like a dreary blanket, mostly thanks to the rain. My phone tells me it's seven forty-five, enough time for me to make it to school before first period ends and my Q rating goes down another tenth of a point.

Fuck it, I think, and I drive in the opposite direction toward Sarah Green's house, past the empty playground with its perfect layer of shredded tire rubber, undisturbed by the scuffs of Keds and Reeboks. Even in the wind and rain, the swings are as still as broken pendulums, and the metal slide is a dull gray, never having been polished by the bottoms of children. I don't remember ever seeing a child inside the enclosure's fence. Kids appear in the morning when the buses come, then in the late afternoon when the buses return. They hurry inside and bend over books until dinner. If they're anything like Anne and Freddie, they eat like hungry soldiers in a mess hall, and bend over their books until bedtime. Most of them are bleached pale, even in the summer months.

Sometimes I think all of childhood has disappeared.

I stop the car in front of the Greens' colonial. Sarah is on her knees, robe fallen open to expose a thin nightgown. She's pulling out the mums she planted only a few weeks ago, fists digging into the earth, flinging mud and roots in every direction. A few clumps of dirt stick in her hair, and a smudge of brown mars her face when she tries to wipe away tears.

"Sarah?" I say, stepping out of my car. "What's going on?"

She doesn't raise her head, and she doesn't answer me directly, only claws at the ground, shredding mums until the brick path is coated with a blanket of yellow petals, leaves, and dirt. "I hate this fucking color. I hate it."

I've always liked yellow. It's a happy color; neither tranquil nor overwhelming. Not in your face, like red, which only reminds me of danger and pain and evil. I think of the butter yellow curtains Malcolm and I hung in the nursery before Freddie was born, the gold of fresh straw they used to feed horses before the farms turned to housing developments, sunshiny yolks smiling up from a frying pan on lazy Sunday mornings.

All of a sudden, yellow is the ugliest color on Earth.

Sarah finally stops her garden destruction and looks up at me. "She couldn't have slid all the way down to seven-point-nine, El. There's no way. You have her in two classes this year, right? Advanced bio and anatomy. She's on time, she's never sick, and she aces everything."

I nod. Judy Green has been at the top of her class since I've known her. "She outranks Anne," I say. "And Anne's good." I'm not bragging, only stating a fact, although if Judy lost more than two points, I suppose I've got my tense wrong.

Now Sarah stands up, pulling her robe around her, belting it with mud-caked hands. She doesn't seem to care that she looks as if she's been wallowing around in a pigsty. Her voice, normally soft, hardens. "Then how did she lose the Q points? Tell me that, El. Did you know something? Did you hold anything back from me?"

"No. Of course not." This is one hundred percent true. I spend half my time at school on weekly reports, prepping for the test, compiling results, and contacting parents of what we call "borderliners"—any student who scores below an A on the previous week's practice tests or who might be in danger of sinking below a Q of nine for other reasons. I've heard of teachers in the green schools, like the one Freddie attends, who lose sleep over the numbers. One-tenth of a point makes all the difference.

Freddie's geometry teacher explained it all to me at our last meeting.

"It gives them a chance, at least," she said, rubbing her eyes. "And if they don't have a chance, it gives everyone in the family time to deal with it. They can spend their last weekends together going on picnics, taking a final trip to see the grandparents, riding a roller coaster at the Six Flags park. All that shit they haven't been doing for the past few years. That way, when the Q sinks below eight and the yellow bus comes, they've had some quality experiences. Memories."

It wasn't always this way.

In the first wave of the tier system, the yellow schools weren't much different from the green and silver schools. They were farther out of town, of course, and they weren't equipped with state-of-the-art science labs or staffed with teachers who had strings of letters after their names. Still, the kids came back home every afternoon.

Until last month, when Madeleine Sinclair made the decision to move the yellow schools. To change the system.

"It'll be better this way," Malcolm said after the girls had gone to bed. We sat on the sofa like bookends, a bowl of popcorn keeping us at a distance. The remote was balanced on my lap, and Malcolm reached over to turn up the volume so we could hear Madeleine's press conference.

"You really think that's a good idea?" I said between handfuls of popcorn. It was the unbuttered kind, the no-salt, no-fat "light" version, because Malcolm liked that better. Me, I wanted the extra grease and salt, but you pick your battles.

"Sure it is, El. You have any idea how crowded those schools have gotten? Not enough teachers, either."

"They're only crowded because the pass rates have dropped," I said. I didn't know whether the tests had gotten harder or what, but I'd suddenly been losing a student every few months at the silver school, and I'd heard the same from my colleagues.

Madeleine, dressed in her usual blue power suit, paused before answering another question. "The fact is," she said, smiling at the press audience, "we're facing overcrowding at our third-tier institutions."

Institutions, I thought. What a fucking word.

That voice, that smooth educator's voice, continued, louder now that Malcolm had upped the volume again. "We're running out of real estate in the urban areas." Madeleine shook her blond bob. "No. That's not entirely true. We've *run* out of room." She silenced an interruption from the audience with a flat palm. "Our cities are overpopulated. Our suburbs are overpopulated. But"—now a smile unfolded on her face—"there's a bright side to everything. A solution."

One of the younger reporters asked what that might be.

"Farmland," Malcolm said, nodding next to me.

"Our farmland," Madeleine answered.

Malcolm tossed another handful of popcorn into his mouth. "That was my idea, actually."

I looked at him. "What was your idea?"

He shushed me with a wave of his hand. "Listen. She's about to explain it."

A close-up of Madeleine Sinclair, now the secretary of education, filled the screen. "We've decided the best route forward is to give our children—all of our children—the room they need to grow."

I let her drone on, talking about how the new yellow schools would have more space, more amenities, more activities, more teachers, more everything. The way Madeleine put it, they sounded more like vacation-lands than schools.

The only downside was that they wouldn't be close to home.

"Families will adjust," Madeleine said, fielding another question from the press room.

I moved the bowl of popcorn to the table and stood up, blocking the television from Malcolm's view. "They're boarding these kids? Where? In Iowa?"

Malcolm stared at me. "Well, yeah, El. And other places around the country. Wherever there's room. Think of it as a kind of Outward Bound. Get the kids out of the crowded city and into the fresh air. They'll thrive."

"More like Downward Bound," I said, not holding back my sarcasm. "Anyway, what you mean is wherever land is cheap, right? And you're telling me this was your idea?"

I went to bed early that night, hoping I'd be asleep before Malcolm came in.

SEVEN

I put Malcolm and Madeleine and the whole stinking Department of Education behind me, and now I'm back on what used to be Sarah Green's neat brick path. It looks like a land mine went off.

"You said she was doing fine," Sarah screams. "Fine! Every single report we got said her Q was almost perfect."

"It was perfect, actually," I said.

"Well, it isn't now. For some reason. Now she's on her way to fucking Kansas?" She laughs, but it's not a funny laugh. "Kansas. To a state school with a year-round schedule." Every one of her words is the verbal equivalent of screaming caps. I don't even try to interrupt.

"Oh, right, they tell us we can come visit once a quarter. Do you have any idea how much leave David and I have to take to fly to Kansas four times a year? And that's if we can get the extra time off work. That's *if* we want to see our own Qs take a nosedive, which means Jonathan's Q gets hit, and he's already in a green school. For a day, Elena. One single day with our daughter. They used to send the kids home for Christmas. Thanksgiving every other year. Summer."

"You were on the board when the new schedules were approved," I say.

Sarah stutters and goes silent. Then, she turns and makes for her front door. Her hair is in wet ropes down her back, and the terry-cloth robe is as sodden as a drowned cat. She spins fast and looks at me, hard. "I guess you'll have more time for your top two percent now, El. Good luck with them."

Her words hit me like a slap in the face, but it's a reactionary slap, a quid pro quo return on the slap I'd just served her.

I remember when the schedule changes happened. Another night on the sofa with Malcolm, another press conference with Madeleine Sinclair in her blue power suit and blond bob and that saccharine smile that makes you feel like you're in kindergarten all over again and need shit explained to you in small words. I remember the reduction in vacation time being another one of Malcolm's brainchildren.

I also remember parents like Sarah and David Green supporting it.

As little as five years ago, participation in the tier system wasn't compulsory, not exactly. Instead, a guideline came from Washington. A suggestion that parents pay close attention to their children's individual needs. This was followed by another, and then by another dozen, all of them coldly clinical and mathematical.

Parents of children with Q scores below eight points are encouraged to consider yellow schools.

Top-tier systems may not be in your offspring's best interest. Don't push them!

A panel of two dozen experts has concluded that tier separation benefits everyone.

Of course, there was pushback—PTA meetings where infuriated parents stood up and interrupted the barrage of suggestions, threatening to homeschool their seventh-graders rather than subject them to the constant pressure of tests. The opt-out culture of parents storming from assemblies and plucking their kids from school had started to take a tenuous foothold.

But only in some neighborhoods. Not in ours. Not in Sarah Green's.

And then the PTA meetings were supplanted by board meetings. The guidelines became directives; the directives included fines for truancy, taxes disguised as penalties, trickle-down effects on siblings' Q scores. Homeschooling requirements became more restrictive than gun laws, and the forms were ever-changing. A line left blank or a code entered incorrectly meant a red *Declined—not subject to appeal* stamp from the school superintendent's office. I wonder sometimes where they found all that red ink.

Women like Sarah Green had their own way, campaigning for a different type of pressure, pressure that came in the form of leaflets with *Do not hire this unfit parent!* and *No benefits for the antisocial!* With enough Sarah Greens on your side, who needs laws?

I stand in the rain under my umbrella and watch Sarah, shoulders slumped under the weight of grief and confusion and hatred, go into her house. She turns back once to hiss at me, "Those yellow buses? They're not supposed to come here, Elena. Not here." The front door slams shut, and the lock clicks, telling me I needn't bother taking those few steps onto the porch and knocking, so I walk back to my car, curse at the defogger for the tenth time this morning, and curse at everyone for taking all of this super-child garbage too far.

As I drive away, I look back one more time at the house. Somehow I don't think there will be much of a garden in the Greens' yard next year.

But then I think, *Maybe she deserves it.*

EIGHT

No one asks what happens to the kids who fall through the cracks—there isn't a reason to. Yellow school graduates manage the local supermarket; they work at costume jewelry kiosks in the few brick-and-mortar malls that are left. They run 7-Elevens and flip burgers now that immigration quotas have been cut again. They do all those jobs no college graduate wants but that still need to get done.

Let's face it. Sarah Green is a snob. She's no different from the Callahans and the Delacroix and the Morrises living down the street. These are families who have self-sealed themselves into a bubble of privilege, whose favorite pronouns are We and They and Us and Them, whose theme song is "Not in My Neighborhood," whose idea of school choice is best translated as *I'll make the choice for you because I know better.* So what if some kid from the city gets shipped off to the equivalent of a vocational school, if a country boy from Nebraska doesn't make the cut to his state university? These are things that happen to Them, never to Us. If I didn't share a house and a bed with Malcolm, and if I didn't worry constantly over Freddie, I'm not sure I'd even know they were happening. After all, how many people watch Madeleine Sinclair's State of Education addresses? The president barely draws fifteen percent of the population for those big talks he gives, so I'm guessing Queen Madeleine gets next to nothing.

As I wind my car down the GW Parkway and cross the bridge into the city, I wonder if we've all been playing the old out of sight, out of mind game. I wonder if we'll keep playing it until the game pieces start coming into view, shifting from Their playing boards to Our playing boards. Like they did this morning, when Sarah Green's perfect teenager was demoted to a pawn.

I'm late anyway, so I pull over in Georgetown, hold my phone up to the meter, and pay for fifteen minutes' rental of prime real estate parking. *Ch-ching!* All done. Somewhere in the radio waves above my head or the fiber-optic lines below my feet, fifty cents move from a bank account in one state to another account in a different state. No one even needs to empty the coins.

At Starbucks, my caffe latte is waiting at the mobile order pickup counter. Two-percent milk, half decaf, light foam, one sugar. Grande sized, whatever that means. The barista-robot chirps an automated *Have a great day, Elena! Hope your drink is perfect!* as I pick up the coffee. *See you tomorrow morning!* she says. Sometimes, the barista-robot is a he. They like to mix things up.

There's a girl at the window, tucked up on one of those deep sofa things with lots of pillows, legs folded under her, reading. She's almost young enough to be in high school, but she's here in Starbucks, and she doesn't look like a dropout or a truant. One of those career-guide bibles that's supposed to tell you what you want to be when you grow up is open on the table, pages facing down, next to a pile of college guides and SAT prep manuals teetering by her coffee, partially obscuring her face. She has a brightness in her eyes, the kind I see in my best students, but I know she doesn't stand a chance in the college admissions game.

She's using a yellow ID card as a bookmark, and no college has admitted a third-tier student for at least a few years, according to Malcolm's latest dinnertime report.

"Hi," she says, catching my eye when I reach the door.

"Hi."

"I was top in my class two years ago," she says. "Numero uno. Gave a valedictorian speech and everything. I mean, it wasn't the best school. Kids from my neighborhood don't go to the best schools. But still. I figured being first would count for something."

I'm so late. But I let the door swing shut and stay. "It's hard now."

She closes the Barron's bible with its lists of statistics for everything—admissions, average SAT scores, demographics, nearby bars, number of athletic fields, all that quantifiable shit. "What do you do?"

"I teach."

"Oh, yeah? Where?"

"Davenport."

The girl sweeps her eyes over me, taking it all in. The suit, the strappy heels, the calfskin purse slung over my shoulder. "Figures. You look like one of them."

"I don't know what that means."

She laughs. "White. Rich. Perfect. Bet you have a super-high Q."

"It's okay." Actually, it's 9.73, but I don't want to tell her this.

"Anyway. I'm trying one more time for college. After that, I don't know what. Used to have a job here, but, well, you know." Her hand moves in a game-show-hostess gesture. "Lost it a few months ago. I still hang out, though." She points at the books. "Reading's not a real popular hobby in my hood."

There's a lull while I wait for the right words to come to me, and another lull when I realize there are no right words for this girl or this situation. I blurt out a lame "What do you want to major in?"

"Math," she says, closing the book. "I'm wicked at math. Go ahead, ask me anything."

My phone pings. It's Rita from school. "I'm sorry—I'm really late this morning."

She looks at the coffee in my hand. "Yeah."

"I'm sorry," I say, meaning it in all the ways, knowing she doesn't believe me, and I open the door.

Outside, the automated street sweepers suck leaves and twigs and debris from Thursday-night college kids off the pavement on the other side of Wisconsin Avenue. The two cars whose owners forgot about street-cleaning day get tickets. Not paper tickets, but in a few minutes one hundred dollars will move between bank accounts for the green Jeep, and another hundred for the yellow Mini Cooper with racing stripes. The parking enforcement drones and meter maid trons move on, up Wisconsin, in search of their prey.

All this automation makes me wonder where they'll put the yellow school kids in another few years when the last of the grocery stores switch to self-checkout and the little Amazon delivery drones buzz up to front doors, plopping their parcels on the porches. Click, buzz, plop. It's supposed to be progress, and I guess we'll be seeing more of it. Who knows? Before I retire, they might even automate teaching.

"Competition," Malcolm says during his dinner-hour updates, almost always for Anne's benefit. "You work hard, you study, you succeed, you get a job."

The problem here is childishly simplistic: The jobs are disappearing and the people aren't. When I pull into the underground parking garage and let another machine scan my car's decal, greeting me with a sunny, if electronic, *Good morning, Dr. Fairchild*, I wonder where all the yellow school kids will be in another ten years. I wonder what we'll do with the people who aren't necessary anymore.

NINE

The high school where I teach isn't very different from the high school I attended almost a quarter of a century ago. There are rooms, teachers, books, and students. It's the students, I think, as I set up books and attendance sheets on the desk in my classroom and pull the blinds up to give us a view of something green, who are too similar. Far too similar to each other and to what they were in my day.

Back then, the autism spectrum wasn't so much a spectrum as a *what the fuck is autism?* question—as bright a blip on the high school radar as peanut allergies, celiac disease, transsexual restroom rights, and out-of-the-closet teenagers were in 1990-something. Changes trickled along, a drop or so at a time. I figured by the time my girls were teens, everyone would have joined in on the diversity dance.

I was wrong. Diversity never made it past a slow, awkward shuffle. As my students come in for one last period of pretest cramming—what we're supposed to call a final review, but what everyone knows is an umpteenth-hour cram session—they're all the same. Straight, mostly white, athletic. And I've never seen such a thing as a trans-friendly bathroom.

Testing days are both rushed and slow. This morning, we rush. I take my classes through their review, getting them ready for the SOLs.

The acronym is supposed to stand for Standards of Learning, an updated version of its former self, but I've been calling it the Shit Out of Luck test for a year now.

Never out loud, of course. And never to Malcolm.

It's the Shit Out of Luck test because two months ago I stood in front of thirty faces. Today I stand in front of twenty-seven. The three empty desks are still here, though, scattered about. No one bothers to remove them, or consolidate them in the back of the classroom. Or maybe that's the plan—to leave the empty desks, the ones that used to be occupied by Judy Green and Sue Tyler and a ghost-pale boy named Antonio who kicked ass at chemistry but couldn't hack it in number theory. Maybe the empty desks are here as a carrot.

Or a stick.

Some teachers have it worse than I do. Nancy Rodriguez, for instance, who teaches advanced programming, lost two students after last month's tests. I've heard Dr. Chen's chemistry class has dwindled from two dozen to a scant fifteen. Talk in the teachers' lounge happens in whispers around them. *Nancy's kids better pass the lab module or she'll find herself teaching in a green school. Chen is pulling her hair out because of the failures.* And so on. As the students advance, the sieve gets finer.

It isn't that the green schools are lousy—Freddie says her teachers are great, even if Malcolm frowns at the idea of faculty with master's degrees instead of doctorates. And I've seen the homework Freddie brings back every afternoon: stacks of heavy hardcover textbooks, instructions for the quarterly science fair projects, annotated bibliography assignments that would have made a college freshman back in my day start filling out course-drop requests. The faculty is good enough that every once in a while a green school student scores out of the ballpark, ends up with a silver card, and transfers to a first-tier school.

Most of the time, though, there's only one way for a kid to go once she's in a green school. Down.

We aren't supposed to look at it as "down," per Madeleine Sinclair's crowd. We're supposed to view it in euphemisms: helpful, appropriate, child focused.

"Money saving" never gets a mention.

So I take my students through their Mendelian genetics; I hurl words ending in -*osis* and -*isis* at them until their eyes glaze over, until I'm confident they know the material backward and forward and upside down, until, when I say "Who's ready for the test?" twenty hands go up. Mercedes Lopez, sitting three rows away and glancing nervously at the newly empty desk every few minutes, is first. She's my only remaining European student. The rest fled while they could.

All the while, Judy Green's desk sits vacant in the front row, pencils and pens and highlighters cleared from the trough on the left side, books gone from the shelf underneath it. Last month, when I asked who was ready for the test, Judy's hand was the first one raised.

And yet her Q fell more than two full points, low enough to send her off on a yellow bus.

This isn't what bothers me, though. What's been eating at me since this morning, since I stood in the rain listening to Sarah scream accusations at me and punch me with words that she should have thought about first, is that even if Judy didn't pass—even if she blanked out during transcription of genetic codes or screwed up the difference between intrinsic and extrinsic musculature—every single one of Judy's tests would have had to be completely blank to bring her down so far.

My students file out and a new batch comes in, the chemistry crowd from Dr. Chen's class in a building across the street. A few of them are like Anne—confident, even haughty. They know they'll pass. Others squint nervously, as if they're trying to visualize the entire periodic table on the backs of their eyelids. One girl—I think her name is Alice—chews on a fingernail. When she takes it away from her mouth, there's a raw, red crescent of blood where she's nibbled down to the quick.

I'm proctoring today, and that means I'm not permitted to speak to the students except for reciting the test rules, which I know by heart.

You have one hour.

You may not speak to any student.

You may not leave the room for any reason.

When time is called, put down any and all writing implements. If you do not, ten points will be automatically deducted from your score.

Once, I added an extra line about cheating. It's not necessary anymore.

It used to be that cheating was an art form. We knew all the tricks: the sticks of chewing gum with chemical formulas written on them, dissolved by teeth and spit if a teacher should pass by; inked thighs under pleated skirts bearing presidents and dates; some genius kid's famous "Inviso-Method," which involved writing your notes on a disposable top layer of paper, hard enough to impress the bottom layer. There were folded-up crib sheets tucked into knee socks, last year's exam copies bought with pooled lunch money, calculators pre-programmed to solve the deadly quadratic equation. If there was a way to cheat, someone invented it.

So maybe competition isn't all that new, but there's no cheating these days, not since that incident a few years back.

I'm not sure of the details. There were whispers, naturally, about the two women from the Fitter Family Campaign, about how they spent a solid hour behind closed doors with the kid who stashed microscopic notes inside the barrel of an automatic pencil. Nancy Rodriguez said he bit one of the women. Dr. Chen told me she heard crying behind the door. What I do know, and what I'd rather forget, is that before the kid's parents made it across town to the school, his Q was recalculated and a machine spat out a flat yellow card.

We didn't see him again. And, of course, there haven't been any further cheating incidents.

One by one, the students take their seats. I hand pristine sheets of lined paper to them and supply each desk with a pencil and a pen. Then I recite my lines and start the slow march up and down the aisles. I hate this part, because it reminds me of touring a museum, shuffling along and shifting my weight, getting a good case of museum-foot. I'll proctor four more tests before the day ends, and by the time I'm home my ankles will be swollen.

By the time I'm home, I'll find out how Freddie's day went. I can't say I'm in a rush to know.

TEN

Dinner is a disaster.

We always get Chinese takeout on testing days because the idea of standing over a stove long enough to boil even a pot of water for spaghetti makes me cringe. The dining table is littered with those white boxes. Rice, spicy eggplant, rice, General Tso's chicken, rice, egg rolls, something called Happy Family Delight, and rice. After Malcolm mentions his broken peace lily for the third time, the only words Freddie says are "Pass the soy sauce, please."

"So," Malcolm says. "How's school going?" He scoops more of General Tso's famous and ubiquitous chicken from the paper container onto his plate, setting the rest between himself and Anne at the exact moment Freddie reaches for it. "Oh. Sorry. Did you want some, too?"

Freddie just looks at me, defeated. On nights like this, it's as if Malcolm has only one child.

Anne stops revisiting every single minute of the five tests she sat for this afternoon and pushes the chicken toward her sister. It's a small act of defiance, but my heart skips all the same. "Go on, Freddie. You first."

"I have a project for government class due next week, Dad," Freddie says.

Malcolm says nothing until I kick him under the table. Then, "Need any help?"

"Maybe. Just for brainstorming. We're supposed to design some kind of social system."

As if we haven't already, I think.

"I need a bit more specificity," Malcolm says drily. If Anne had been as vague as Freddie, she would have gotten a teasing smile.

I ignore my husband and coax my daughter. "Go on, sweetie."

But she doesn't go on. Instead, Anne comes to her rescue. "I have the same project. It's about social institutions. You know, trying to come up with a place to put everyone based on their Q scores. The Fitter Family Campaign's sponsoring it, and there's a prize for best project." She smirks. "Actually, there are two prizes this year. The winner gets a summer internship at the FFC headquarters in her home state."

"What if a guy wins?" I say with one eyebrow raised. It's as if Anne hasn't contemplated the possibility of her coming in anything but first.

"Then it's *his* home state. But only if he wins." She throws me a wink.

"That's my best girl," Malcolm says.

Freddie sinks a few inches lower in her chair.

I kick his foot under the table, harder this time, and he turns to give me a *what was that for?* look. Christ, he's oblivious. Or maybe not. Maybe he really doesn't care that Anne gets ninety percent of his attention while Freddie stares at her plate, pushing rice grains into abstract patterns with chopsticks, one at a time. She makes a feeble attempt to interrupt, gets a "Hush up a minute, hon, I'm listening to Anne," and gives up.

"Malcolm," I say. "How about we let Freddie tell us how her day went?"

Freddie blanches, shakes her head, and goes back to decorating her plate with rice mandalas. Malcolm looks grateful.

"I bet her day went just fine," he says, passing another wrapped egg roll to Anne. "If she's anything like her sister, she sailed through." He isn't actually speaking to Freddie, only about her. So I give him a third under-the-table kick. "Right, Frederica?"

Malcolm's never taken to Freddie's nickname, something he points out each time he addresses her.

"Sure, Dad," Freddie says in a clockwork voice. Then, "Can I be excused?" She doesn't wait for an answer before pushing out her chair and going down the hall to her bedroom. No. "Going" isn't the right word. She skulks or slinks or scuttles. Some onomatopoetic thing. Something a primitive nocturnal animal would do.

Anne gets up and follows her. "Be right back, Dad."

When she's out of earshot, I shake my head at him. "Anyone would think you were the one who had the umbilical cord sixteen years ago. Anyway, the yellow bus came today," I say, peeling the wrapper from an egg roll.

"Huh."

"That's it? 'Huh'?"

He shrugs. "I thought I told you, El. There were some schedule changes. Memo went out a few weeks ago." He takes the egg roll from my hand. "You don't really want another one of these. They're all grease."

What I want to say is, *Get your paws off my fucking egg roll.* Instead, I go back to the real subject. "Do you even care who it picked up?"

"Who?"

"Judith Green from up the street."

Malcolm's eyes widen a few millimeters, but otherwise his expression doesn't change.

"You know. Judy? Anne's best friend since she was five?"

"Oh. Right," he says. "I think I remember her."

Okay. I take the egg roll back and forget about peeling off the oily

49

outer layers before sinking my teeth into it, just to show him I don't give a crap. "You *think* you remember her. For chrissake, Malcolm, she was here last weekend for a sleepover. We made chocolate chip pancakes on Sunday morning, and the girls asked you for help with their homework. So don't fucking tell me you *think* you remember."

Anne's back. "Remember what?"

"Language, El. Language." Malcolm slides his eyes in my direction.

"Don't lecture me." I'm hot now, hotter than I've been in a while, but I pause, take a few of those deep yoga breaths, and cool myself down before speaking. "There's no way Judy failed her test last month. No way."

"Wait a sec," Anne says. "Judy failed? That's impossible. Judy's a fucking rock star. Oh. Sorry, Mom. Freaking rock star." There's no tutting or reprobation from her father. "Anyway, no way Judy bombed." She leaves the room, iPhone in hand, fingers working madly at the keys.

When we're alone again, I glare at my husband. "Like I said."

So what does Malcolm do? He shrugs. That's it. Shoulders up, shoulders down. And he pinches another piece of eggplant with his chopsticks.

I used to love the man sitting across from me. I loved his wit and his smarts and his *I'll always take care of you* attitude, and I looked up to him. I traded something for this man, something I thought I wanted, and still do.

In hindsight, it was a shitty trade.

ELEVEN

THEN:

I was in my studio apartment at Yale on the last Saturday of September, finished with classes and ready for the weekend. New England had started turning pretty with its annual leaf-mosaic show, and I'd planned on taking the car out of shitty New Haven and driving farther north for the weekend. I had not been planning to wake up and lurch to the tiny subway-tiled bathroom.

An hour later, after a quick trip to the Rite Aid down the street, I was still in that bathroom, sitting on the icy porcelain of the toilet, shaking the pee stick, as if by shaking it I could knock one of those blue lines out of the little window and turn a plus into a minus, change a baby into a nothing.

I'd split up with Malcolm in early summer, partly because my mother persuaded me that a break might be a good thing, partly because I didn't want my first boyfriend to be my only-and-forever boyfriend. And partly because of Joe.

We grew up together, played kickball in the street and made mud pies in a ditch behind my parents' house. Joe was normal, except for a fanaticism about anything with an internal combustion engine. When we got our licenses, he fixed up an old Mustang, a wreck of a thing he rescued from Mr. Cooper's junkyard. When he turned seventeen, Joe had the hottest car in town. He also had the lowest grade point average in our high school, and SAT scores a hedgehog could have beaten.

He wasn't exactly Joe College, but he was a good guy, taking me to movies he swore weren't dates, buying me gallon-sized tubs of fake-buttered popcorn while some teen-scream villain with razors for fingernails flashed in the on-screen shadows. At sixteen, I was more interested in museums than movies, but I still let Joe talk me into a Friday-night replay of a decades-old film that he once again swore was Not. A. Date. Until he tried to turn it into one. He shivered once next to me when Freddy Krueger danced murderously into the dreams of unsuspecting Elm Street teenagers, and I realized Joe didn't like the flick, either. But I knew then why he had picked it.

So we sat, shrinking back in our seats, tucked against each other, giggling at the absurd bits and gasping at the cheesy horror.

I told Malcolm about the movie the next day, deliberately leaving out the awkward almost-romance. He rolled his eyes and asked why I was wasting my time with that type, with someone who could never amount to anything more than a subpar grease monkey, with someone who would only make me miserable. He drove the point home by always stopping for gas at the station where Joe worked, and the subject never came up again. I saw the black grease under Joe's fingernails, the tattooed dragon coiling around his biceps, the future of him undefined and not very desirable.

Joe still called, sent emails, caught up when I came down from Connecticut on school breaks. He got me through a bad patch of depression, spent hours on the phone with me when exam anxiety wouldn't let me sleep, told me stupid jokes on the nights I didn't think I'd ever smile again.

That summer, everything changed.

I'd just gotten home from Connecticut, temporarily back in my childhood bedroom. Maryland was already sticky with humidity, and my parents' house felt close with it after spring in New England. Winston, our dog, seemed also to feel it, so I fetched his lead and went out the front door, starting down the street toward the wooded path heading west.

I heard the Mustang's eight cylinders before I saw it. It was a cool sound, a leonine purr I remembered well.

"Hey! Fischer!" the voice called. I remembered it well, too.

"Hey, yourself!" I called back, raising a hand in a wave.

Joe pulled over and parked, killing the purr, letting the beast rest, and we walked along with Winston. Then he did the strangest thing.

He kissed me.

What I did next was even stranger—I kissed him back. And I didn't kiss him the way I kissed Malcolm, lips slightly apart, tongue withdrawn, eyes open. No, I went in deep and hungry, tasting him. Swapping spit, as kids would say. As Malcolm would never permit.

"What was that for?" I said, twisting, trying to get some space between us so I could talk.

"Just wanted to know what it felt like to kiss you," he said.

"Why?"

"No good reason." Joe leaned in closer. "Maybe I like you."

"What do you like about me?"

"Well, you're beautiful," he said, his lips a breath away from my own.

"That's not enough." He was still leaning, and I was inching back now, keeping my distance. Physical beauty wasn't supposed to drive decisions. Malcolm had shoveled that line in one word at a time through high school.

Joe laughed. "It's not the only reason, El. And I don't mean you're only beautiful on the outside."

A runner rushed up the path toward us, and we did that thing people do when they're caught, instinctively separating ourselves, adopting some ridiculously unnatural pose that told the whole story. The woman, who I'd seen before in the woods, ran on, but not before shooting a smile my way.

And, like magnets, Joe and I closed in on each other.

"Do you like it up there?" he said. "At Yale?"

My parents and grandmother had asked the same question only a few hours before. The answer I gave Joe now was the same. "It's okay."

"Then why stay?"

We were side by side, shoulders and thighs touching as we leaned against a fence rail, watching Winston burrow his way into the dirt. Joe's pinky finger wrapped itself around mine and squeezed. I wanted to tell him about the pressure, about the nights I spent alone in the library, wishing I had someone to take me to the movies. But I didn't have to.

"Don't go back, El," he said quietly. Whether he meant to Yale or to Malcolm, I wasn't sure.

Joe might not have made the grades in high school, and he had as much use for standardized college entrance tests as a cat does for a set of roller skates, but he wasn't stupid. "This whole country's getting crazy," he said. "And it'll get worse before anyone figures it out. Come down to the islands with me. We'll get a boat. Maybe two. Maybe a couple of kids to go along with the boat."

I didn't make any decisions about quitting school and escaping to St. Thomas, but I did quit Malcolm for a time. The next time I saw Joe's Mustang, curvy and red and smooth from the kind of waxing only young men have time for, I was in its backseat. And kissing wasn't the only thing we did. It was a heavy car, but not as heavy as Joe's body on top of mine, not as heavy as the even breaths I drew in and pushed out, not as heavy as the rain that pounded the soft top or the thunder that clapped along to our rhythm. We went slow and fast, and then faster and slower. After two times, we rolled, and I lay with my head on Joe's bare chest, listening to his heart like it was the only sound in a still and quiet universe.

And then we did it all over again because when you're young and crazy in love, the body has a way of resetting itself as many times as it wants to or needs.

In September, I went back north, driving my little VW Rabbit, missing the hardness of the Mustang and the hardness of Joe's body. And now I was here, in a subway-tiled bathroom holding a pee stick with its accusing blue cross. If I turned it, the cross became an X, and I imagined it was my entire life that was being crossed out.

I threw the testing stick into the trash bin, pulled up my pajamas, and climbed back into bed, thinking I'd call my mother. As I reached for the phone, it rang. The caller ID announced Malcolm. I let it go to voice mail and fell asleep.

Three hours later, I played the message.

He was driving up for the weekend.

He was taking me to the Cape.

He wanted to ask me a question.

On the first Saturday of October, I'd taken care of things. It was easier than I thought, allowing myself to stretch out on that gurney in the student clinic, watching the anesthesiologist as she gazed into my eyes and said something that sounded vaguely like *She's nearly under*. Not worrying anymore about what kind of child a mechanic and a college dropout could possibly raise.

Joe never knew about any of it. He knew only what I wrote him in my letter, the one he never answered.

I've decided to marry Malcolm. I'm so sorry. I love you, Joe.
I love you crazy. But I don't think we have a future.

I tore the sheet up and rewrote it, leaving out everything after "sorry."

TWELVE

"Freddie kicked me out," Anne says when I meet her in the hallway, halfway between her room and her sister's. "What's up with that?"

I want to tell her what's up with that is her father's empathy deficit, but instead I tell her to help Malcolm with the dishes and go down the hall myself. The sight in my daughter's bedroom stops me short.

Freddie is packing a suitcase.

It's the old green one, the hard-shell Samsonite that O.J. used to kick around on television, the one Malcolm and I took on our honeymoon to Bermuda. I don't know where Freddie even found it.

Her room, usually arranged with the help of a T square, has morphed into a disaster zone. Think New Orleans after Katrina. A few patches of shag carpet peek out through gaps in underwear, jeans, hair scrunchies, winter socks, and almost everything else that used to live in a drawer or a closet or a hamper. I'm ready to call in FEMA.

"Freddie?" I say, careful to keep my voice steady. "What are you doing?"

As if I need to ask.

She sits on the floor and starts a process of unfolding and refolding, getting the creases in pants' legs exactly right, measuring the distance between T-shirt sleeves until she's satisfied they're symmetrical. All the while, she's rocking to some inaudible rhythm. It isn't really inaudible; there's music going on inside Freddie's head, in a dark space I can't quite reach. The best thing when she's like this is to sit down across from her.

So I do that. And I start rocking, matching her time, being a mirror image metronome of Freddie. After a few minutes, she's back with me, back in the now.

"I bombed," she says in a flat monotone.

"You can't know that, honey."

Someone knows it, though. While we gorged on Chinese food in our dining room, a machine, or a bank of machines, in the Department of Education tallied thousands of scores. Qs are being adjusted at this very moment, matched with student ID numbers. Soon, phones and tablets will start pinging. Some families will celebrate. Others will be shopping for new uniforms over the weekend. Still others will make last-minute plans to visit relatives, pack favorite items of clothing in old suitcases, spend their last Sunday together in tears.

This is all supposed to be good for the children. Good for the families. Good for society.

I lean over and wrap her in my arms. She's wooden. I feel like I'm holding a doll.

"Come on," I say. "Let's go have some ice cream."

This elicits a crack of a smile, and Freddie's eyes shine. Good. Somewhere underneath that stiff exterior, there's still my little girl.

"Chocolate?" she says.

"Sure. And vanilla and strawberry and cookie dough. Anything you want, honey."

The thing I love best in the world happens next: Freddie's crack of a smile turns into a grin.

Then all the phones start pinging.

THIRTEEN

I'm okay.

I'm okay I'm okay I'm okay I'm okay.

If I say it enough, it'll be true, right?

Malcolm and Anne are in the den, eating ice cream. Well, Malcolm is eating nonfat organic frozen yogurt sweetened with Splenda while Anne devours celebratory spoonful after spoonful of rocky road mixed with strawberry. Neither of them knows what I know.

The problem, I think, is that I've got a husband who's so intensely wrapped in his überintelligence bubble that imagining any world outside that cocoon is impossible. The idea of failure in our family doesn't enter into Malcolm's equations of reality, and Anne lives in the kind of blissful oblivion that only teenagers can live in.

This is about to change.

"Malcolm," I say quietly.

He looks up, and I don't need to say another word.

I want to, though. I want to say a million words, all beginning with F and ending with UCK.

"Impossible," says Malcolm.

Possibilities are only measurable before an outcome, I think, but I don't say anything, only hand him my phone with the message from the Department of Education and wait while he reads. It doesn't take long—the department is ruthlessly parsimonious in its alerts. Child's name, child's ID number, child's current tier, and a single, life-altering number: 7.9.

"It's a mistake," he says, getting up from the sofa. "I'll sort it out."

"You do that," I say.

He's on the phone in five seconds, talks for another half minute. Toward the end, the only words he says are monosyllables like "Oh," "Right," "Okay."

My glance shifts from him, to the hallway leading toward Freddie's room, and back to Malcolm. He's the same as when I met him over twenty-five years ago. Same angular, often emotionless face; same square-set shoulders, as if he's preparing for a wrecking ball to hit him and plans to hit back just as hard; same dark blond waves of hair framing his face, although there's gray curling around his temples and at the nape of his neck. The glasses he wears have gone through a few more thicknesses over this past quarter century, but otherwise, Malcolm's the same.

It must be me who's changed, because when I see him now, I don't see anything to love.

"We need to fix this," I say. "Now."

His call has ended, and I corner him in the kitchen. He's turned his back to me and pretends to be fiddling with a grease spot on the counter. "Malcolm? Did you hear me? We need to fix this."

I grew up in a family of quiet men and women, people who didn't shout over one another at Sunday dinners, didn't try to shut one another up to get their point heard. Mostly, tense situations called for calm voices and steady nerves.

Malcolm's absolute silence, on the other hand, isn't a calming force. It's jarring and violent, this stone wall. There's too much room for wonder and speculation.

When he finally answers me, he's almost inaudible.

"We're not fixing anything, Elena."

My full first name is supposed to be a signal that the conversation is over. I don't agree.

"What if it were the president's kid? Or a senator's? Are you telling me they'd sit back and watch their child board a yellow bus on two days' notice?"

This gets to him, and his eyes narrow. "Sometimes the rules are bent."

"Broken, you mean."

"Bent, Elena. Everyone's treated equally."

I pour a glass of wine, all the way up to the rim, and drink it down an inch. Maybe I'm building up some Dutch courage. Maybe I want to piss off Malcolm. "Bullshit. Don't give me that 'everyone is equal' crap."

Anne comes into the kitchen with a bowl of ice cream that's melted into soup. "What's going on?" she says. "You guys having another husband and wife fight?"

She gets a sour smile from her father and an exasperated sigh from me.

"We're leaving," I tell her, changing the subject. Let Malcolm deal with that hardball. Let him figure out who the "we" is.

"What?" Anne spits the word. "Leaving for *where*?" She doesn't wait for me to answer. "But I've got homecoming in a couple of weeks. And the math club. And the forensics team finals. And—"

I cut her off. "And your sister isn't going to a federal boarding school. Period. The end."

Her mouth opens, the jaw working up and down, up and down, while not a sound comes out of it.

"Go to your room, Anne," Malcolm says, then he turns to face me, placing a hand on my arm. It's not a gentle touch but a restraining weight. "Do you have any idea how much jeopardy my job would be in if we took off? I'm supposed to set an example, not be a poster boy for rule dodging. I work in the goddamned Department of Education."

"I meant the girls and me."

What emerges from his throat is a bark of a laugh, an explosive negation of my statement.

And then, less explosive and more sinister: "You're not taking my daughter from me."

Daughter. Singular.

"You don't want Freddie here anymore, do you?" I say. "You don't want her here at all."

Malcolm says nothing, which really means he says it all.

I pull my hand away and drain my glass of wine. Malcolm gives me the eye, and I pour more until the bottle is nearly empty and the glass is brimming again. "Do you know how much jeopardy our family will be in if you don't work this out, Malcolm?"

But my words have no force in them, and Malcolm only smiles.

FOURTEEN

I leave Malcolm stewing in the kitchen and go to Freddie's room with my wineglass and a mountain of chocolate-vanilla-strawberry. If only it were that easy, leaving. Walk out the door with a few suitcases and a credit card and the keys to the Acura. And Freddie and Anne, too.

Nothing is easy these days. The Fitter Family Campaign created obstacles I never saw coming, which is a testament to my own optimism. Or stupidity. Who knows? Maybe optimism and stupidity are siblings.

Headlines from the past decade flash in front of me in the dark of the hallway.

STUDENT PERFORMANCE UP SINCE INTRODUCTION OF TIER SYSTEM

DIVORCE RATES PLUMMET—INCREASED WAITING TIMES TO THANK—KIDS SPEAK OUT!

EDUCATORS ENJOY INCREASED JOB SATISFACTION, SAYS NEW STUDY

COUNTRY ON FAST TRACK TO HIGHEST HAPPINESS QUOTIENT IN OVER A CENTURY

**PRENATAL Q + REPRODUCTIVE FREEDOM =
INFORMED CHOICES FOR WOMEN!**

STAND BACK, CHINA—AMERICA SOARS LIKE AN EAGLE

And so on, and so on, and so on.

No one remembers anymore how bad things had gotten, how we'd nose-dived into a second-rate economy, how college degrees had become as worthless as the fake sheepskin they were printed on, how the elementary schools had stagnated through years of anorexic budgets and overcrowding and teachers' union strikes. They need reminders.

That's where Madeleine Sinclair's monthly State of Education addresses come in handy. Where Petra Peller's ever-evolving genetic testing propaganda helps to squelch any fears before they boil up to the surface. Where the Fitter Family Campaign's endless rallies and public service announcements—*Do you want to go back? Do you want single parents and latchkey kids again? Do you want to worry about your children's future while paying for* other *people's children?*—serve as frequent pokes to anyone who might require a refresher course in how far behind we fell in the game and how far we've come.

If all this isn't enough, we've got other incentives for playing along. No one knows this better than Moira Campbell two houses down.

I catch a glimpse of Moira's place from Freddie's bedroom window. The porch light burned out months ago; the blue glow from the television went dark a day after the bus came to take Moira's two sons away. Once a week, Moira comes out to check her mail, and on Saturdays her car rolls out of the garage, disappears down the street, and comes back an hour later. I'm guessing Saturday morning is Moira's grocery shopping time, but I can't be sure. I never see her with groceries.

And there is no Mr. Campbell. Not since he moved out last year. They were always arguing, the Campbells. Always skipping out on neighborhood parties at the last minute. Moira had a headache; Moira was getting home late from work; Moira left town for a family emergency. The excuses were different, but the reason was always the same—Moira and Sean Campbell, like most couples with a rocky marriage, didn't socialize. They put on a show for a while; Sean hung around the house pretending to be a husband, and the word on the street was that they were sticking it out for the kids' sake. When Sean finally left, Moira would hang out his laundry on the line in her side yard. A few pairs of boxers, some T-shirts, whatever. Just enough to keep the illusion going.

The illusion didn't last long, and the Fitter Family's child welfare representatives—gray-faced women in gray uniforms, clipboards in hand—started coming around, trolling the neighborhood, asking questions. A month later, a gray van arrived, and Moira's boys clambered in, suitcases in one hand, while Moira cursed and threatened from her front porch.

"We're doing fine!" she screamed at the gray women. "One parent is as good as two!"

The Fitter Family Campaign disagreed.

Moira went to court, not once but three times. She ended up representing herself because no lawyer would take her case, not as a single mother. She lost before the hearing even started.

"They told me you have to get the fitter parent to testify," she said after the third day in court. "Can you believe that? The fitter parent— meaning the one who earns more, the one who takes less annual leave, the one with the higher Q rating. I can't even find my ex-husband, let alone get him to show up before a judge. Fucking laws."

I felt for Moira then. I feel for her more now as I realize that Malcolm, with double the income I bring in and half the late days, will always be the fitter parent. Most men are—even the ones who aren't.

So now, sitting in Freddie's room with wine I don't want and ice cream she won't eat, the idea of leaving enters my mind, snakes around for a few delicious seconds, and then departs, replaced by a hopeless question. How long could I keep up the subterfuge? A month? A year? More likely, I'd be discovered by the end of the week. My Q rating would drop, and I'd lose my job.

And that would hurt Anne. The thing about Qs is this: They seem to be inheritable.

Malcolm, though. Malcolm could work it out. He's got access to the databases, and he could fudge Freddie's numbers. By the time the yellow bus arrives to pick up Freddie on Monday morning, we could have a fresh set of Qs, back in the eight-point-something range.

That fantasy lasts all of a minute.

"Okay, little miss," I say to Freddie. "Bedtime."

"Stay with me for a while, Mom?"

I answer her with a hug, and she brightens, but it's a temporary light that shines in her eyes. "And then tomorrow we'll go see Oma and Opa, okay?" My parents are going to flip a wig when I tell them. They've always hated Malcolm, and by tomorrow afternoon, they'll hate him even more. Not as much as I do, but enough.

The light grows a bit steadier as Freddie settles back against my arm and smiles up at me.

She's asleep in no time at all, a heavy presence next to my body. Through the door, the television murmurs as Malcolm watches yet another hour of C-SPAN. It's a mush of words, but the punctuated "Q this" and "Q that" comes through all too clearly.

I'll have the same ugly dreams, dreams of dancing Qs with long, reaching tails that describe swooping arcs. In each curled tail I see a child, a teenager, a person.

I see them strangling. I see them like this in the quiet of night, and I wonder if Freddie sees them, too.

FIFTEEN

When I wake up, it isn't Malcolm next to me in bed but Freddie. She's all preteenager limbs, and her arms and legs wrap around mine like squid tentacles, squeezing me. I'm not in my bed, and there are pink flowers on the border near the ceiling, so I must have fallen asleep in Freddie's room.

"Mom?" she says, her voice syrupy with sleep.

I love her like this, calm and relaxed, all the anxiety of the day yet to squash her under its pressure.

"Yes, baby doll?"

"We still going to Oma and Opa's house today?"

I hold her close, wrap her pink blanket tight around us. "Absolutely."

"Is Anne coming?" she whispers. Already the thickness has gone from her voice. I can hear the twinge of fear and worry in it, like needles.

"Maybe not." *Definitely not*, I think. Malcolm will keep her home and have a lovefest about how wonderful Daughter Number One is. "Let's get you dressed and hit the road, okay? I'm going to take a shower."

Her hand locks onto my wrist as I slide out from under the bedclothes. "Can you take one in my bathroom? And sing something?"

"Sure, hon. Sure."

Under the hot water, wet brush working through hair that's become long enough to start being annoying, I sing a medley of Beatles' tunes. Mostly their old stuff, before dope and mysticism turned the Fab Four into the Just Plain Fucking Weird Four. I know it all by heart, and the words come out automatically, which is good because while I'm soothing Freddie, I'm also planning what I'll tell my parents when we get there. And whether I'll have the guts not to come back home.

After Malcolm's threat last night, I know the consequences of choosing Freddie over Anne, if only until I can sort out a new option. It's a horrible choice, one I would have imagined unthinkable, but it's not the worst one I've ever made. Not by a long shot.

When I come out of Freddie's room, a quart of conditioner weighing down my hair, I'm shivering because I forgot to fetch clothes from my own closet first. I dress quickly, and out in the kitchen Freddie's holding up last year's Wonder Woman costume.

"Can I wear this to Oma's house?" she says, eyes pleading with me. She is already inside the kid-sized red boots and has on those shiny arm bracelet things, which are really coated in plastic, but to Freddie they're all-powerful. I wish they were.

Malcolm only shakes his head at the scene. "Shouldn't she have grown out of that nonsense by now?"

"She's nine, Malcolm," I remind him. "Nine. And it was just Halloween, for chrissake." Then, to Freddie: "Of course you can, but you still have to wear a coat over it." When she comes back five minutes later, Freddie has the costume on—cape to boots.

Malcolm shakes his head again.

I leave him in the kitchen without a word and go to my closet again, swap out the purse I've been carrying for a Dooney & Bourke satchel I could fit most of Brazil into, and start loading it with the barest of clothing essentials. Underwear and bras go in the bottom of the bag, an extra pair of jeans and a sweater, and the crap from my other purse on top. It doesn't look full. Not too much.

Out in the kitchen, Malcolm is making an egg white omelet with low-fat cheese, crumbled tofu, and barely cooked kale. His version of a power breakfast. I make a promise to stop at McDonald's for a sausage and egg biscuit for me, hotcakes and hash browns for Freddie. Anything she wants.

"Where you going, El?" he says, watching me button my coat.

"What do you think? I'm taking Freddie to see my parents."

"Why?"

Where. What. Why. Our marriage in *wh-* questions. "It's what people do on the last weekend. Anyway, we'll be back later."

Anne comes in, grabs a handful of granola from a bag in the cupboard, and starts crunching. "Can I go?"

"You can if you sweep up those crumbs," I say.

Malcolm, as usual, comes to the rescue. "Anne's staying with me. And don't nag her, Elena."

So we're still doing the full-name thing.

I force a smile. "See you around five, probably. Unless they ask us to stay for dinner, which they will. There's a ton of leftover Chinese in the fridge if you want it." I duck back into the hall. "Ready, Freddie?"

"Freddie's ready!" she chirps, running out to the kitchen. It's an old joke, and a silly one, but there we are.

Malcolm takes one look at my overstuffed bag and says, "Going on a trip?" Then he shakes his head, slowly. One shift to the right, back to center, one shift to the left, back to center.

Shit.

My husband is smart. More than smart. When we hooked up in high school, all I could think was, *Don't let this one get away!* I didn't.

But, Christ, how I wish I did. I wish I'd unhooked him and thrown his smug, handsome self back into the pond for some other fisherwoman to catch. I wish I'd cast out a line and reeled in someone normal and nice. I knew someone normal and nice. Once.

Don't, El. Just don't.

"Let me get my coat," he says, taking the omelet off the fire.

I swear I hear him chuckling.

SIXTEEN

There's no arguing with Malcolm, which is why I'm now sitting in the backseat of his oversized BMW crossover SUV, minus one Egg McMuffin, with Freddie next to me, laser-killing zombies on her phone. Malcolm insisted Anne sit up front because of her car sickness, but I know better.

"Be nice to see Sandra and Gerhard after all this time," he says, rolling up the window. "And your grandmother."

It's a bald lie. The animosity between Malcolm and my family is mutual, even if the active hatred scales tip toward Malcolm's side.

I decide to call him on it. "I don't know why you're coming with us."

He raises his face in the rearview mirror, the bridge of his nose and those chocolate eyes. It's obvious he's smiling. "Don't want you and Freddie to go off on your own," he says. "Not on a nasty morning like this."

The drive to my parents' house takes an hour. Freddie is asleep by the time we reach Baltimore, leaving me with a silent Malcolm, a sullen Anne, and thirty minutes of secondary roads stretching out ahead of us.

"Elena," he says. "You know I'm not stupid."

Yeah. I know. Malcolm has been informing me of that for over twenty years.

He keeps going. "Your family. They're—what's the word?—unpredictable." Only he doesn't mean this. "Unpredictable" is Malcolm-speak for "not interested in playing by the rules."

"They just don't like the system," I tell him.

I can only imagine how my mother and father would have reacted to the Fitter Family Campaign or the new educational system or any of the craziness that's run through our country like shit through a goose if they still had me back home. Knowing my dad, he would have blown up half of Washington if he thought it would do any good; I don't think he would have cared if he ended up in pieces himself. The only reason they put up with Malcolm is because they've got a major crush on Anne and Freddie.

"That's what I meant." He lowers his voice. "And your father called me a Nazi last Thanksgiving."

"He did not."

"I was there, Elena."

Freddie asks, "What's a Nazi, Dad?"

Before Malcolm can go didactic, I take over. How to condense a decade of nasty history into a digestible sentence? "Someone who thinks he's better than everyone else. Someone who wants to control things."

Malcolm points at the air with his finger. "See? That's what I'm talking about."

The next words out of his mouth are "Freddie, shut that stupid machine off or mute it or whatever. It's giving me a headache."

"Okay, Dad," she says. And whatever zombies or aliens she's been killing off go silent.

When we pull into my parents' driveway, Freddie and Anne clamber out of the car, run to the porch, and come within a breath of knocking my mother backward. Dad comes out, and there's a four-way group hug that sends the porch swing rocking violently.

Today is going to be hard, I think. So much love can only bring fantastic amounts of pain. Whatever else might happen today, Freddie will be coming home with us. For all of thirty-six hours.

She knows this, and she doesn't. Somewhere in my daughter is a filter made out of steel. Or titanium. Or Kryptonite. Reality comes and goes for her, and at this moment, the only reality for Freddie is the smile on her Oma's face and the soft pressure of her Opa's hand on her back and promises of ginger cookies with warm milk at the kitchen table.

"What a surprise, *Liebchen*," my mother says, tousling Freddie's hair with one hand, now wild with static from the winter hat, and caressing Anne's cheek at the same time.

Freddie beams at her and squeaks a cheery hello. Even Anne lights up at the sight of their grandmother.

That Malcolm isn't mentioned is absolutely no surprise to me. He exists to my family in the way a crutch exists to an accident victim—a necessary, but thoroughly unwanted, prop. When he joins us on the porch, the temperature drops a few degrees despite the smiles.

"Malcolm," Dad says, not offering his hand.

"Gerhard."

I can feel the mercury level plummeting further as Malcolm dispenses the obligatory greetings. It seems suddenly warmer when he walks through the door and into the hallway.

Mom presses us inside, out of the cold, and pats Freddie once on the bottom. "Cookies in the kitchen, girls." Then she and Dad turn to me when Malcolm is out of earshot. "Why the long face?" Mom asks.

I tell them everything in three short sentences. Freddie failed. Freddie's on a yellow bus. Freddie's going away.

"*Scheisse,*" Mom says. "*Scheisse, Scheisse, Scheisse.*"

Four Germanic *shit*s in one breath is unusual, even for my mother,

73

but I don't shush her up. Given the circumstances, her words fit the bill.

I shed my coat and swap my shoes for a pair of fuzzy slippers my mother keeps in the hall closet. They feel like home, which is where I want to be right now. We go into the kitchen, the heart of this house, and Mom tells me my grandmother is upstairs. "She's not feeling well, so she probably won't join us for lunch."

"When has she ever?" Malcolm says to me under his breath. He's at the kitchen island with a glass of beer. My mother, who can hear a sparrow fart during a thunderstorm, glares at him.

"You're not serious about sending Freddie off to one of those schools," my father says, slicing cold cuts. He punctuates every other word with a stab of his knife. "Monthly testing in the first grade was bad enough, but I thought we left segregation behind a while ago."

Malcolm ignores the stabs. "All for the good, Gerhard."

Dad stops slicing. "Giving a nine-year-old a lower—whaddaya call it, Q?—because she fails a test is supposed to be good? What are they testing them on anyway?" In a sweeter voice: "Girls, how about you go find Polly and give her a treat?" The girls disappear out the back door with Milk-Bones; Anne looks over her shoulder nervously before shutting it.

"Do you know, Malcolm"—my father starts up again—"how many children were imprisoned in this country's so-called state schools in the twentieth century?"

Malcolm sets his glass down, a little too loudly. "No one put kids in prison, Gerhard. And don't you dare go filling the girls' heads with your misinformation."

My father straightens, pulling himself up until he's every inch of his six feet. I don't think I've ever seen him this tall. Or this mad. His nostrils, at the same level as Malcolm's eyes, flare. It wouldn't surprise me at all if the next words out of his mouth were something like "How about we take this outside?"

Mom has been icing a cake with chocolate buttercream, Freddie's favorite, and takes the heat in the kitchen down a notch. "It isn't misinformation, Malcolm. Where I grew up in Massachusetts, there was one of those schools not so far from Boston. They called it the Fernald School for Idiotic Children. Seriously, idiotic children? Sounds like a paradise."

"No one's complained so far," Malcolm says. My father doesn't say a word, but his fists tighten, and the muscles in his forearms stand out like cords.

"No one ever does until it happens to them," my mother says, offering me the icing knife to lick clean. "You know the old story about boiling the frog? If you put the frog in a pot of boiling water, he'll jump out." She silences Malcolm with a hand and smiles. "If, on the other hand, you put the frog in a pot of cold water and turn up the heat one degree at a time, well, before long you'll have a boiled frog. And he'll never know what's coming." Then, taking my father's hand in her own, she says, "Our parents saw the frog boil in Germany. One degree at a time."

The back door swings open and Polly races in behind the girls, tail wagging. The conversation shifts to a lighter topic.

But the air in the kitchen still weighs heavy.

SEVENTEEN

I leave my family in the kitchen, four people I love and one I don't, and head back to the front of the house, to the stairs leading up to my old room. Copies of diplomas hang in the same place they always have, a staggered staircase arrangement of overembellished fonts and hastily scrawled signatures of deans and registrars. Yale first, then Penn, then Johns Hopkins—my pedigree in three frames.

My feet move automatically, up the first five steps, past this testament to my accomplishments. For a few seconds, I'm in grade school again, running up these steps two at a time, latest drawing clutched in one hand, a smile as wide as the Chesapeake Bay spreading across my face. At the time, I thought, *I want to be just like Oma*. I thought, *I will be just like her*.

The noises from downstairs are familiar: my parents dancing between English and German, talking about how tall their granddaughter has grown since summer; Freddie giggling at the unfamiliar gutturals and fricatives, trying to mimic them; Anne speaking more fluently. And Malcolm's feet pacing as he decides whether sitting down would put him at some emasculating disadvantage on the familial battlefield.

"Leni?"

The voice floats down from the top stair, at once frail and forceful. I turn toward it.

No, that's not right. It *pulls* me, reeling me in on invisible lines.

"Leni?" it says again. The nickname Oma gave me forty years ago is one I've never liked. It reminds me too much of that old filmmaker, the one with the unpronounceable last name and the legacy of propaganda choreographed to Wagner arias. My grandmother assures me there are more than two women named Leni in the world.

When I reach the final step, Oma holds out a hand, palm up, silver rings turning all the wrong ways on fingers that have grown too lean. No. Lean is a kind way to put it. My hundred-year-old grandmother looks something like death as she leans on her cane, her free hand gripping the banister for extra support. When I reach out and she falls into me, she weighs as much as a sigh.

I say the first thing that comes to mind. "They're taking my baby."

"I heard." She taps her left ear. "They gave me new ears a few weeks ago. Cost a fortune."

Then I'm crying. We melt into a puddle of arms and legs on the top stair, this old woman cradling me like she did when I was a sick child. There's a nasty taste rising in my mouth as I think of Freddie's future mapped out, of a yellow bus coming to drive her along a path that's anything but a yellow brick road, of my daughter about to be lost to a system I helped create—one stuck-up bitchy comment and one shiny gold privilege card at a time.

Oma waits until I've stopped heaving, then speaks. "Tell me about these yellow buses. Where do they go?"

"Kansas." The voice that says this word isn't my own. Malcolm has stopped his absent pacing and parked himself halfway up the staircase. "Hello, Maria," he says. The words might sound kind from anyone else's lips. "You look well."

"I look like death," she says. "There's no need to lie."

His eyes seem to agree with her, and he cringes. Not much, but enough for me to catch the distaste in his eyes. Still, I'm thankful he hasn't used one of his more colorful words: *old, feeble, burden on your children*. My foot, a few easy inches from his gabardine-encased groin, might just find its way to an unpleasant target. The thought makes me smile.

"Well," he says, "I'll let you two catch up."

"You do that, Malcolm," I say.

And he leaves, returning to ignore my parents and his younger daughter.

"Still the happy married couple," Oma says. It's somewhere between a statement and a question, and I don't miss the sarcasm in her voice.

"Not really. What happened to you? You look like you haven't eaten in a month." I take one of her hands in mine, examine the brittle, ragged nails, the cracked skin stretched taut over knucklebones. Oma's hair has changed, too, since I last saw her, and when I brush a lock from her unshadowed, unlined eyes, a few strands come away in my fingers before settling on the stair runner.

She's shedding, I think. *Like a malnourished stray.*

"I've lived too long, *Liebchen*," she says.

"Nonsense."

"It's the truth. I've lived too long, and I've seen too much. Now help me up, *Liebchen*. I want to show you something while we're alone."

Oma and I walk down the upstairs hall to her room, a room that used to be mine, with windows overlooking the back garden and, farther past it, the endless rows of new houses. With my help, she arranges herself in a chintz wing chair, and asks me to bring over the ottoman for her legs. Her ankles have disappeared altogether, they're so swollen.

So this is what old age looks like.

"Oh, Oma," I say.

She waves a hand in the air, a delicate gesture but dismissive all the same. "Enough of that. Go open the cedar chest in the corner and bring me the blue box—no, not that one. The bigger one, nearer to the bottom."

I do as I'm told, resting the box in her lap. It's tied loosely with fraying twine, and she tugs at one of the ends until the bow is nothing more than a pile of curled string. The loops make me think of fat Qs, their tails tentacles.

"You lift the lid for me," she says, her hands falling limply to her sides as if they have had enough work for one day.

And so I do.

Inside the box are neatly pressed and folded layers of material, blue wool and white cotton. A black necktie lies coiled at one side, its edges worried by dry rot. I can't imagine why Oma wants me to see her old uniform, not after all these years.

"This was your school uniform?" I say, fingering the coarse blue wool of the skirt.

"It was a uniform," she says. "But not for school." Oma still pronounces the soft *sh* at the beginning of the word. "Take it out if you like. The shoes are in a bigger box in the chest."

I unfold the items one by one, first the white poplin blouse, which against the bedspread reveals itself to be not white but an aged yellow. I lay the skirt with its center pleat over the blouse's tails and uncoil the necktie. It's brittle, and fine black powder rains down on my hands.

"Now the shoes, *Liebchen*. The marching *Schuhe*."

"Oma? Are you okay?"

"The *SCHUHE*, girl! Get them." She strikes the floor once with her cane, hard.

From the heavy second box I take a pair of stiff black lace-ups. When I set them down on the hardwood, the sound gives away their secret—on the heel and toe each is a horseshoe-shaped metal plate, like a tap.

"You see now, Leni?" Oma says.

I don't see at all. Unless my grandmother is trying to tell me she was in a strange kind of militaristic tap-dancing troupe in 1930-something. My hands run over the material, sensing the different textures, feeling the round edges of the blouse's buttons. Each one is embossed with letters.

"What's BDM and JM?" I say. "Your school?"

Instead of answering, she orders me to sit down. "I'm going to tell you something, Leni. Something I have never told anyone. Not even your father."

"Okay." The sound of her voice makes me wonder whether I want to know.

Oma relaxes back into the chair, loosens the grip on her cane, and starts to talk.

"I knew a girl when I was young. She wasn't poor—her family was quite wealthy. Her father worked as a doctor, and her mother taught mathematics in the *Gymnasium* in my town. And Miriam and I were very good friends." Oma's eyes begin to shine. "Very good friends. Like sisters." Her eyes shine even brighter, and I don't ask whether she still knows Miriam, or where Miriam is. "My father and my great-uncle made me join the Bund Deutscher Mädel as soon as I was old enough. I think you know what that means, yes?"

I work out the German. "Band of German something."

"In English, they called it the League of German Girls." She nods toward the clothing laid out on the bed. "My father bought me the uniform and the shoes. I didn't like it at first, but for my birthday that year he made me a present of the special taps and he sent me to the shoemaker to have them put on. And you know what?"

"No."

"I liked it. I wore the uniform every day to the activities after school and to the evening meetings. After a while, I started wearing it to school also. As did many of the other girls. Will you get me some juice from the little fridge?"

I find a can of apple juice and pour it out. Oma sips greedily, and her voice takes back some of its smoothness when she resumes talking.

"School became very different. After the uniforms. Girls who used to skip the rope and play other games together began to separate. My father told me I was not to speak to Miriam while I was wearing the BDM clothing." She laughs the kind of laugh with no humor in it. "It did not matter. Miriam had long stopped speaking to me."

There's a long pause.

"What happened to Miriam?" I say when the pause has stretched out until it's no longer comfortable.

"I don't know." Oma's eyes flick once to the window before coming back to me. "No. I do not know. After, I joined the local Glaube und Schönheit group, and I began to study art." Another laugh. "Faith and beauty. It is funny that none of my art ended up being beautiful." Her eyes sweep the far wall of the room.

I follow them.

Most of Oma's paintings are shades of gray and black, abstract depictions of walls and fences, the images of separation. They make me wonder what kind of art I would have created had I listened to my heart instead of my husband.

EIGHTEEN

THEN:

I sat in the back room, where my father had knocked a new window through the wall when he made me a studio of my own. The studio wasn't mine anymore, not full-time, but I used it when I came back home during summers, or when I escaped the chill of Connecticut Februaries for the—slightly—more temperate weather of Maryland over spring breaks. This room was warm in the winter with its humming radiators, cool in the summer when the wind blew through the screen of the open window, and damn near perfect on this November day.

I should have been poring over art history texts, boning up on the Pre-Raphaelite masters before Thanksgiving vacation was over, but the blank canvas called out to me, almost begging for color.

Malcolm came by in the morning, also back from college. He kissed me lightly and took my left hand. "You really want to wear your ring while you paint, El?" Then, looking at my work in progress: "What the hell is that?"

"First," I said, "the ring's washable. Second, this is art. Like it?"

A shake of his head told me he didn't. Not one bit.

"Good thing I got you out of the postmodernist world and back into the real one, hon." He bent his head, first to the right, then left, then back to middle. "What's it supposed to be?"

"Sex."

"Good sex or bad sex?" Now he was nearly upside down, trying to make sense of the swirls of red and orange.

"Good," I said. And blushed.

He sat in the chair my grandmother often occupied. It didn't fit him well, not with its size or floral-patterned chintz. But then, nothing ever seemed to fit Malcolm Fairchild, not naturally. He simply adapted the world to his own ways, forcing it to fit.

"I've got news," he said.

"Good news or bad news?"

"Excellent news."

I put down my brush and wiped my hands on a rag. I had news, too. Oma had exchanged emails with a former colleague down at the Savannah School of Art and Design. We were driving to Georgia on Saturday to talk about graduate school. I started to tell Malcolm, and we started to speak at the same time. We laughed.

"You first," he said.

"No. You go first."

It was always like this between us, more so in the year we'd been engaged.

Now he stood and took my paint-smeared hands in his own. "I've decided on a master's program."

"Okay—"

"Aren't you going to ask me where?"

His pout was almost cute, so I took the bait. "Where?"

"Penn!" Before I could say anything, he went on. "They've got a rock-star ed school, El. Combine that with poli-sci, and I can write my own ticket. And—if you still want to think about my little idea—

83

a great life science program for you. We could get an apartment downtown, save up, and get married like we talked about."

We had talked about it. But between the summer and now, other things had happened. I'd been painting more, stretching myself into new forms. I'd gotten a piece into a juried show in New Haven. I'd been invited to Savannah. "I—"

Malcolm held his hands up. "Wait. Just wait until you hear me out, honey."

I waited.

He took a magazine out of his coat pocket and flipped it open to an article in the middle. "Science, tech, engineering, and math. They're pouring money into it, El. Guaranteed bucketloads. And by the time I'm where I want to be, there'll be more money for the top-tier STEM schools. The only thing is you have to be good enough to teach at one. And you have to stay good enough. But you will. I know you will." He hugged me then, a long hug. "My brilliant wife-to-be."

I think it was fear that swayed me, fear I'd never paint anything worthy of a real gallery, that I'd be stuck teaching like Oma. Did I want to watch and wait for one of my own students to strike gold in the art circuit, see myself occasionally mentioned—if it was mentioned at all—on a line in someone else's biography? I saw an older version of myself, living on the generosity of my own children, and I didn't like this vision.

We had lunch with my parents and my grandmother. Oma seemed surprised when I waffled on the subject of Saturday's trip down south. I manufactured a lie about a project I needed to catch up on, making it sound as if I'd have to stay glued to textbooks for the weekend, which meant I ended up staying away from my studio. The unfinished canvas was still there on Sunday when Dad drove me to the airport, and Oma's smile as she kissed me goodbye couldn't hide the disappointment in her eyes.

Four days after Thanksgiving, I switched my major from art to life science.

It had been Malcolm's suggestion. "Only a suggestion. You can be anything you want," he'd said. But when I thought of the money I could make teaching in one of the new silver schools, I leaped at it. No more struggling, no more pinching pennies to cover the electric bill. We'd fit into the world, and make the world fit us. We'd create our very own master class.

NINETEEN

Oma finishes her apple juice and leans back into the chair, obviously tired.

"You must stop thinking about these Qs. Or," she says, "perhaps you must learn to think of them in another way. Think of them as questions you need to ask. And think about whether you want to send your daughter to one of these new schools."

"They're not the same thing as the—" I don't know how to say it, so I don't. "As the places where you were born."

"You don't think so, *Liebchen*?"

"Of course not." It's laughable, really. Oma has a good heart, but she's always been prone to that certain hyperbole that comes with age.

She waves me away, as if she senses my ridicule and sees the disbelief in my eyes. "I'll tell you more. When you are ready to hear it. Now, I am ready for my nap. Please put those . . . things back for me."

From the kitchen, Mom calls me to lunch, and smells of *Rouladen* and seasoned *Blaukraut* waft up.

"Okay, Oma. After lunch, I'll come back up," I say, leaving her in the chair and folding up the uniform. My grandmother is already asleep by the time I put everything back into the cedar chest and pull her door closed.

When I reach the top of the stairs, I see Malcolm staring up at me from below.

"Get your coat, Elena. And Freddie's and Anne's," he says, as if he's speaking to his admin assistant or the kid he hired as an intern a few months ago. And then, before I can say a word: "Now."

I've never been afraid of Malcolm, never been intimidated by him the way others are, the way Freddie is when he uses "Daddy's scary voice," as she calls it when he's not around. Still, my body shrinks back against the wall, my limbs weak and almost jelly-like. Because his voice *is* scary in its definiteness.

Funny how I never realized this before now.

"We're having lunch, Malcolm. My mother's cooked it, and we're eating it." For effect, I add, "Now." I want to walk toward him while I speak, but my legs aren't up to the task. Not yet. So I square my shoulders and lift my chin, a small gesture that tells him I won't be backed down in this Mexican standoff.

It doesn't work.

Malcolm disappears into the little vestibule at the front of the house and reappears with three coats and three pairs of shoes. "We'll eat at home today. And tomorrow. Just the four of us." He sounds pleased with the prospect, and I wonder if he's imagining I buy into his bullshit the same way I used to. Back then, I did buy into it. I gobbled up his snobbery and swallowed it whole, like some urban whore turning tricks in a cheap room, selling herself for cash, a fix, approval.

We stare at each other for a long minute, and I know he's been listening from the bottom of the stairs. Nothing to do now but bundle up and walk out the door with him, this husband I'm told I need. This husband I loathe.

Or.

I could refuse. I could put my foot down and stay here with Mom and Dad and Oma, turn back invisible hands on an invisible clock and live the life I used to live, but differently, with only Freddie. But Anne catches me musing and gives me a pleading look. She's my daughter as much as Freddie is. I can't unconceive her, and I can't give her up.

"What's this?" Mom has come tripping into the living room, apron still on, a cloud of flour dust sparkling around her in the shaft of afternoon sun. Freddie's behind her, holding twin apron strings and giggling.

I love Freddie this way.

"Malcolm wants to go home," I tell Mom, and Freddie's giggles stop, like someone has just thrown a switch.

"Before lunch? I've just sliced up half a salami." If there's a true evil in the world according to the Gospel of Sandra Fischer, it's an over-abundance of already-sliced cold cuts. My mother, a child of a child of a long-ago depression, hates waste. "Stay. Have lunch. You can go home after."

Freddie is down on the carpet, an old frayed and sun-faded remnant from my mother's first home, before Malcolm has the chance to open his mouth. She's started her rocking routine, shutting out the world around her, keeping all hurt at bay.

"Christ," Malcolm says. "Again?"

And then, loud and clear and horrible, he says the worst thing I can imagine.

"This is why she needs to go, Elena. She's not right in the head."

Every limb in my body seems to respond at the same time. My feet carry me down five steps in what feels like a single movement. My left arm arcs backward, part of me and not part of me at once. My mouth opens and forms the syllables of "bastard" as a fist I didn't know I was capable of strikes Malcolm squarely in the jaw, slanting off, hurting.

Malcolm says nothing, only pushes a bundle of coats and shoes into my chest. They're heavy, but not as heavy as my rage.

"You fucking son of a bitch," I whisper.

And I know now that, one way or another, we're over.

It takes me thirty minutes to get Freddie's coat and shoes on.

Malcolm waits in the vestibule, tapping his Bruno Magli–clad foot and scowling. My parents and Anne stand quietly in a corner of the living room, deliberately not making anxiety-inducing eye contact with Freddie, although Dad turns toward the front door every few seconds to toss an icy glance at Malcolm.

"It's all right, baby," I say in my soft voice, a voice that struggles to emerge as my ugly voice, the one I want to use toward my husband, boils up and battles for control. "Ice cream at home. And then we'll watch the movie about the princess, okay?"

Ice cream and princesses are the last fucking things on my mind. Brass knuckles and Amazon warriors, though, yeah.

Finally, Freddie's settled.

"Go on and kiss your Oma and Opa now." I want to bring her upstairs to kiss her great-grandmother goodbye, but Malcolm has already opened the front door, letting a chilly breeze in. As if it weren't cold enough in the house.

Now it's my turn to make the rounds. They're less permanent, as I know I'll be seeing my parents and grandmother before long, probably next weekend. Probably sooner than that, since the thought of spending one more second than necessary with Malcolm tastes like yellow bile.

It's cute how wrong I am, and how I don't even know it. Not yet.

I shrug my coat on and trade soft slippers for my hard leather shoes, imagining them as combat boots I'll need for the ride home. Malcolm leads our unhappy little parade out to the car: him, then Freddie and Anne, then me.

And then a blur of terry cloth and gray hair emerges from the doorway. My grandmother.

She's almost running toward me on two legs and a cane, reaching out to the coat on my back with her other hand, clawing.

"Don't let her go, Leni. Whatever you have to do, don't let her go to that . . . place." Another word lingered on her lips. Nearly another week will pass before I understand the full weight and meaning of the word she stifled.

"What am I supposed to do about it?" I say. "It's the law."

Oma yells to Malcolm to wait with a force that surprises everyone. She pulls me close and asks me one question: "Do you want Freddie in a prison?"

"What?"

"You heard me."

"No."

Malcolm, already at the driver-side door, honks. The sound of it hurts my bones.

"No," I say again.

Oma squares herself, bony shoulders rising as if she's preparing for battle, as if she's back in her old uniform giving marching orders to younger girls. "Then you'll have to go with her," she whispers, and she kisses me full on the lips, hard, like she did when I was small.

The horn blares again.

TWENTY

My grandmother has to be exaggerating, I think, as Malcolm winds us back the way we came. Has to be.

I know about the state schools from documents Malcolm has in his study, from still pictures that flash on the screen during Madeleine Sinclair's weekly broadcasts. They aren't home, but they look clean, and the kids in them smile their way through jump rope and hopscotch and team sports. Visiting parents lay out picnic blankets on thick patches of green and snap selfies to bring back home to grandmothers and aunts. The adults, the teachers, pause at each cluster of families, stopping to chat and answer questions.

Still, my own grandmother is comparing our yellow schools to work camps.

I don't talk to Malcolm on the ride home because I don't have anything to say. I also don't expect he'll break the silence, but that's exactly what he does.

"You need to climb aboard the commonsense train, Elena." His eyes are fixed ahead of him, on that double yellow line (*yellow bus,* I think), and his knuckles shine pale white as they clench the steering wheel. On his right cheek there's a purplish bruise blooming. No blood, though. I kind of wish there were blood.

"I don't think I like the commonsense train anymore, Malcolm," I say between clenched teeth. In the side mirror to my right, I can see Freddie in the backseat. She's counting telephone poles. Or mile marker signs. Counting something, anyway. It's just as well. Anne has put her phone away and sits silent, listening.

Malcolm taps the wheel with his fingertips. If he were anyone else, I'd take it as a nervous twitch, but he isn't anyone else. He's Malcolm Fairchild, PH-fucking-D, and Dr. Fairchild never twitches nervously. He's only tapping out the words he's about to say before they escape his mouth.

About fifteen minutes from home, we turn off the main road, and the tapping stops.

"Your grandmother is old and prone to exaggerate."

"Maybe. But I don't want Freddie going to a state school."

Now he slams his palm against the steering wheel. "Do you even stop to think how"—he jerks his head back slightly, toward Freddie—"breaking the rules for her would affect me? My career?"

My back's up now. "I don't know, Malcolm. Do you stop to think about your own daughter?"

"It's for the best."

"For the best," Freddie echoes from the backseat. "All for the best. Best, best, best." Then she goes silent again and returns to counting telephone poles.

"See what I mean?" says Malcolm.

When Freddie was five, I thought she was on the autism spectrum, maybe far off to one side of it but still on the spectrum. She simply wasn't paying attention, wasn't focusing. Several hours of testing and consulting, and several hundreds of dollars later, our pediatrician shook her head.

"Asperger's?" I asked.

"That's still on the spectrum, so I don't think so," she told me. "I'd be pushing the envelope with that diagnosis."

"Then what's wrong with her?" I asked. Even now, I want to bite my tongue when I hear myself saying it. *Wrong.* Like my daughter is some broken mechanism that needs to be fixed.

Dr. Nguyen laughed, not unkindly, and glanced toward the kids' play area, where Freddie was building a tower of blocks. "Nothing's wrong. Freddie's a little anxious, that's all. She'll grow out of it."

"Am I—are we—supposed to do anything? I mean, sometimes she curls up and blocks the world out," I said. "Plus, she repeats things. Like an echo."

Again, the doctor chuckled. "What do you want to do? Treat her like glass?" She put a hand on my arm. "Treat her like a little girl. That's what she is. Maybe a bit nervous." She scribbled an illegible prescription on the pad from her desk. "We'll try a low dose of Paxil for now. It's a serotonin reuptake inhibitor."

I knew what that was, and I didn't like the sound of it. "You think she's depressed?"

"No. No, I don't. I think Freddie worries more than some children her age. And the worry means her head is full, and a full head means she has trouble paying attention. We're going to target the worry, not the attention-paying, okay?" Dr. Nguyen looked at her watch, and I knew it was time to go.

Now, in the car, I turn to Malcolm. "What if she just needs a higher dose of meds? Can we try that? Can't you get some sort of—I don't know—stay or whatever you call it? Get her retested next month." Even as I said the words, I knew this scheme would never work. It didn't matter whether Malcolm agreed or not. If Freddie felt the pressure of another testing day in four weeks' time, who knows what kind of meltdown would ensue? Also, I hate the desperation in my voice. The begging. "Never mind."

Besides, I want to steer the conversation away from tests before another fight happens. Freddie's been holding her head above water, barely, but always able to keep her Q score hovering around 8.3. Of course, Malcolm doesn't know about the hours I spend with her at my parents' house before the exams, doesn't know about the extra dose of selective serotonin reuptake-whatevers I dose Freddie with. It's better for all of us if the word "test" is absent from our conversations.

I come back to my grandmother's question. "What if I asked for a transfer?"

Malcolm's knuckles relax somewhat as he turns the car into our driveway. My tone must have done it; he must think all the anger has drained out of me because he's doing that thing with his palm flat on the steering wheel. This is Relaxed Malcolm. Not someone I see much of. It makes me wonder how much he and Freddie have in common.

"Transfer where? You don't like the Davenport School anymore?" He kills the engine and gets out, not bothering to come around to the side door. "There's another silver school, but it's farther away. It would double your commute."

"I was thinking about one of the green schools. Or even a state school." I untangle Freddie's coat from the seat belt and let her run off by herself to the back door.

Malcolm only stares at me.

"Well?"

"Out of the question, Elena."

"Why?"

"For one thing, Anne and I need you at home. Which is the only reason I'm letting you off the hook for that scene you pulled earlier." He touches a finger to his face casually, as if I'd thwacked him with a kid glove instead of laying on my left hook. "And then there's the other issue."

I already know what the other issue is. *The Other Issue*, if I say the words the way Malcolm pronounces them. The Other Issue is that if I left, I'd be in the same position as Moira Campbell down the street.

Malcolm's protected from the gray women with the clipboards, the ones who troll neighborhoods in search of "unfit" families. He pulls enough in annually that he'll be able to keep custody of Anne and Freddie. I don't.

As usual, justice boils down to how high you can keep your Q rating.

As usual, your Q depends on how quickly you've climbed aboard the commonsense train.

TWENTY-ONE

Instead of sharing Malcolm's bed tonight, I share Freddie's again. It's a twin, and I have to curl my arms and legs around her so we both fit. The result is something womb-like, me wrapping myself around my daughter's thin frame as if I could draw her back inside me and shut out the world. As if I could unweave reality one strand at a time and turn it into a prettier tapestry.

She stirs and snuggles closer. Maybe Freddie's trying to crawl back inside, too.

Then, out of the blue, a question. "Do you love Daddy?"

I can't lie. And I can't tell her how things really are. So I dodge. "I did once."

"But not anymore."

Out of the mouths of babes come brutally honest truths.

Before I can answer, Freddie asks another question. "Why did you love him?"

The bedtime story I could tell her would start like this: Once upon a time, Elena was a stupid little shit. I could tell her about the games Malcolm and I used to play when we were a shade past Freddie's own age, how we tore the school population into good, better, and best with our silly colored-card idea.

Guilt has a foul taste to it. A sewer-like taste, black and rotten, rises in the back of my throat.

Freddie's voice, small as it is, snaps me back to the now. "Maybe you'll stop loving me, too."

"No, honey. Never."

She drifts off to sleep, that glorious place of escape where nothing can hurt us. I stay awake and stare at the darkness over me, tossing her nonquestion around for hours. At midnight, I've had enough, and I go upstairs to my office.

The first search string I type in returns pages and pages on the Bund Deutscher Mädel. There's a second part to the name, and I don't need Google to translate it for me.

In der Hitler Jugend.

My grandmother was a Hitler Youth girl.

I click on images, and within seconds copies of Oma's uniform flash up on the monitor. Inside the uniforms are girls, blond and fit and beautiful, smiling broadly at the camera. There are photos of girls marching, skipping rope, running across sandy beaches. There are photos of girls lined up like soldiers, heads held high as if they are looking into their own futures.

There are photos of girls with their right arms raised in salute.

Oh, Oma, I think. *Did you know? Did you know where it would all end up?*

These are pictures I don't want to look at, but like the gory scenes in a horror film, I can't help but stare at one after the other, sifting through slideshows in archive sites, wondering if one of the blondes is named Maria, if one of them had a childhood friend named Miriam. I'm so lost in thought I don't even hear him behind me.

"What are you doing, Elena?"

Malcolm is in the doorway, just two steps away. I close the browser windows quickly, but it's too late. I should have been facing the door, should have pulled up school reports or grading spreadsheets or solitaire. Anything but this blank laptop that reveals I have no answer to his question other than the truth.

So I say nothing.

I expect him to lecture me, tell me my grandmother is filling my head with propaganda and sensationalism, but Malcolm acts as if I've done nothing wrong.

"Come to bed. I'm having breakfast with Alex tomorrow, and you're joining us," he says.

"I'd really rather spend the day with Freddie, I think."

He smiles. "You can do that. After breakfast. We'll be back by ten."

I hate Malcolm's tennis pro/doctor friend Alex. He's smarmy, and he looks at me as if I'm something to eat whenever he's at our house.

"I don't want to," I say, trying to think of an excuse.

A firm hand grips my shoulder. "I don't care. You're coming to breakfast, and we're spending the day together. All of it." He pauses, and his smile turns sour. "I can divorce you like that," he says, snapping his fingers. The sound in the sparsely furnished office is crisp and clean, a breaking sound. He doesn't need to spell out the rest, mention the words "sole custody" or "demotion." With his left hand still on my shoulder, Malcolm reaches around and shuts down my computer. End of discussion.

It's two in the morning when we pass Anne's and Freddie's bedrooms on the way to our own. Behind each closed door, there is crying.

TWENTY-TWO

I don't know where the weekend went.

They say time is constant, steady, always moving at the same pace. But that's a bald lie. Any child knows time slows down in the days before Christmas; any bride knows time speeds up during a wedding reception. And any mother knows time flies in the years after she gives birth. Eight pounds become forty pounds become a hundred pounds. If they could just stay little till their Carter's wear out, like the jingle sang.

Freddie's suitcase is light for me, but her muscles strain when she tries to pick it up.

"Roll it, sweetie," I tell her and pop up the extension handle. The sound of wheels as she pulls it across a bare patch of hardwood floor is like thunder.

Anne takes over, showing her younger sister how to roll the suitcase. Her iPad has been off since Saturday, and I haven't heard a word about which boy has which Q, or the homecoming dance. Or really anything at all. She's stayed glued to her sister all weekend, which somehow makes everything worse.

Malcolm, who's made the generous paternal gesture of going into work late on Monday morning, gives Freddie a hug and pats her head.

"Be a good girl, now, and study hard. We'll come visit at Christmas, okay?"

The way he puts it, anyone would think we were packing off our youngest daughter to an elite Swiss boarding school.

"Okay, Dad," Freddie says. Her eyes don't match the stiff smile she's plastered on. They're wide, like the eyes of a frightened dog.

My hall clock chimes its six thirty bells at the same time as Anne's iPad and the alarm clock in the kitchen ping their own warnings. Reluctantly, Anne shoulders her backpack and goes to the front door. She'll come home to a family of three this afternoon, and she knows it.

"I feel sick today," Anne says. The silver bus outside idles, and the fembot voice calls out in her machine voice, *Davenport Silver School students, this is your final call. Davenport Silver School bus is ready to depart. Final call for Davenport Silver School.*

"Anne," Malcolm says, and that one word pushes my older daughter outside.

Now we wait. The green bus rolls up to the end of the street as Freddie watches through the window, silent. And we wait some more.

"Time to go, Freddie," I say, and we walk out the front door together, Freddie hunched and focused on each mortar line between the bricks of the path leading from our house.

The scared girl, the one Anne said was fine a few days ago but who looks anything but fine today, leans against a car, arms folded and head down. No crimson pleated skirt and jacket today, no backpack bursting with books. An olive green soft-sided suitcase sits on the sidewalk next to her. Sabrina.

Whoever drove the girl today waits in the car, a steel gray SUV, new-model Lexus. I think it's a woman from the size of the shape, but it's hard to tell because that shape is hunched over, head bent onto the steering wheel, shoulders moving in a jagged rhythm. Sabrina stares down at the sidewalk, a yellow card clenched in her fist.

They get them out right away, those yellow cards. Freddie's arrived yesterday by courier in a padded manila envelope addressed to the Fairchild Household. In the upper left corner was the sunshiny emblem of the Fitter Family Campaign, a silhouette of three figures with something that looked like a halo around the smallest figure's head. To me, it was more like a crown of thorns.

Another thing I know about Sabrina: She's gone from a silver school to a state school without passing through green. Kind of like getting booted out of heaven and finding yourself tumbling all the way down to the eternal inferno, skipping through the slight hope of purgatory. As Judy Green did last week.

This new and sudden shift in the way things work makes me more uneasy. We have rules, systems, well-oiled machinery that, even if some of us hate the product, at least we know what the machine spits out, when and where the widget drops onto the production line. Yellow buses make their rounds once a month, always on the Monday after testing day. Silver school kids who fail bump down to green schools. This is how the machine works.

The machine didn't always function this way. All buses were the same color. All children went to the same schools. People went to graduate school and studied what they wanted instead of what they were told was necessary for the greater good.

Before I let Malcolm persuade me to switch to the more lucrative field of life science, I sampled everything college offered. Philosophy, literature, classics. There was a poster in my Latin class of an elephant who had just taken a dump with *Stercus Accidit!* at the bottom in bright yellow letters—the professor's idea of a Latin joke. But now that I think of that poster, I realize the image was completely wrong. Shit doesn't happen all at once; no invisible elephant unloads a pile right where you're about to step. What happens is this: Some bunny rabbit lets a little pellet drop. Then another one. Then another. You don't worry much because the bunny's cute and the pellets are small, easily brushed away.

Stercus accidit. A little bit at a time. Usually while we're not paying attention. Like my mother's story about the frog in the boiling pot.

"Hi," Freddie says as we approach the waiting car.

"Hi," says Sabrina.

And now we wait again.

Behind us, Mrs. Delacroix's curtains shift slightly to the left as she sets herself up to watch the morning's events. In the houses on either side of hers, things are less subtle. Blinds roll up with an audible snap. Mrs. Morris pretends to be dusting a windowsill. Mrs. Callahan sprays Windex on the same pane five times, rubbing at squeaky-clean glass with a new paper towel after each squirt. Every one of them joined Sarah Green's social engineering campaign some years back.

Enjoy the show, ladies. Fuckwits.

Freddie takes out her phone and starts tapping chickens across traffic-filled roads, her way of escaping into another reality. I let her play— anything to prevent one of her meltdowns. Sabrina continues staring at the sidewalk as if it were a work of art. The figure in the SUV's driver's seat steps out, lights a cigarette (it takes her three tries before she finally makes the flame meet the end of it), and looks at me hard.

"You're that Fairchild asshole's wife, aren't you?"

"Yes." I don't add, *For the time being.*

Sabrina's mother draws heavily on her smoke, exhaling in my face. "That's for him, bless his heart."

You have to grow up in the south, or at least spend time there, to get the fact that "bless your heart" isn't exactly a polite way of wishing someone well. Quite the opposite, actually. I wave a cloud of smoke away and stand next to Freddie as the yellow bus rumbles around the corner. More indistinguishable shapes of various sizes press against the windows.

"Get back in the car, Sabrina," Mrs. Sabrina says. "We're going home. And I don't care what happens to your brothers' Q scores. We'll move. We'll go somewhere sane." She says this last bit with her eyes on me.

Sabrina only stands there, looking down. She shakes her head once, then twice. "I have to go, Mom."

"No. You. Don't."

"You don't understand. I do have to."

"Enough. Come on, girl," Mrs. Sabrina says, pushing her daughter inside and pulling her seat belt on before running around the front and getting in herself. The engine purrs to life.

There's an elementary physics lesson; I know of it from proctoring years of tests. The idea is this: To effect change, you require force. And force is exactly what comes pouring out of the Lexus as Sabrina tumbles out of the car, shouting at her mother to go away as the yellow bus blasts its first sharp honk into the neighborhood.

What happens next happens fast. Sabrina running to where her suitcase sits on the sidewalk. Mrs. Sabrina stalling the Lexus's engine as she tries to reverse. Sabrina scrambling toward the yawning door of the yellow bus, stumbling. Mrs. Sabrina leaving the car, careering blindly in the direction of her daughter, grasping for purchase on Sabrina's jacket and coming away with fistfuls of air.

It's as if the girl wants to go.

For a ridiculous moment, I'm thinking of that old movie with the Child Catcher, wondering why anyone would want to board his horrible little wagon with its iron bars while desperate mothers are screaming in the streets.

Mrs. Delacroix and Mrs. Morris and Mrs. Callahan are still at their windows, watching. I yell at them to mind their own business, and there's a clattering of window blinds as, one by one, the women roll them down. There's something in the sound of those blinds being released from their prisons with the flick of a finger. Something that sounds like a collective sigh of apathy.

Suddenly I'm back in another school board meeting with Malcolm, six-year-old Anne at home with the babysitter, listening to the questions and complaints coming from the audience of concerned parents, tired teachers, and frustrated community ombudsmen led by Sarah Green from up the street.

My kid's teacher spends more time on the ones who can't read.

I can't do another round of summer school this year. I just can't.

Do we really have room in the budget for more sign language interpreters and ESL specialists?

And, finally:

Can't we just put them somewhere else?

The second time the bus honks, Freddie begins to shake her head with such violence I'm worried her neck might snap. Can that happen? Is it physically possible to break your own neck?

I don't know. But I know one thing. I'm taking her back inside.

TWENTY-THREE

And now I discover why my husband stayed home this morning.

Before we've crossed the street, Malcolm is outside, hands buttoning up his coat as he walks toward us with the kind of smile he reserves for his older daughter.

"What's this?" he says, scooping Freddie up into his arms. "What's all this about?" When Freddie doesn't respond, he coaxes her. It's a sound like wooing. "There, now, Frederica. You can tell me."

She snuffles once, a deep and choked inhalation of tears and snot and phlegm. Malcolm's smile fades, and his eyes register disgust I wouldn't think possible from a father.

"I want to stay here with Mom and Anne," she says finally.

My own eyes plead with Malcolm from behind her. They say, *Fix this*. They say, *I know you can*. When he speaks, I almost believe he's heard me.

"Now, Frederica," he says. "You can stay with us if you really want to. It's all up to you."

I nearly ask him who put the drugs in his coffee this morning, then think better of it. Freddie has relaxed and quieted, and a wide smile lights up her face as Malcolm carries her to the front porch, away from the idling yellow bus, sits her down on his lap, and begins to speak.

"Do you know what 'progress' means, sweetheart?" he says in his best lecture voice—not too hard, not too soft. A Goldilocks voice. The kind that burrows into unsuspecting ears and defeats defenses without any weaponry.

Freddie nods, sniffs again.

"What does it mean, honey?"

"It's when things get better."

"That's my girl. And we want things to be better, right? We don't want things to get worse."

She nods again.

"Now. If you stay home, they'll take points from Anne's Q score."

I can't believe what I'm hearing. "Malcolm? What the—"

He glares at me. "Don't make me make this worse, Elena."

Freddie's eyes widen. "A lot of points?"

"I don't know. Maybe a little, maybe a lot. You don't want that to happen, do you?"

Oh, Malcolm.

Freddie shakes her head.

"Of course you don't. Anne's got college to think about. And your college years are still a long way off." He sits her up straight so she's facing him. "Now. You love your sister, right?"

"Malcolm, I swear," I say. "Stop this."

He doesn't stop. He keeps going. And he makes it all worse. "You and your mother would have to go live with Oma and Opa."

My daughter doesn't see the wickedness, doesn't realize what's about to come next. The smile on her face changes to trembling lips as she listens to her own father explain.

"You wouldn't see Anne anymore," he says, looking at me, daring

106

me with his eyes to interfere, knowing I'll stay quiet. He's won this round. A knock-down, drag-'em-out finale.

"Never?" Freddie says.

"Never. You don't want that to happen, do you?"

A fast shake of her head.

"And we're all going to do what's best for everyone, okay?"

Another nod.

"Good girl." He stands, takes Freddie by the hand, and wheels her suitcase back across the street to the bus. Mrs. Sabrina is still there, looking blankly up at a backseat window where a cloud of condensation has obscured her daughter's face.

Freddie gives me a final hug and climbs aboard. She takes a seat in the back, near Sabrina, wipes a clear patch with her palm on the window, and waves to us. I can't remember the last time she smiled at her father.

"Oh, Malcolm," I say, smiling on the outside only as I wave to my daughter. "What the hell have you done?"

"Just what you wanted, Elena."

TWENTY-FOUR

The popular girls stood in the short line on Monday, hipshot and chatty, lips shining with gloss. They compared notes on the weekend's parties and football game, adjusted hair that didn't need adjusting every five seconds, and cast sultry, unteenage looks at whichever boys were choice of the week.

I hated every single one of these girls. At the same time, I wanted to be them. I wanted to be part of the "us" crowd, not part of the super-geek, bring-your-own-lunch, never-get-invited-anywhere crowd that sat together at a corner cafeteria table. Jimmy Fawkes, Cheryl Comstock, Roy Shapiro and his pimply girlfriend, Candice Bell— sixteen-year-olds who had nothing in common other than straight As and the shared hatred of the pretty, popular people.

This Monday, though, with Malcolm to my left and Cheryl to my right, I was happy. I was waiting for the shit to hit the fan. When it did, it would hit big-time.

Malcolm sniggered and elbowed me in the side just as pretty Margie Miller reached the lunch counter, tapping her plastic tray with bright pink fingernails. I figured her brain was hurting from trying to decide which flavor of nonfat salad dressing she wanted on her rabbit food.

Well, Margie was in for a surprise.

The new ID cards had rolled out that morning, distributed during homeroom while all the Margie look-alikes flirted with their weekend conquests, and the undesirables like me had their noses in a textbook, cramming for the day's geometry test. I watched Mrs. Parsons hand them out—gold, green, and white—and watched Margie and her crowd slide their new white cards into purses and pockets. The handouts Mrs. Parsons gave out with them ended up on the floor or in a trash bin.

"Watch this," Malcolm said, elbowing me again as Margie ordered.

She had her ID card out, ready to scan, when the lunch server shook her head. "Other line, dear."

Margie looked around. The other line snaked around the far end of the counter, along the wall, and back to the rear of the cafeteria. There might have been a few kids past the doors. It was hard to tell.

"No way," Margie said. "I've only got a half hour before cheering practice."

This time I sniggered along with Malcolm. Roy Shapiro reached across the table and slapped me a high-five. They all knew what was coming, even if Margie didn't.

"White-card holders in line two," the server said. "This line's for the gold and green cards only. New policy."

Margie shook her head. "Starting when?" By now, the cafeteria had gone quiet; only a murmur made its way through the longer line, from front to back, and again in the opposite direction.

"Didn't you get the handout?"

"Freaking ridiculous," Margie said to the other girls in line with her. She twirled, her blue and white skirt belling out, and marched off, tray in hand, fingernails no longer clicking.

Twenty-five minutes went by. We were all back at our corner table after speeding through the express lane, lunch bags forgotten, eating the fruit salads and cheeseburgers and Rice Krispies bars that usually disappeared before our eyes while we were crowded out of the lunch line. On top of a gold ID card, I had extra babysitting money and bought the last of the mixed salads for Candice and myself. I didn't even want the salad, and judging by Candice's fresh sprouting of pimples, she didn't go for the greens, either. But I bought them anyway. Just because I could.

For the first time, I was first.

Margie finally made it to the counter. "Mixed salad, please. Non-fat ranch." She checked the slim little watch on her slim little wrist. "And I've only got five minutes." A chorus of "me toos" came from the girls behind her. Margie might have been at the end of the line, but she made sure there were still people behind her.

The server exchanged a look with one of the other lunch staff, who threw his hands up in a *tough luck* kind of gesture. Next to me, Candice helped herself to a third Rice Krispies Treat and tittered. Margie shot her a look, then turned back to the counter and pitched a fit.

"Do you know who my father is?" she said. "Do you?" Then, to the rest of the cheerleader-skirt crowd, "This is unbelievable."

It didn't matter who Margie Miller's father was or what position he held in the legislature. He might make a noise at the state level, but right now, and right here, we were at the local level, where the only thing that really mattered was that Margie's grades had gotten her a white card, and white cards had to wait.

It was a glorious fuck-you to all of them. From us.

TWENTY-FIVE

When humans find themselves in extreme situations, in personal trauma, a mechanism clicks on. A switch is thrown. Even the most introverted open themselves up and bare their souls.

I don't know Sabrina's mother; I've only seen her shadowy outline behind the wheel when she drops off her daughter. But when the doors close, sealing shut the mouth of the yellow bus, this nameless woman and I hold on to each other as if we were the last two humans on Earth. This time, when she lights another cigarette as the bus pulls away, she doesn't exhale a cloud of burnt tar in my face.

"They say we can visit," she says to no one in particular. "Once a quarter. For a whole five hours."

They did say that. In the same envelope that held Freddie's yellow card was a single-page handout outlining the rules. I recite them in my head.

Dear Parents:

Please do not send the student with electronic devices, including portable phones, cameras, voice or image recorders of any kind, tablets, laptops, and flash drives. These will be confiscated during check-in and held in lockers. We find that working in an electronics-free zone gives your student the freedom to reach his or her academic potential. Also, please do not send your student with cash, jewelry, or other valuables.

We kindly request that parents and other family members refrain from calling or emailing the school. Our mission is to serve your children. Staff are unavailable to devote resources to communication with parents, except in the event of a family emergency. In-person visits outside of scheduled visiting days cannot be accommodated.

Visiting days are scheduled once per quarter. Your date and further details will be mailed to you within the next two business days.

Thank you for entrusting us with your children,
Mrs. Martha Underwood, Headmistress
State School #46

No names for the state schools, only numbers, almost one per state. I had no idea there were so many.

Mrs. Sabrina turns out to be Jolene Fox, although she looks less vulpine and more like a deer in headlights now, with her eyes wide and her pupils dilated.

"I don't understand," Jolene says between shallow drags on her third cigarette. "They're not supposed to go to state schools if they don't pass the silver-level tests. I mean, it was bad enough when we got the envelope, thinking there'd be a green card inside. But we didn't expect yellow. Not yellow." She pauses, wincing at the sun. "It's funny. Yellow used to be my favorite color. Now I'll have to change the curtains because I can't stand the sight of it."

"You all right driving? Want to come in for some tea?" I ask, immediately taking it back because Malcolm is giving me the evil eye.

She shakes her head, crushes the half-smoked cigarette under a Bally pump, and jangles her key fob nervously in one hand. Lexus SUV, Swiss shoes, monogrammed Tiffany key chain. No daughter, though. So much for the cocooning effects of money.

The only thing left to do is trade emails, so we spend a silent moment tapping in letters and numbers and @ signs before I head back into my own house. Malcolm has already gone inside, but not before the bus drives off with his child, who I can visualize on that yellow bus, head bent to the cold glass of the window, counting trees and telephone poles and mile markers.

I don't know whether there's a word for what I am now. Many come to mind, all of them with a negative cast, but none seems to fit; none spells out the horror-grief-anger-loss-sadness-hate that I feel. There should be a new word, a new concatenation of sounds and syllables to describe the desperation inside me. It might sound like *thlug*. Or *frake*. Or a scream.

"Did they make a mistake?" I ask Malcolm as I nuke my now-freezing coffee and take it back to the window where I can hold vigil over Jolene. These are the most words I've spoken to my husband since yesterday morning when he blackmailed me into going to breakfast with him and Alex. Even then, the most I could muster were a few one-word answers to Alex's questions about the girls.

He looks up from his phone. "About what?"

"About that girl. Last week she was in Anne's school. Now she's got a yellow ID card."

It would be too much bother for Malcolm to join me by the window, so he speaks from the dining room chair, where his computer and coffee and ego are keeping him company. "Maybe she failed everything on Friday," he says.

"Anne says she was doing fine. Great, even."

Malcolm's only response is a noncommittal shrug.

Across the street, the Lexus's driver door opens. Jolene sits, half in and half out of the car, and lights up another smoke. It's seven in the morning. I have a feeling this is going to be a two-pack day for her.

"I'm taking a mental health day and going to my parents' house," I say, texting a message to Rita.

This gets Malcolm's attention, and he turns toward me. The bruise on his cheek has developed a yellowish corona. "You're coming back, I assume." It isn't a question.

"Of course."

Malcolm doesn't care if I come back, if I stay at my parents', if I grow a beard and run away with a traveling circus. This much is obvious from his tone. Without me in the way, he and Anne can have their own private little dinner parties; he can fill her head up with ideas about his brave new world of education.

He throws a coat over his shoulders and walks past me on the way to the front door. "Just don't spend so much time with that grandmother of yours that you screw up your teacher assessments tomorrow."

Did I really love this man once upon a time? "I won't screw them up."

The front door shuts with a definite slam, separating more than the outside from the inside, and I sit in Freddie's bedroom. The pillow on her bed still smells of my younger daughter, and I bury myself in it, breathing in the last of her. Everything is a shade of candy pink or moss green or butter yellow in this room, soft colors that should comfort me but don't. Dolls watch me silently from their perch on the little shelf I whitewashed last year, reproach in their black eyes. A stick of bubble gum—strawberry, I think—has fallen between the nightstand and the bed rail. I pick it up and hold it, imagining Freddie's small fingers unwrapping the foil, folding it into quarters the way she always does.

I shouldn't be so selfish. I'm not the first woman, not the first sister or mother or wife, to sit in an empty bedroom with nothing but colors and icons for comfort. Women have been losing their children since they've been having them. Cholera. Cancer. War. None of it fair.

A phone chirps from the kitchen counter, interrupting my grief, and I stupidly think, *This is it. This is when they tell me there's been a mistake.* Relief comes to me and dissolves in a matter of seconds. There's no salvation waiting on this phone, no cheery voice about to inform me of a glitch in the system. I leave Freddie's room reluctantly and shut the door behind me.

The phone isn't mine or Freddie's but Anne's, and it shouldn't be here. It should be glued to Anne's palm like it always has been. There's a text message alert from one of her friends, a girl who has visited our house for study sessions on more than one Saturday afternoon.

Hey. U OK?

This is the latest in a long chain of back-and-forths, and I'm about to put the phone down when I see Anne's last responses.

STFU!!!! accompanied by a crying emoji. Not the laughing-crying one, but the other. The one with real tears and a sour face. And after that, a terse **I H8 U.**

I shouldn't scroll through them, but I do. Otherwise, I'll worry. Otherwise, I'll wonder all the things.

The friend—who I imagine isn't a friend anymore—started this conversation on Friday night with a simple text: **Prolly better this way 4 Freddie**

Of all the ways I've thought about how "this way" is for Freddie, the word "better" hasn't come up. Not once. But this isn't what raises my blood pressure.

She's not like u

Maybe she's a moron

Like in ur dad's books

The words make my eyes sting. And they explain why Anne left for school without her phone.

I'm up the stairs, coffee forgotten on the kitchen counter with the message-filled device. The office I share with Malcolm in the back room is more his than mine, a square of space carved out for my laptop and a few files from school. Mostly, I leave work at work, bringing papers home only when necessary. I ignore my own space and go straight to the floor-to-ceiling shelf to the left of Malcolm's desk.

There's the canon of learning theory and cognitive development, from Köhler to Piaget to Montessori, on the top shelf. I remember reading a few of them when Anne was young, but I don't remember any mention of morons in the descriptions of Gestalt psychology or the Montessori Method. My fingers move across the spines of these books, then to those on the next shelf down, and finally all the way to the bottom shelf, partially hidden by a file cabinet and a wastebasket. I slide the first three books out and start paging through them on the floor between the desk and the wall. I don't even know what I'm looking for.

Maybe she's a moron. Like in ur dad's books.

I start with the oldest one of the three, the one with a cracked cover and foxed pages that can't be part of Malcolm's graduate school leftovers. Even the smell of it is old, a dank and dusty old of the sort you find in forgotten basements of libraries where mold reigns. When I open it, the book falls flat to a page in the center.

A chart I remember seeing in an undergraduate psychology survey course fills the right-hand page; dense narrative is on the left. In bold at the top are two words announcing the theme of the chapter: *Scientific Support*. I read the first paragraph.

It's difficult to use the term "science" in the same sentence with

116

phrases like "Henry Goddard, Director of Research at the Vineland Training School for Feeble-Minded Girls and Boys" and "the greatest threat to civilization is in feebleminded individuals spreading their defect to future generations," but I continue along, referencing the bell curve on the facing page as I read.

There's no arguing that a thirteen-year-old with a mental age of two is an outlier on any intelligence measurement scale, but the casualness with which the term "idiot" got tossed around in the first part of the twentieth century is shocking. I check out the chart on the next page, a handy key to the categories. Less than seventy falls into the general category of "feebleminded," with idiots at the bottom, imbeciles just above them—but still below fifty, and morons in the purgatory of fifty to sixty-nine.

Another page lauds Alfred Binet as the genius behind the one-hundred-point system, but he gets only a quick mention before the focus shifts to Henry Goddard and the broadening of standardized testing and the advantages of identifying mentally deficient children at the earliest opportunity. The name Goddard strikes a bell, and I close my eyes in an effort to visualize where I've seen it. On a car? No, that's not right. On something with wheels, though. Something larger than a car.

A bus. A silver bus.

Quickly, I scan the shelf behind me for what I need. Three over is a large D-ring binder labeled *Silver School Inventory* with the current year. White tabs with bold black labels, each a state, separate the pages. I want the Ms.

They're listed by county, and I let my fingers move down pages until I find Montgomery. And I read.

Davenport
Fernald

Galton

Goddard

Harriman

Laughlin

Noll

Sanger

Thomson

Almost all of the names are unfamiliar, or they were unfamiliar before a few minutes ago. Automatically, I turn toward the first bookshelf, pushing the wastebasket out of my way and heaving the file cabinet a few inches forward, enough to read two of the titles.

**Feeble-Minded in Our Midst: Institutions for the
Mentally Retarded in the South, 1900–1940**

**The Kallikak Family: A Study in the Heredity of
Feeble-Mindedness**

Other books aren't books but journals. Inside a 1912 volume of the *Boston Medical and Surgical Journal* is a bookmark, and the pages separate on their own to the text of an oration by Walter Fernald. Its title is enough to make my morning coffee rise up in a wash of bitterness: "The Burden of Feeble-Mindedness."

What the shit?

Malcolm's computer is off-limits—something to do with security clearance—so I fetch my own laptop from my own desk and kneel down among the scattered books and journals, ears cocked like a wild animal's for any sound from downstairs. My hands are shaking so badly I fail twice at the right password, and the little box shakes a schoolmarmish *no no no* at me each time I press return. On the third try, I hit the button to show what I'm typing, reading over the string letter by letter. It's correct—I know it's correct—but the box still shakes, like a wagging finger.

A wagging finger belonging to my husband, telling me it isn't only his computer that's off-limits.

He's locked me out of my own laptop.

TWENTY-SIX

I'm about to use my phone as a last resort when I decide to call my parents instead, and in fifteen minutes I'm in the car, on my way north and west.

Madeleine Sinclair's saccharine voice answers the interviewer's question on a public radio talk show I used to enjoy, back when the guests were people who had more interesting things to say. I remember Queen Noor of Jordan talking about the importance of cross-cultural dialogue, Ursula Le Guin confessing the writing challenges that come with motherhood, Ray Charles waxing nostalgic about watching the Grand Ole Opry as a child. That was then; this is now.

"And we have exciting projects in the pipeline," Madeleine adds. "Projects that will take the Fitter Family Campaign to the next level."

"Fuck your Fitter Family Campaign," I say to the radio as I weave through rush hour traffic, eager to escape the chain of metal coffins rolling along I-66 and reach empty side roads. So far, Madeleine Sinclair's projects have taken my family to two exciting new levels: I fear for my youngest daughter, currently sitting on a yellow bus, alone, counting telephone poles on her way to Kansas; and I'm experiencing a renewed disgust for my husband.

If that isn't exciting, I don't know what is.

I shut the radio off and think about what I'll say to Oma or, more importantly, what I want Oma to say to me. She has more to tell, and I'm ready to listen. Or I think I am.

There was a point in my teens when she and I stopped talking, around the time Malcolm and I experienced our first clumsy fumble in his car, after we had made the step from "least desirable" to "in crowd." Oma didn't like me very much then.

I tried to tell her about how awful things were in the before times, when I flushed red with embarrassment if our gym teacher insisted we practice cartwheels, when my feet got tangled up in a jump rope, when I teetered and fell on my ass before completing even one evolution of hopscotch. Name a playground game—catch, capture the flag, hide-and-seek, tug-of-war—and I sucked at it. I didn't come home with skinned knees and bruised elbows, but I still felt the sting of scraped skin and the throb of ruptured blood vessels. They were invisible wounds, but real to me.

My mother, ever clinically sensible, applied the best salve she knew.

"You don't have to be exactly like them, Elena," she would say. "You're better in your own way. You're smart."

Yes, there was that.

I took her words to heart, grinning smugly each time I finished a test first and walked my paper up to the teacher's desk with thirty minutes to spare, each time the national aptitude reports came in and my scores shone with dark bars and ninety-ninth percentiles. I taught myself insults in Latin and ancient Greek, used them whenever some mush-brained cheerleader flopped next to me in her short little skirt on the day of a game.

Eventually, I found balance, fell in with the smart overachiever set while still finding time for things like makeup and trendy shoes.

Fell in with Malcolm.

Now that Madeleine Sinclair isn't penetrating my personal space, the car is too quiet. I set the Bluetooth to connect with my phone and ask my pal Siri to play me something upbeat. Siri screws it up and throws Lucinda Williams's "Joy" at me, which is fine. If I can't have upbeat, ferocious and angry will do.

I've got so much of both.

I put the song on repeat and by the seventh time Lucinda tells the world she's going to Slidell to look for her joy, I'm pulling into my parents' driveway and parking behind their Volkswagen.

After two days of Malcolm hovering whenever Mom or Dad called, I'm itching to have a conversation with them that doesn't consist of coded messages and subtext.

The day is cold for early November, but not as cold as yesterday. Still, I feel the chill of it, a blanket of icy air clinging to me, seeping through my pores and worming its way into my very bones as I walk up the porch steps.

"Well, I say fuck the lot of them," my mother says when she opens the door. Then, with only slightly less bitterness in her voice, "I'm sorry. I just can't say anything nice about these people. And your father. You should have heard him on Saturday afternoon. The air in the house turned blue he was cursing so much. Come on, let's have a glass of beer. Oma's not well, but I think she wants to talk to you."

Lucinda Williams failed me. Before we even get to the kitchen, I'm a hot mess of tears, sick with everything. Dad sits me down in his big chair, pours two fingers of *Kräuterschnapps* into a small glass, and holds it up to me. The smell of sugar-sweetened herbs and alcohol drowns out everything for a moment; my mother's long fingers stroking me like I'm a beloved pet takes me back to nicer times. It's a temporary reprieve, but I savor it.

"You want to stay with us tonight?" Mom asks.

I nod and blub and somehow manage words that sound like consent. "I have teacher assessments tomorrow morning, though. At nine."

"It's all about money, you know," my mother says. "All of it. When I was still teaching, I submitted a request for extra funds. You know what the review board told me?"

"I can guess."

"Three hundred seventy-five percent. That's what they told me. In other words"—she makes a goodbye gesture with her hand—"no more money. A three-hundred-seventy-five-percent increase in cost per child since 1970. Just before I retired, they started talking about orders of magnitude in spending increases." My mother lights a cigarette, ignoring the tut-tut sound from Dad. She sucks in smoke and blows it out in a heavy sigh. "So I'm in this meeting one day, and these people in suits start throwing around numbers. This percent of gross domestic product, that much spent per student, this much wasted—*wasted*—on teacher salaries, flat performance levels in math and reading and science. The way they said it, the whole school system was broken and I was part of the problem."

"Blood pressure, Sandra," my father offers. But his eyes tell me he's enjoying Mom's rant.

"Malcolm always said we were overspending," I say.

Mom didn't seem like she could have gotten any hotter a few moments ago, but she proves that wrong now. "Overspending? We spent some money and guess what we got? Higher scores in minority student groups. Better integration of talented kids who once upon a time would have been withering away in special ed classes because they didn't give the right answer on a math test. That's not overspending. That's smart spending." She pauses, looks at me hard, and goes on. "Then we've got the überclass. You know, I was in a PTA meeting and parents were screaming for the tier system. They loved the idea. Mostly because they figured it only applied to the Mexican next-door neighbors' kids. Or the special ed crowd. Never to their own precious prodigies." She shakes her head. "It's like a funnel, Elena. A god-damned, ever-widening funnel. But at least we got the population problem under control."

She's right about that. Ten years ago the geography pundits were predicting an explosion. Miami, New York, Chicago, and L.A. were on a fast track to overcrowding. "If we keep on," they said, "we're looking at New Delhi proportions. Right here in our own country."

"Anyway, now that we've got that Sinclair bitch as hellcat-in-charge of education, the money thing's getting worse. For example—"

But I already know the examples. I know Madeleine Sinclair has more power than the president. I know she has a bottomless pit of funding from the top two percent and the backing of so many more—the child-free families complaining about taxes, the white supremacist assholes worrying about an immigrant takeover, tens of millions of aging baby boomers who cheered when their property taxes were cut, parents like Sarah Green who never thought the yellow bus would come for them. The Fitter Family Campaign is pure genius, taking questions and fears from everywhere, from all directions, and answering them with a single stroke of a directive-signing pen.

An irregular tapping from the back room announces my grand-mother, who has apparently moved her lodgings downstairs. "Leni?"

I turn.

"Hi, Oma."

"I have something to say about your teacher tests."

"You heard that?"

"You remember I told you I got new ears," she says, settling onto the sofa with help from Dad. "Now if I could only have new bones to go with the new ears." She laughs, but no one else does. "Come sit, *Liebchen*. They sent your girl away, yes?"

"Yeah."

Oma levels her eyes with mine and grasps both my hands in hers, squeezing with a force I didn't think possible for someone so frail. "You must go to Kansas and get her back."

TWENTY-SEVEN

There was a news story not long ago about an irate father who drove to one of the yellow schools. Bonita Hamilton, America's least popular investigative journalist ("That Hamilton woman. She needs to climb aboard the commonsense train," Malcolm said over Sunday breakfast), had written up the piece in the *Post*. The man drove out of the city, over bridges and rural roads, before pulling to a stop outside the school his daughter attended. *He stopped, he parked, and he walked in. Or, I should say, he tried to walk in,* Bonita wrote. *He was turned away. Now here's a question: What if this were your child?*

I remember a few outbursts, a letter to the editor, a follow-up opinion piece by a retired academic asking if this was where America wanted to be. Malcolm sniffed when I mentioned it. "You have to wonder what kind of a parent lets their kid slip so far down. The schools are there—and God knows we pay enough for schools these days—to pick up where the parents fail. What the hell are we supposed to do, Elena? Let every angry mother and father try to run the show?"

My grandmother's hopes of me walking into Kansas State School 46 are just that. Hopes. "I don't think I can walk in there and fetch Freddie out," I say.

Oma pushes away the tea my mother offers and demands schnapps. Dad gets two words of protest in before realizing he's lost the fight, and returns from the bar with a short glass of the same thing he gave me when I arrived.

"Ah. Bitter and good," Oma says, ignoring me. "And now I am going to tell you all a little story."

I don't want a story just now; I want my parents' computer, I want to look shit up, and then I want to go to bed and forget everything that happened since I woke up this morning. But Oma's eyes tell me to stay put and listen. How foolish of me to think she had lost that commanding way she always had. When my father gets up to put golf on the television, Oma vetoes it with a sharp rap of her cane. "This is about you, too, Gerhard. So sit down." She says this in German, perhaps to make Dad understand she means business.

And then she begins to talk.

"I am old and I am going to die soon, and when I die, this story will die with me," she says. "This is what I have always wanted for my family. To let something ugly die and to bury it. *Aber.*" But.

She tells us in English words and German words, words that develop colorful pictures and clear sounds in my mind as I listen to stories of young girls in uniform. Their heads are high and proud, even the youngest ones in the Jungmädelbund, only ten years old, stand with haughty self-importance as they are photographed at rallies, demonstrations, marches. Starched blouses barely ripple in the breeze, and the pleats in the navy skirts are crisp as the girls parade down streets and riverbank paths. There are echoes of a hundred steel taps on concrete, click-click click-click click-click, and young virgin voices rising in soprano and alto notes. They are the future, a man tells them. They are Germany, and they are perfect. And they march as if they know this.

The voices turn harsh, becoming low, menacing growls in schoolyards, outside shops and synagogues. Hands that spend evenings sewing and playing piano pick up stones. Maria Fischer, now just fourteen in the year 1933, walks past her friend Miriam's house without so much as a glance toward the girl standing in the doorway. She does this every day, until there's no more Miriam to ignore.

"Do you see now?" Oma says, inviting my father to refill her glass. When he does, and after she has sipped greedily from it, she continues, and I see the scene she paints pull itself together in detailed strokes:

Now we are in a building, a three-story beige block with a decorative mansard roof and flags waving in salute at the building's right and left. Two men enter its doors, both gray and bearded, almost lookalikes. One speaks English with an accent; the other as I might, the flat and intonationless English of this country. The first, the one with the accented speech, has a little girl's hand in his own. He smiles at her, telling her stories of the rich Americans who offered money to help finish the construction, and of the meetings that will fill its rooms in years to come.

Oma sinks back into the sofa's cushions, her gray eyes glassy. "I remember that day," she says. "We went to Berlin to see this new institute named for Kaiser Wilhelm. I must have only been seven, perhaps eight. My father had business appointments and left me in the care of a great-uncle. This uncle took me on a tour, and he introduced me to some of his work colleagues." She pauses. "It was all rather boring for a young girl, but in the afternoon he took me to tea and told me he had a surprise for my birthday. All little girls like surprises, so I brightened."

"What was the surprise?" I ask.

"A trip to Switzerland," Oma says. "To the city of Geneva. I had never been to Switzerland, and when my uncle asked Father's permission, I begged him to grant it. In two weeks, we boarded a—"

I see a train now, chugging furiously from village to village in the green of late summer, a small, pinafored girl sipping tea in the dining car. Her attention is torn between the adventure on the inside of the train, the smoke curling past the windows, and the cities they pass. Mannheim. Karlsruhe. Baden-Baden. The long journey makes her tired, but she resists sleep, wanting to take every moment in and hold it. Then, the blue-mirror lakes of Neuchâtel and Léman, as the train rolls toward the city of Geneva.

My father interrupts. "Mutti, what does any of this have to do with Elena going to Kansas? I'm sure Geneva was a wonderful trip." He looks at me pointedly. "And one Sandra and I have heard about before. But—"

Oma quiets him with a raised hand. "Listen to me, Gerhard. And you will understand after I have finished. I am tired now, and my throat hurts me."

Dad backs down, but he shakes his head at me.

"I met many people during those three days in Geneva. Uncle had meetings each morning, but in the late afternoons he would fetch me from the hotel where I stayed with a hired governess. 'We are going out now, Maria,' he would say, and so we did, always to a pretty tearoom with white linens and crystal chandeliers and cream cakes. There were professors from America and doctors from Italy and England, all of whom thought me very charming. But my favorite new person was an American lady. She came each afternoon and was very kind to me. I remember Mrs. Sanger said I would have beautiful, perfect children."

This time, I interrupt. "Margaret Sanger? What was she doing in Geneva?" Sanger, as far as I knew, had been working on rolling out birth control in the States.

Oma laughs. "Oh, Leni, there were hundreds of people in Geneva that summer. You see, it was the World Population Conference. And

Mrs. Sanger, she organized it, and she asked my great-uncle to be a speaker. Father's uncle was very important. He managed the Kaiser Wilhelm Institute for fifteen years."

"What was that? A hospital?" I ask.

This time when Oma laughs she goes into a fit, her body folding in on itself, until my father gently thumps her on the back and my mother replaces the schnapps glass with a tumbler of water. I don't know which frightens me more—seeing her in obvious pain, or knowing that the laughter is the kind of laughter we do when there's nothing to laugh at. When she recovers, she explains.

"There were sick people in that place. For the most part, the men and women who worked there. Also the men and women who helped them. Magnussen. Mengele. That American, Charles Davenport. It has always seemed strange to me that a man named Eugen"—she pronounces this "OY-gain"—"would be the director of such an institute. So now you know, Gerhard." She shrugs slightly when she addresses my father.

Dad shakes his head again. "What do I know?"

Oma, who has been sitting listlessly on the sofa, straightens and leans forward. "That your great-great-uncle was one of the men behind the extermination of millions of humans. His name was Eugen Fischer. Yes, you are wondering now why I kept that name, and that is another story for another time. I must go to bed now."

The room's temperature seems to drop. My mother and father exchange confused glances as they help Oma to her feet. I tumble names around in my head—monsters from a not-so-distant past, activists painted as heroes. Solutions that promised fitter families and ended with finality for so many others.

Before Oma closes her bedroom door, I say, "It wouldn't happen here, Oma. This is the United States."

"Oh, my darling girl," she says, sighing. "Where do you think my great-uncle Eugen got the idea?"

When we're alone, Mom speaks softly. "She's getting worse, Gerhard, isn't she? First those stories about her friend Miriam, then that business about the uniform."

"She told you about that?" I ask. "She said she hadn't mentioned it to anyone."

Mom clears away Oma's empty glass and fetches three for us, pouring a fat dose of schnapps into each. She doesn't touch hers, only paces the room with her hands clasped behind her back. "She's told that story a million times, El. Each time, it changes. The uniform belonged to another girl. Or she found it at a garage sale. Or she bought it on eBay. The latest story is that it was hers." She turns to my father. "I'm so sorry, but I think it's time to have another talk with her doctor. We've been putting it off for too long."

"What about the great-uncle?" I say. "Another invention?"

"I don't know. Probably." Mom stops pacing, then starts up again. "The last time she told us about Geneva, she rambled on until she could hardly speak. Dr. Mendez tells us to humor her, so that's what we do." Her shoulders rise and fall, a sign there's nothing more to be said on the matter. "All right. Who's going to help me peel potatoes for dinner?"

I volunteer, and for the rest of the afternoon, we talk about more pleasant things than failing daughters and senile grandmothers. Still, a cloud of doubt and worry hangs over me all through the hours.

TWENTY-EIGHT

It wasn't that I didn't believe my grandmother, but I stayed long hours into the night reading web page after web page, looking up the names I'd found in Malcolm's old books and journal articles. At one o'clock, when my head swam with names and places and dates, Mom came downstairs and forced me to bed. My father, worried about the next stage of his own mother's life, hadn't said much during dinner, or afterward. He only phoned Malcolm to announce I'd be spending the night and that I'd go straight to school for my testing session in the morning. The phone call was short, not especially sweet.

Now, driving east with a low autumn sun in the exact spot I need to direct my eyes, wary of the wet carpet of leaves on the backroads, my head is punishing me for the late night. And the *Kraüterschnapps*, of which there might have been one glass too many. That guy on the morning radio show doesn't help, either. How the fuck can anyone be so awake and cheery at seven o'clock? I slap the volume button and shut him up.

I planned it out last night after a few drinks, a half carton of ice cream, and a video interview with a man I watched on YouTube. It was an anecdote about the man's grandmother in Munich who stood in front of a line of soldiers on a railway platform when her best friend got loaded into one of the waiting boxcars, suitcase in her right hand, star on her left breast. They wouldn't let the German girl on the train, but damned if she hadn't tried, hadn't been willing to leave her own family behind for the sake of someone she cared about, even if it meant eating and sleeping and pissing in a windowless boxcar for who knew how many days and nights. Knowing everything I know about history, I'm not sure I would have been as insistent. It's too easy to think of yourself as the one who stands up when everyone else sits down, but I wonder if I have it in me to be that selfless.

Still, here I am, driving to my soon-to-be-former place of employment, ready to screw up every test question, ready to manufacture my own demotion, ready to be put on a bus and go to my younger daughter. It's a hell of a choice, deciding between Freddie and Anne, but it's one I need to make. Anne's sixteen; she'll be fine with Malcolm for the few remaining years he can keep her to himself.

The wrinkle in this shitty plan hit me late last night. I could be demoted to a green school. Although, with what I have planned for the morning testing sessions, it's more likely the board of education will put me in an asylum. No, that's not the worry. The worry is that even if the board sends me packing, there are now nearly fifty state schools scattered about the lesser populated regions of this country, giving me almost no chance of being placed in the same school as Freddie.

For that, I'll need Malcolm's help, even if said help comes without him knowing.

First stop is home, but only after texting Malcolm to see if he's gone into the office yet. A two-word, all-caps message pings back almost immediately: **TEACHER TEST**. Not the information I wanted, but I've learned over the years that I'm never going to get what I want from Malcolm, not even a relevant response to a text message.

Our driveway is empty when I pull in, and my dashboard clock tells me Anne's silver bus has already come and gone. I don't bother changing out of my jeans—testing days are casual affairs as far as the dress code is concerned—and head straight for Malcolm's desk in the upstairs office we share. The room is part workspace, part Office Depot warehouse. Two printers, multiple reams of copy paper stacked next to them, binders waiting to be filled with the latest hole-punched reports are all crammed into every shelf and spare bit of surface area.

I know what I'm looking for, though, and where to find it.

Malcolm's letterhead from the Department of Education is in the second drawer down, nestled next to envelopes with the same logo. I slide out three of each and rummage around for something—anything—with his signature on it. Then I fire up the copier and print out the three sentences I typed early this morning, using my husband's best *you will do as I say* voice, on Mom's laptop. The memo, now on Malcolm's own letterhead, looks good. I slip this forged document and an accompanying envelope into a folder.

The clock downstairs chimes half of the Westminster Quarters. Eight thirty. Time to go.

I think of my mother's last words to me before I left this morning: "Do you really want to do this?"

I wish there were another answer, one that rhymes with "no" instead of the one I gave my mother:

"I have to."

Five blocks from my school, I take a minute to look over Malcolm's letter, signing his name with sharp, pointed strokes, and finishing the signature off with a bold double underline. Nice and aggressive looking.

The park where I've stopped my car is notable for two contrasting visitor types. The first is a dwindling batch of older men who cocoon themselves in blankets and crumpled newspaper, adept at a quick disappearing act should a police cruiser roll by. The second group couldn't be more different: wiry twenty-somethings with stripped-down racing bikes between their legs and messenger bags slung slant-wise over their backs. These are the ones I want.

With a single twenty-dollar bill from my wallet in one hand and the envelope addressed to the principal of the Davenport Silver School in the other, I walk to the friendliest-looking bike courier in the group. He's only friendly by bike courier standards—these kids are sharp and swift and take no prisoners, running red lights and dodging frightened pedestrians around the labyrinthine streets and avenues of Washington, DC. If the twenty doesn't convince him, I'll pay forty.

But the twenty turns out to be enough. He listens to my instructions, taps a note and location into his phone, and rides off with his messenger bag on his back. If all goes as planned, I'll see him again this afternoon in the school's central offices.

Not that he'll show any sign of recognizing me.

The life sciences department of the Davenport Silver School is tucked between two of the ten streets that form the spokes of Dupont Circle, housed in a Beaux-Arts mansion that was once a club for Washington's wealthiest women. They donated the building and its grounds to the Fitter Family Campaign ten years ago, and the FFC turned the old club into a school when they grew out of it. I park in the underground lot next door, sign in at the front desk, and walk up the wide staircase to the ballroom-turned-auditorium, where a few dozen of my colleagues sit in nervous silence.

Dr. Chen, the first-year chemistry teacher, clicks her pen to the beat of an inaudible metronome set to allegro. Drs. Stone and Stone, the married couple who handle advanced placement Spanish and French, exchange smiles in their seats toward the back. The smiles seem forced, as if ghost-like hands are tugging at the corners of their mouths. I have it in confidence that the female Dr. Stone nearly suffered a breakdown after her last test. Dr. Chen, despite her envious ability to recall the entire periodic table of the elements, slips a pill into her mouth, chasing it with what looks like water but what I think might have slightly more numbing properties.

Everyone has a right to be on edge. The academic portion isn't enough to freak out twenty-some people with terminal degrees, but the administrative section—five pages assessing our understanding and absorption of various new policies handed down from the federal Department of Education—is maddening. Our doctorates haven't prepared us for Madeleine Sinclair's ever-evolving plans for the future of learning. And the document I forged this morning only raises the stakes for my colleagues. I'm glad they don't know what I know, that they have no idea the words I wrote—just a few little words—have the power to condemn them to something far worse than demotion to a green school. I try to swallow my guilt. It tastes bitter.

Normally, I would study throughout the month and pull a weekend-long policy cram session immediately before the test. Normally, I would not have put my daughter on a bus to a tier-three school twenty-four hours prior to a battery of grueling assessments. Even if I didn't want to bomb today's test of mental endurance, I know I'm grossly unprepared for a three-hour assault on my over-worked brain.

Perhaps that makes things easier, having the decision out of my hands, especially since I don't have a clue as to what the next few days will bring.

While we wait for the proctor to come in with stacks of blue books and the usual recitation of rules against collaboration, talking, and the use of electronic devices, I practice breathing in and out in a steady rhythm, and I think about my grandmother.

Oma didn't reemerge from her room for dinner, although she called me in twice during the early evening. Each time, she seemed ready to tell me something. Each time, she started down a winding path of stories with an extensive cast of characters until my mother came in and insisted on rest.

I looked them up. Most of her stories were verifiable, although whether they were Oma's stories or co-opted tales she'd cobbled together and made into her own is a different question. Mom insists it's the latter, that Oma isn't all there anymore. Were there institutions for the so-called feebleminded here a century ago? Absolutely. There were also Jim Crow laws and insane asylums, neither of which I imagine will be experiencing a renaissance. I put thoughts of prisons and Dickensian workhouses out of my mind, smiling a little at the ridiculousness of it all. Freddie's in a boarding school, and I'm going to take her out of it.

It will be three short days before I realize how absolutely wrong I am.

TWENTY-NINE

I've been staring at the same blank page for over an hour. My pen, now with a mind of its own, writes one sentence.

There. That should get the attention of the assessment board.

Not that they'd care. There are plenty of would-be teachers lining up to take my place; plenty of people willing to switch tracks and sell their souls to snag a position at a silver school. If there aren't enough willing souls, the Fitter Family Campaign will offer more money from its bottomless bucket.

The testing room begins showing signs of anxiety around eleven. Skirts and trousers rustle as legs are crossed and uncrossed. Leather shoe soles slide and tap underneath desks. Hands run through hair as if to stimulate brain cells or pick answers from the cobwebs of memory.

We've been here for two hours now.

The proctors have brought in small bottles of spring water, tissues, and energy bars. One by one, we're escorted out of the room for turns in the lavatory. No one looks up from their blue books; no one exchanges a glance. We simply sit and shift, like bits of stew in a pressure cooker.

There's a moment when I want to turn back the pages, fill in proper answers, make an honest stab at passing this exam. This is when I think of Freddie.

She's never spent a night alone, not even on a sleepover with friends. I hated to keep her from childhood rituals, but I worried. I worried Freddie would have a meltdown. I worried she would wake up in the dark hours unable to orient herself, wondering why the books on another shelf didn't match her own. I worried she might cry out, and one of the other girls would taunt her about it in school the next day.

Would I have chosen differently ten years ago?

I nearly did. In the end, though, I faked Freddie's test results, choosing a number high enough to make Malcolm happy and low enough to hedge my bets.

It may have even been a true number. Freddie's problems, to the extent she has any, are exactly what Dr. Nguyen diagnosed. Nervousness, stress, anxiety. All manageable. Of course I made the right choice.

I'm not sure I made the right choices in the years after that, coddling Freddie and keeping her sheltered, prepping her for each test until I was satisfied she wouldn't end up too far below the false quotient I created before she was born. Now I worry I screwed it all up, laid patchy groundwork for a situation no one could see coming. My protectiveness backfired, leaving my girl unprotected.

I scribble more nonsense on a blank page of my blue book, put my pen down, and raise my hand.

I'm done being Malcolm Fairchild's brilliant wife.

THIRTY

I was getting funky with Malcolm after giving Anne her night bottle and tucking her into the bassinet on my side of the room, just in case she got the midnight munchies. The same old song played in my head. If he pushed one way, I'd sing along with his rhythm; if he ran his mouth over my body, I'd match the music to the lapping waves of his tongue. Mostly, I'd stay there with him, but a part of me often slid from underneath his body, stepped onto the carpet next to our bed, and danced a little jig.

Do you love me? I sang inside myself. *You know, now that I can dance, and all that other shit?*

I wasn't a very good dancer, which didn't matter at all, because Malcolm was only ever interested in one thing. Not my tits or my ass or how well I went down on him, either.

I used to try fluffy little baby doll negligees, satin merry widows, even webbed body stockings that gave me that rather interestingly sadistic Spider-Woman look. Malcolm shook his head at all of them.

"Take that off, El," he'd said the time I came to bed in a red teddy so sheer you could see my organs through it. "It demeans you." What he meant when he said this was that he wasn't interested in my body, and I thought that was hilarious and not hilarious at the same time.

So there we were, back when sex still happened, pumping and bumping in the night under ten-thousand-count Egyptian cotton sheets he said were the Absolute Best, which was key, because Malcolm was all about the Absolute Best. Well, one of us was there. I was somewhere far, far away. In a nicer place, thinking about a man who once kissed me and said I was beautiful. I was thinking about messy sex, rock-and-roll sex, crazy crazy *I can't get enough of you* sex in the back of a Ford Mustang.

I always stopped at that point because I wanted to hang out there in the car, not in my subway-tiled bathroom in Connecticut, not in the library where I finally wrote Joe my last letter, and definitely not in the sterile clinic where I took care of things so I could have a better life. If I didn't stop, the nicer place I traveled to turned gloomy.

Malcolm's body hovered over mine, shuddered, and went still, the weight of him pressing down on me and trapping me.

"God, I love you, El," he said, and I asked him the question, asked him what he loved about me. It came out as a joke, a spur-of-the-moment pop question: "Do you love me for my body or my mind?" I said.

"What do you think?" Malcolm said, rolling over, tracing my body with one hand, whispering so as not to wake the baby.

I wasn't sure how to answer, whether to get the question right and win the big prize of a wide Malcolm smile, or say what I wanted to hear. I wanted him to think I was beautiful. We're not taught that, we girls and women. We're taught to look for men who want more than just a pretty face. Make sure he's interested in what's upstairs. The body goes; the mind stays. Love is cerebral.

Yeah.

We're supposed to believe all this, to want it, to crave men who love our minds more than our flesh, men who are blind to our outer beauty and see only our inner, cerebral gorgeousness. All the women we've ever trusted tell us this is what's good and right, and I suppose if I had to pick, I'd rather have a lover with eyes that saw deep inside me, past the laugh lines or the sagging bum or the matching set of stretch marks. The thing of it is, why should I have to choose? What's so fucking wrong about wanting to be wanted? In all the ways.

Malcolm stirred next to me and threw an arm over my waist, and there was sleep in his voice when he told me how much he adored his brilliant wife. For me, there was no sleep. I was thinking.

I was thinking he'd rather have sex with my ears. That way he'd be closer to the part of me he really loves.

THIRTY-ONE

My boss sits tight-lipped and narrow-eyed behind her desk. Before she speaks, she pushes around bits of paper and office supplies, straightens the name sign that says *Dr. Marjorie S. Williams, Principal.* Then she does it all over again, pushing, straightening, avoiding looking me in the eye.

"What the hell is this, Elena?" she says, tapping my blue book where I wrote *I DON'T CARE* in capital letters, large enough to cover an entire page.

I have no answer other than the one I wrote.

"Is there a problem? Is everything okay at home?" Dr. Williams's voice is softer now, soft being a relative term where silver school principals are concerned.

"No. And yes," I say. I don't mention Freddie's sudden transfer to State School 46. "We're fine. I just had a bad day."

She takes a brief inventory of my face. "It looks like you had a bad year from where I sit. Not a smart move before testing day, Elena. And now I'm in a shitty position."

I like Dr. Williams. But at this moment I want to tell her she needs to rework her definition of shitty. Instead, I sit, still as stone, hands in my lap. A sideways peek at the wall clock tells me it's time.

As if on cue, the blond kid from the park comes in, shown the way by my boss's secretary. He's sweaty now, despite the cool autumn weather, spandex and Lycra clinging to a body wiry from constant use. He's so on time, I think FedEx should give up its fleet of planes and just hire bike couriers. He looks past me as if we've never met while Dr. Williams signs the tablet.

And then he's gone.

"Hang on a second." Dr. Williams slides a letter knife under the flap. It's a small sound, and at the same time, it's huge. A rip of paper that might as well be the gates of hell opening up.

I hold my breath, waiting for her to read the directive I wrote only this morning.

"Oh," she says. "Oh, dear."

As she scans the type a second time, and then a third, I read Malcolm's letter along with her.

Effective immediately, a new policy is in force. Any teacher failing his or her monthly exam shall be transferred immediately to a state school in need of additional staff. You are hereby directed to transfer any failing faculty from the Davenport Silver School to State School #46.

Signed, Malcolm Fairchild, Ph.D., Deputy Secretary, United States Department of Education, blah blah blah blah.

I breathe again.

"I'm so sorry, Elena," Dr. Williams says, putting Malcolm's letter to one side and turning to the computer on her desk. She sounds as if she means it. As she types letters and numbers and codes, she talks to me. "There's been a change. A few minutes ago, I was sorry as hell to have to send you to a green school."

I feign complete ignorance.

She sighs, and her entire body, usually stiff and erect and full of presence, seems to sigh with her. "I can't do that now."

"So I'm staying here?"

"Um, no."

Careful, El. Don't ham it up too much or she'll get suspicious. "I don't get it. Silver school, green school. It's not like there's anywhere else to go, right?"

The printer on my left spits out two copies of a form. Dr. Williams pushes herself up, rubs at eyes that look as if they don't want to read anything ever again—directives, forms, exam booklets of normally high-functioning faculty—and takes the pages. She keeps one and hands the other to me.

"Wrong," she says, picking up Malcolm's letter. "New policy. You're being moved to State School"—she glances down at the number on the page—"forty-six. It's in Kansas. Your new identification and instructions should arrive sometime this evening by courier."

In the years I've been working under Marjorie Williams, I've never seen her waffle. Never heard a tremor in her voice or found her at a loss for words. She's a hard woman. Fair, but hard. I guess it's built into the high school principal template. So when she puts a hand on mine and says how sorry she is, I'm not sure how to react.

"I'll need your silver card, Elena."

So I give it to her before I turn to go.

I don't know what will happen over the next forty-eight hours. Not exactly. But I can predict with all the clarity of a genuine medium what will happen tonight when my new yellow identification card is delivered to our house.

Malcolm will hit the roof.

And I'm okay with that. I'm so okay with that, I laugh all the way to my car.

From a distance, it must look as if I'm crying.

THIRTY-TWO

Once, a boy named Joe kissed me and said I was beautiful.

I don't know. Maybe I was. Am. Was.

There's a little swell now where a flat belly used to be, a few more laugh lines or frown lines or stretch marks, some spider's-web strands of gray curling around my ears. Malcolm has never mentioned any of these.

Tonight I feel neither beautiful nor brilliant, only tired. For the first evening, we're a table of three instead of four. Only Anne and I seem to notice the vacant seat to my left. I wonder if my husband will notice when there's another empty seat tomorrow.

Malcolm talks about work, addressing the air between us; Anne mouths "Can I be excused?" to me. I nod yes, and she leaves the table for her room.

"Where are you going, Anne?" Malcolm says. "You've hardly touched your food."

"Homework, Dad." It's the one answer he can't argue with.

"Let's all go play some tennis this weekend," he says.

"Sure," I lie. Might as well keep playing the game until I can't anymore.

Our clock chimes out three times. Seven forty-five. Malcolm says something about the vinaigrette I made being my best ever. I've been teleported into a weird alternate universe, some twin world full of domestic intimacy and marital bliss and weekend tennis plans, absent the threats of divorce and custody battles. I go to check on Anne, wondering if Malcolm will even realize I've left the room.

"I miss Freddie," she says.

Anne has always been casual about the system, and I understand why. She's like one of those kids today who can't imagine a world where everybody smoked, where crystal ashtrays and silver table lighters were considered appropriate wedding presents. Her entire school history has been filled with tests and transfers and broken friendships. Caitlin's in math class on Friday but not on Monday. Barbara won't be coming over anymore to play video games and eat raw cookie dough out of the container. The girl next door who used to babysit is no longer available.

Children are resilient, I think. And that's good in so many ways— they fall down, they dust themselves off, they get back up and do it all over again. But resilience brings a sort of callousness with it, an acceptance and tolerance that piggyback along. In Anne's eyes, what happens to failures is nothing more than the way things are. A situation to be shouldered and shrugged over. Until now.

The doorbell rings.

"Yeah. Me too," I say, hurrying out of her room. "Be right back."

Malcolm is in the kitchen doing his preinspection of dinner plates before they go into the dishwasher. "Can you get that, El?"

The courier tonight is the same woman who delivered Freddie's yellow card on Sunday night, and the padded envelope shows the same Fitter Family Campaign logo, the happy little sunshine family in the upper left corner. I'd like to take a Magic Marker to it. Or a flame torch. Since the envelope is addressed to me, I sign the courier's tablet.

"Sorry, ma'am," she says before she turns to walk down the path to her waiting car. As if she knows.

I prepared for this before Malcolm came home.

In my right pocket is an old Metro pass, hard plastic like a credit card. There's probably ten bucks left on it, but I won't be using the Metro anytime soon, so I turned it into a prop with a bit of silver paint from our Christmas decoration stash. It's a shitty facsimile, but no one's going to see it up close.

"Who was that?" Malcolm asks, drying his hands and folding the dish towel carefully in thirds. It looks nicer that way, sure, but nice doesn't mean dry. I let it go.

"School stuff," I say, waving my fake silver identification at him. I've already torn the envelope and pocketed the yellow card that was inside. "They updated some system over the weekend, and we all got new cards. Something about a security breach."

To my surprise, all he says is, "Good. Can't be too careful about security these days. Want to watch a movie, Anne?"

So it worked.

The rest of our evening is pleasant and horrible, pleasant because instead of Madeleine Sinclair force-feeding us more of her Intelligence-Perfection-Wisdom crap and talking up the benefits of a twenty-first-century master race of prodigies, Malcolm and Anne are watching an old Jimmy Stewart movie that we all agree is one of his best. The evening's horrible because I'm in the kitchen imagining Anne returning from school tomorrow afternoon to find my car gone, my closet half-empty, and a note stuck to the fridge she'll find as soon as she starts rummaging for a snack. *Sorry, but I'm abandoning you.* It won't say that in so many words, but it might as well.

Anne sniffles once from the living room, and Malcolm's arm reaches around, settling on her shoulder. "We'll be fine, honey," he says. "You'll see."

Stewart acts out another comic line, stands tall and lean and a little gawky on the television. He reminds me of Joe: clean, honest face, warm eyes—even in grainy black-and-white—and a touch of self-consciousness that I find endearing. He's no macho man, no *People* magazine's Sexiest Man Alive contender or Nobel Prize finalist, but neither was Joe. My old friend-turned-nondate was just a good guy. Well, okay. Joe was strong and sexy. But he was other things, too.

I only miss him when I think about him. Which is often.

Lying in bed next to Malcolm, who says he's dog-tired tonight, I fantasize about Joe. Maybe not even Joe himself, but a good guy, a Jimmy Stewart, a man who might run his hands over me tentatively at first, who would kiss me softly before trying anything beyond first base, and then, once things started smoking, would take me to the moon and back. I think about how much I'd like that, and how, at forty-something, those are nothing more than fantasies, experiences I'll never have again.

As soon as Malcolm's breathing slows and deepens in its steady sleep rhythm, I creep downstairs to the kitchen. There's still a half bottle of cava in the fridge from dinner. I don't bother with a glass; I take it into the TV room, curling up sideways on the sofa. And I cry.

For all the reasons.

THIRTY-THREE

This Wednesday morning is exactly like last Wednesday morning except for Freddie's absence. I get up, shower, pull on a plain blue jersey dress and boots. I putz around in the kitchen. Bread goes into the toaster; bread pops out of the toaster, transformed. Yogurt and muesli and juice wait on the counter. We eat, and I smile around a mouthful of toast.

Just another school day, that smile says. *See you all in the afternoon.*

"What's for supper?" Anne asks, accustomed to me planning out meals in three-day chunks.

"Pasta," I tell her. It's not a lie. I'll leave the box of rigatoni next to the stove with a can of crushed tomatoes and herbs and garlic next to it. The only detail I omit is that Malcolm will be cooking it, not me.

He leaves first, raincoat over one arm in case it rains, keys to his car in the other hand. We act out the same scene from all the other mornings of our marriage: a peck on the cheek, a "Have a good day," and an exchange of smiles.

Anne runs out the door not long after Malcolm's car vanishes around the curve. "See you later, Mom."

"Later, honey," I call, resisting the instinctual urge to bolt down the driveway and throw my arms around her.

Later. I wonder when that will be.

With the house empty, I accelerate into a sort of turbocharged mode, the kind of organizational frenzy everyone experiences when a mother-in-law calls to say she'll be popping by in ten minutes. Clothes and shoes and underwear find a new home in a suitcase that smells vaguely stale after not having been opened in five years. I throw my makeup bag and brush and comb on top of the pile, zip it up, and heft it. Not too bad, room for a few books that will keep me company on the bus and maybe find their way into usefulness at State School 46. From the fridge, I grab two bottles of water, two apples, and a sandwich I made at three this morning. Then I think of Freddie, and add a few bags of oatmeal cookies to the snack pile.

My suitcase, briefcase, and lunch put me at my limit.

The instructions that came with my new identification card are clear—and not recommendations:

Three pieces of luggage per person, to include: one suitcase of carry-on dimensions, one personal item such as a handbag or briefcase, one clear plastic bag for soft drinks and snacks. No alcohol is permitted in any of your luggage.

I'm not sure I like the idea of going from regular wine drinker to teetotaler overnight, but the letter's tone, clipped and precise as a nun's in a Catholic school, makes me skittish.

You will present yourself at your designated meeting point (see attached) no later than 9:00 AM on your date of transfer. Upon arrival, go directly to the check-in desk to be registered.

You must carry your identification card at all times.

You will. Go. You must. All imperatives without even a "please" to soften their stiffness.

Automatically, I reach for my coffee mug and raise it to my lips. Not automatically, I set it back down when my hand starts to shake. Everything about this morning tells me it's not the right time to give myself the caffeine jitters.

Malcolm left the radio on when he left for work, and now an interview with Petra Peller comes on the air, invading my kitchen.

"The Genics Institute," Petra says, "is proud to announce the acquisition of a new subsidiary, WomanHealth, Incorporated. As you know, WomanHealth has been a champion of informed family planning for over a quarter of a century. WomanHealth is here for you," she went on. "More importantly, we're here for your children. For your children's future. Even if those children are unborn."

I'm thinking something more along the lines of, *What the fuck is an unborn child's future?* Unborn children don't have futures.

Which is exactly Petra's point.

"Think of the stress of education," she says. "The pressure it puts on our little ones, our tweens, our high schoolers." She pauses for effect. "I'm just so proud to share our plan with you, a plan that will leave no child behind. Not one."

"How are they planning to work that miracle?" I say back, turning toward the radio so quickly I almost lose my balance.

Petra clears it all up for me in a few sentences. "Beginning next month, WomanHealth will offer no-cost pregnancy management services to any woman referred by the Genics Institute. Your income won't matter. And by any woman, we mean any woman, regardless of where she is in her term. If you don't like your baby's Q score, we're here to help." There's smiling in her voice, and little mm-hmms of approval from the interviewer.

The words "no child left behind" take on fresh, terrible meaning: It's impossible to leave a child behind if the child doesn't exist.

Petra's voice—prerecorded, I'm guessing—comes back in a public service announcement tone: *Are you single? Unemployed? Worried about your financial future? No college education? Miserable about your Q score? Come on down to WomanHealth for your free consultation!*

The next part targets a different audience:

Do you have everything except a child? Tired of feeling like you're being outbred? Is it time to start the family you deserve? WomanHealth is here for you!

A radio voice reminds us this program has been sponsored by the FFC. As if anyone needed reminding. The same voice, void of any identifying dialect markers, introduces the brave women who have offered testimonials. N from Vermont says her piece, then A from Dallas, and a teenage-sounding girl identified as Z from St. Louis. Z can't be much older than Anne.

To hell with the caffeine jitters. I nuke the cold coffee.

"I was on the streets," Z says. "Like, not knowing what would happen tomorrow. I heard that WomanHealth was helping people like me, so I went in to talk to them. Yeah, I guess you could say they helped take care of my future. They told me—"

Z from St. Louis is cut off. Another voice replaces hers.

"This is H from Washington," the radio voice says, "telling us about her experience with WomanHealth."

"It was just a mistake. I got pregnant, and no, I wasn't married. WomanHealth saved me."

I kill Petra's voice with a finger, and scratch out a note on the pad usually reserved for shopping lists. It isn't my best effort, but those damned Westminster Quarters chimes are singing out their time-to-go song. And for this, I think short and sweet is best.

Dear Malcolm and Anne,

I'm so sorry, but I can't stay here anymore. Please don't look for me. I hope to be home soon.

Love, Elena/Mom

A magnet, one Malcolm bought me from a long-ago trip to San Francisco, does the job of holding my words until someone comes home later today. After a last look around, I load the car with my three pieces, check for cash in my wallet, and start up the Acura, which I'll dump at the nearest big-box store parking lot before going the rest of the way on foot. Cabs are no use to me; cabs keep records. My house, the house where Freddie and Anne played as toddlers, where Malcolm and I once sat up late discussing books and music and all things erudite, lingers for a few seconds in my rearview mirror as I drive away.

And then it disappears, along with my forgotten coffee in the microwave.

THIRTY-FOUR

Inside a brick building on the fringes of one of Washington's less chic neighborhoods, the two women at the check-in desk are a study in shades of drab. Their name tags say Mrs. Parks and Mrs. Flowers, neither of which image they conjure up. Mrs. Parks teeters on a wooden stool behind the desk, a tall, insect-thin shape of a woman, while Mrs. Flowers takes our identification cards one at a time, scans them, and checks off names on a clipboard.

"Sit down and wait until you're called," Mrs. Parks snaps at the woman behind me as she prints out a ticket and hands it to me. "Don't lose this."

I turn, and the woman isn't a woman at all, but a girl really, pink skin dotted with freckles, a thick froth of red hair, eyes that likely haven't seen much of the world.

"Sorry," she says and moves to a row of chairs against the wall as Mrs. Flowers scans my card, checks my face against the photo on her computer screen, and puts a red tick next to my name.

"You," Mrs. Parks says, pointing her chin at the young woman. I take a step backward, because it seems that chin is about to poke me in the eye. She aims it toward me next. "Go. Sit."

"You forgot 'Stay,'" I tell her.

"Stay." The eyes peeking out from above her horn-rimmed glasses show no sign of getting the joke. "You," she says again.

I roll my suitcase to an empty chair at the same time the girl-woman stands. "Ruby Jo Pruitt," she tells Mrs. Flowers when she reaches the desk. "Good morning."

"Identification."

Ruby Jo fishes her yellow card from a tired leather hobo bag slung over one shoulder. And she promptly drops it. "Sorry."

"Pick it up, girl. I don't have all day."

"You don't gotta be so mean, you know," Ruby Jo says, bending to pick up the card. Those eyes that haven't seen much are shining. "Here."

Mrs. Flowers scans, looks, and ticks. Mrs. Parks prints another ticket, reminding Ruby Jo not to lose it. "Take your seat. Next."

In the past five minutes, more people have come into the room, mostly women, a few men, an entire spectrum of colors and ages and body types. The only free seat is the plastic chair, a relic from an old high school cafeteria, to my right. Ruby Jo takes it, setting her duffel bag between her feet. Her shoe brushes mine.

"Sorry," she says, rearranging herself, trying to make her body smaller than it already is.

"Don't worry about it. At least you didn't scuff one of their shoes," I say, nodding in the direction of Mrs. Flowers and Mrs. Parks.

"Yeah. Prolly woulda crushed me like a june bug if I had. How you like them two, huh?"

Ruby Jo's got one of those voices that most people can place on a map. It's tinged with the hues of Appalachia, probably southwestern Virginia or West Virginia, the kind of dialect that screams poor, un-educated trailer trash. Looking at Ruby Jo's dress and shoes, I might be on the right track about poor, but I'll leave the trailer trash judg-ment to people like my husband.

The slip of paper Mrs. Parks gave me is nothing more or less than a ticket. On the left is my origin and destination, printed in black. On the right side, there's a barcode. The time at the bottom states an 11:00 AM departure. If we drove straight through, we'd cross the Missouri-Kansas border in about seventeen hours.

Seventeen hours on a bus. Shit.

"Where you headed, ma'am?" Ruby Jo's eyes, the ones that haven't seen much of this world, move toward my ticket.

"Kansas," I say, holding the slip of paper up. I've got nothing to hide.

"Me too. Never seen Kansas. Never seen a place that's all flat like that. Never seen the ocean, either, come to think of it."

Like I said, eyes that haven't seen much.

I put Ruby Jo in her early twenties, too young to have her doctorate, so, unlike me, she must be coming from a teaching gig at a green school. She also must be either out of her mind or have some unflappable call to the teaching profession to have gotten into the education game so recently. Looking her over, my best guess is the unflappable call, but there's another possibility.

Not many younger men and women pick teaching these days, not voluntarily, not like they did when Anne was starting school. There's too much goddamned pressure now. It got to a point about ten years ago where the education departments at most universities saw enrollment rates spiral down to nothing and attrition rates skyrocket. Word was out to steer clear of teaching as soon as Madeleine Sinclair's predecessor passed his Senate confirmation.

So what's to be done when there's a demand but not a supply? What's the procedure for that? For the Department of Education, backed by the muscle and money of the Fitter Family Campaign, there were two answers: finance and force. A carrot and a stick, to put it in simple terms.

As it turned out, the stick worked better.

Even with scholarships and stipends and promises of high salaries, pensions that would make a career navy admiral turn green with envy, it still wasn't enough to fill college classrooms with prospective teachers.

So started the draft.

Mrs. Parks and Mrs. Flowers bark out another set of orders to the now-crowded room, and I wonder if they were on the committee that identified me as a potential educator and shunted me into the box I've been living in.

"I figure you for an English teacher, ma'am." Ruby Jo says "figger," not "figure." It's new to my ears, but endearing all the same.

"Nope. Biology and anatomy. You?"

"Chemistry."

You're kidding, I think, and as soon as the words are in my head, I regret them. They sound too judgmental, too needlessly surprised, too much like Malcolm. Instead, I say, "Organic or inorganic?"

"A little of both," Ruby Jo tells me. "You think maybe we can sit together on the bus ride, ma'am?"

I take a look around the room. Every man and woman here seems miserable, like they're about to be loaded onto a cattle car to a state penitentiary. Ruby Jo, though, she's got a bit of spark.

"On one condition," I say. "You stop calling me 'ma'am' and start calling me Elena. Deal?"

"Yes, ma'am," she says, and her face opens into a broad smile that warms me like a summer sun.

THIRTY-FIVE

THEN:

"Maybe you should try talking to her," Oma said. We were in the kitchen at my parents' house, and I had just come home from school.

"Why?" I said. Today's topic was the new girl in my third-grade class. She was small and dark and shy, but that wasn't the problem. The problem was Rosaria Delgado didn't speak more than ten words of English. The problem was compounded when our teacher made us partners for a science project and I ended up tied for the lowest grade in the class. "I got a C because of her."

"So, what? You're going to make her feel even worse by treating her like a piece of old cheese? Leni, I am ashamed of you."

I stood there, arms folded in a defiant nine-year-old snit, watching Oma smear butter on toast. She offered me a slice, and I turned up my nose, even though I wanted it.

The things we do for spite.

I never spoke to Rosaria again, and I made sure my friends didn't. It was easier than I thought, making up stories about Rosaria Delgado's family and where they lived. We sneered at her outfits and mimicked her accent. If our teacher put one of us in a group with her, we ignored her input and did things our way.

We did this from January until June. In September, Rosaria didn't come back.

We'd won.

Oma didn't seem to think so. "Here is a question, *Liebchen*," she said. "What if she were your daughter?"

I didn't have an answer for that. Not at nine years old. So I made one up, just to make her think I wasn't backing down. "My children are all going to be perfect." And I stormed out of the kitchen with my best nine-year-old attitude, thinking, *So there*.

THIRTY-SIX

Here's a thing I've learned:

Never trust any of those mapping apps.

It isn't that the apps are wrong, but they don't account for re-fueling stops, rest stops, unclogging-the-onboard-toilet stops, food stops, change-of-driver stops, or letting-off-the-passengers-whose-final-destination-is-Missouri stops. Nor do they foresee unexpected snow in the mountains, a tire blowout in southwestern Pennsylvania, or the roadwork that reduces I-70 to one slow-crawling single lane of rush hour traffic on the outskirts of Columbus, Indianapolis, St. Louis.

To put it kindly, our trip from Silver Spring, Maryland, to ten miles outside of Columbia, Missouri, is twenty hours of blue burning hell.

And, as Ruby Jo puts it, "We ain't done yet, honey."

We've napped. We've eaten apples and stale microwaved apple pies from fast-food restaurants. We've taken turns watching each other's bags when one of us goes to the bathroom, which, by the time we reach Columbia, Missouri, has begun to smell like the bottom of the monkey cage at the National Zoo. We've traded stories and shoulders to rest on, played that old license plate game, and stared out the window at streetlights, telephone poles, cornfields, nothing. We've cried.

In twenty hours, Ruby Jo Pruitt and I have become friends.

"So," she says while we're in line at what I hope will be the last burger and fries joint I see for the next decade, "how come you're here?"

I tell her everything there is to tell. Freddie's transfer, my intentionally screwed-up teacher test, doing a runner from my home like some desperate refugee. In turn, I get Ruby Jo's story.

"I flunked," she says. The "I" comes out like an "Ah." "Flunked it good and well and honest. They asked some question like could I comment on the effects in the global chemistry community of some son-ofabitch old guy who got the Nobel Prize in 1925. I just couldn't do it. I mean, does that—pardon my French—horseshit really matter?"

"No. It doesn't. And let me get this," I say, forking over a ten-dollar bill for eggs and cheese on biscuits. The food smells like old grease and sweat, but at least it's not a hamburger this time. I order two salads as an afterthought and hand the girl at the cash register another five.

"You know," Ruby Jo says between bites of her biscuit when we're back in the bus, "they don't do biscuits here like they do where I come from."

"I bet they don't," I tell her. I've had real southern biscuits, the kind made with lard and Martha White self-rising flour, the kind that tricks your tongue into thinking you're eating a cloud. What we're eating could be used as a weapon.

Ruby Jo tells me about her scholarship and her high school sweetheart and how she almost set her chem lab on fire when she made plasma with two halves of a green grape and a microwave. "Fascinating stuff, them plasmas," she says.

My face must have taken on the shape of a question mark.

"No. Really. All you need is a little grape and one of them cheap microwaves. You got your ions in the grape, right?"

I nod. It's not my field, but I follow, like any well-trained and overeducated citizen. Also, I know Ruby Jo is doing her best to distract me, to stave off another crying jag.

"Look, any living thing has ions," she goes on. "So you get yourself a living thing that's the right size, about a quarter wavelength of the stuff your microwave puts out, like a grape. Then you gotta cut it and make sure it's still connected." She breaks a piece of tomato from her fast food salad so only the skin holds it together. "This little section here acts like a sort of antenna, right?"

"Right," I say.

"Now you got your ions and your electrons and your energy, and everything gets all excited and bursts into flame!" I recoil into my seat when she says this. "Wanna hear about my manganese dioxide and hydrochloric acid experiments?"

To be honest, I'm not sure I do.

Ruby Jo doesn't wait for an answer before explaining how to make chlorine gas, or how to create explosions with gummy bears, or how she wrote secret messages to her girlfriends with lemon juice. "There was one girl in my school who had real strict parents. I reckon they were half off their rockers. Anyway, when they took her out of the fourth grade to homeschool her, I'd send her blank pieces of paper and she'd read 'em when she did her ironing chores. Then she'd sneak a note back to me the same way."

Somehow I don't think I could do as much damage, or be as sneaky, with biology and anatomy. What would I do? Send secret messages in blood and bones?

Ruby Jo's made up of ions and electrons and chemicals, too. She's got more energy in her than—as she would put it—a rutting jack-rabbit. It strikes me that the bus we're on could have made it from Maryland to Kansas on Ruby Jo Pruitt power. She keeps talking, changing from one subject to another, keeping the conversation alive and keeping me sane. Finally, she stops and asks me a question.

"Think you could teach me to talk nice like you?"

"What's the matter with the way you talk?" A list of epithets, every one of which I've heard from Malcolm's mouth, floats up in a cartoon thought-bubble: cracker, yokel, redneck, hillbilly, white trash. Never mind that "hillbilly" might even make some sense, since half of the Scotch-Irish Protestants who set up home in the mountains named their firstborn sons after William of Orange. Maybe more than half. All these words Ruby Jo has probably heard at one time or another. I wonder how much they sting.

"You know. Like what them folks from town call poor white trash."

"Yeah. I know."

"Hell, I mean, we *are* poor. My granddaddies worked in coal mines and came home black as midnight for a sack of nothin'. But poor ain't dumb." Ruby Jo gazes out the window at another crappy, depressed town. "Well, not all the time, anyway. But the way I talk, that's the first thing people think."

I want to tell her accents are pretty much fixed once a kid hits her teen years, but Ruby Jo beats me to it.

"Look at Madonna. She's from Michigan, right? But now she sounds all English."

"Sure, hon," I tell her, thinking Madonna's linguistic affectations probably necessitated a small army of dialect coaches. "We can work on it if it's important to you."

Another smile, another one of those happy-warm-sunshine feelings floods through me.

When we reach the Kansas state line, there are only three of us left on the bus. Ruby Jo, me, and an older woman who keeps her head down and her mouth shut.

"About five hours to go," the driver says.

Five hours to go. Five more hours until I see Freddie.

THIRTY-SEVEN

Kansas is flat as a pancake. No, it's flatter than that. It's so flat, it might as well be concave. And I've never seen as much corn as I have in the past few hours. I can't think how anyone could possibly use this much corn.

We turn off about fifteen miles west of nowhere, onto a gravel road leading up to double gates. A low sun slices through the window where Ruby Jo's head is resting. When the bus swings wide to the left, the light moves across the iron rails of the gates and rests on a small hut. A gatehouse.

"Looks grim," she says.

"Grim" is a nice word for what this shithole looks like.

"Just like my old granny said it would." Ruby Jo shades her eyes and peers out toward the gatehouse.

"Huh?" I ask, but she hushes me.

A man heaves himself up from his chair behind the small building's window, pulls open the door, and swaggers out, beer belly swaying in a rhythmic plop-plop over the beltline of his uniform. He's dressed in gray, and the two patches on his left shoulder are familiar. One is the sunshine-happy Fitter Family Campaign's emblem; the other is the Department of Education's tricolor peace symbol with the words *Intelligentia, Perfectum, Sapientiae*. From where I sit, the guard doesn't look intelligent, perfect, or wise.

"All right, people. I need to see tickets and ID cards," the guard says, like he's addressing a mob of anxious concertgoers at Madison Square Garden instead of three high school teachers at the entrance to a crumbling complex of nineteenth-century buildings in Winfield, Kansas. He climbs aboard, checks the bus driver's manifest, and looks us over, one by one. "Mm-hmm. You first."

The old woman with the bent head stands and picks up her purse. She's not too steady on her pins, but neither the driver nor the guard seems to give a shit. I stand up, tossing the bunched-up fast-food bag on the empty seat next to Ruby Jo, and walk toward the front of the bus.

"I didn't call you, lady," the guard says. "Sit down."

I really hate being called "lady." *A lady* is fine. *That lady in the green coat* is fine. *May I please speak to the lady of the house* is fine. But this fat slob isn't fine calling me anything other than Dr. Fairchild.

"How about you sit down," I tell him, "since it seems that's what you do all day anyway. And I'll help this woman get off your bus. Sound good?"

I've learned about bullies in my lifetime. Any teacher has. The taller they stand, the taller you have to stand. And, even without heels, I've already got a good six inches on Mr. Beer Belly here. He backs off, as if no one's ever spoken back to him, as if no one has stood her ground.

Good.

But I wonder why this should be so surprising to him.

The lady with the bent head is Mrs. Munson, she tells me. Mrs. Munson. What a name. Still, if her legs don't work so well, her mouth makes up for it. "You tell him, honey."

Once Mrs. Munson's on the ground, I climb back aboard and collect my briefcase and the snack bag. All that's left in it are the packs of cookies I took out of the kitchen cupboard over the fridge and brought along for Freddie.

Twenty-eight hours ago.

It's always interesting to think of yourself as a ghost, an invisible fly on the wall, an unseen observer.

So I do that now, and picture myself in my own kitchen at four o'clock yesterday afternoon. Anne is home from school, backpack stuffed with books, stomach whining with the late-afternoon munchies. Teenagers are like hobbits: breakfast, second breakfast, that odd prelunch snack the Brits call elevenses, lunch, and so on. They're all their own private little internal combustion engines.

She's in the door, having let herself in with the key Malcolm and I entrusted her with only last year. Shoulders slumped with the weight of books—more slumped with the weight of other, less tangible things—Anne unloads her books on the living room sofa, washes her hands in the kitchen sink like her father's told her to do since she was six. Right now, at this moment, everything is normal. Nothing has changed.

Her mother will be home in thirty minutes. A half hour at most. There will be banter and bickering and reminders that this house feels empty.

Or not.

Anne kicks off her shoes, shrugs out of her Harvard Crimson school jacket, goes to the fridge. She does this automatically, as she does every afternoon. At first, her mind is so intensely tracked on food she doesn't see the note. Why would she, when yogurt or fruit salad or a slice of Swiss cheese calls to her like a wind-tossed plastic bag calls to a sight hound? It's only when she goes back to forage for something else and put the wrapped hunk of cheese where it belongs that she closes the fridge door a second time and sees my note.

For the next five minutes, she'll read and reread my scribbled apology, the news of my leaving, in the same way a jilted GI rereads a Dear John letter from his stateside sweetheart. Confusion mixes with disbelief and denial. *It can't be. She's not really gone. This is a dream, a nightmare, a lie.*

Mothers don't just walk out.

In my imagined fly-on-the-wall position, I can see her tapping numbers into her phone, screwing up the sequence, trying again when the first call is answered by a hair salon. Then, "Dad? Mom's gone." And again, the cycle of confusion and denial starts.

Wives and mothers don't just walk out.

I want to materialize in my kitchen, take Anne in my arms, and tell her I'm not gone, not really, but then Ruby Jo tugs at my coat sleeve because it's time to collect our suitcases from the belly of the bus and start the long walk from the double gates to the low redbrick building that says *Administration* on its facade.

"I don't have a good feeling about this place," Ruby Jo says.

And we walk on.

THIRTY-EIGHT

The path leading up to the admin building might have been laid three-quarters of a century ago, and weeds older than that poke out through the crevices and cracks. Mrs. Munson nearly trips on a nasty tangle of withered vegetation, and I take her suitcase. It's the nonrolling kind, the hard-backed Samsonite that went out of style in the seventies. And it must have bricks inside it.

"Just a few books, dear," Mrs. Munson says.

Of course, the fat guard is back in his gatehouse now, probably watching crap TV and stuffing his face with corn chips. Every step I take with the heavy Samsonite makes the path seem longer.

We pass a small parking lot to the left, partially hidden by a line of scrubby hedges in need of a serious trim. On our right is a dense row of conifers masking what used to be a playground, but when I look closer, it's overgrown, a jungle of sagging tire swings and rusted monkey bars. Not a single kid plays in it, even though the school day must have ended at least a couple of hours ago. I find it eerie.

"Maybe there's a new one out back," I say, not really believing it.

"You reckon?" Ruby Jo says. "Get a look at this place." Then, under her breath, "Just like Granny said."

"You keep saying that. Why?"

"Tell you later." She points a freckled chin, scrunched with worry now, toward a spot in the path ahead of us.

I don't know who I was expecting. Maybe another fat guard; maybe Mrs. Martha Underwood, the headmistress; maybe even Malcolm. He could have taken a last-minute flight from Washington Reagan to Kansas City and waited for me.

All the possibilities tumble around in my mind: Malcolm calling my school—my *former* school. Malcolm snooping around the teacher database for clues. Malcolm pissed off as he sits on a cramped plane. Malcolm driving out here to pick me up and take me back home before I get the chance to see Freddie.

"Rules are rules, Elena," he would say.

But the figure walking toward us isn't fat, isn't a woman, and isn't my husband. His long, easy strides, not rushed but not slow either, belong to someone else I know.

Next to me on the path, Mrs. Munson draws in a sharp breath. "Wow," she says when she recovers. Ruby Jo seems not to notice the man as he reaches forward for the Samsonite, his fingers brushing mine as he takes it from me.

"Thanks," I say, though I groan a little on the inside.

I'm not a weak woman. I work out, running treadmills and hefting free weights a few times a week. I don't need a man to carry my luggage or put me on a pedestal or worry over whether I might break a nail. But man, that fucker was one heavy suitcase. I'm glad to see it go, less glad to see the face of the person who takes it from me.

"No problem," he says. Hanging from one tanned and tennis-muscled arm, the Samsonite might as well be stuffed with feathers. "This is yours?"

"No. It's Mrs. Munson's," I say, pointing to the older woman, who hasn't closed her mouth since the man showed up. "I didn't expect to see a familiar face here."

Alexander Cartmill is one of those men who is handsome and knows it. I spent Sunday at breakfast watching him preen himself between sips of decaffeinated cappuccino while Malcolm bragged over last week's tennis scores.

"I'm out here doing some doctor business for the week," he says, extending his free hand to Mrs. Munson.

The three of us follow him through lengthening shadows cast by the admin building. He could be forty, I think. Or fifty or thirty-something—it's always so goddamned hard to tell with men. They don't change like we do, don't go through the same desexing hormonal flips and flops, don't grow hair where they shouldn't and watch their waists thicken into nonexistence. He offers help taking the rest of the bags up the steps, but I hold on to mine, as does Ruby Jo.

She falls back a few feet and whispers to me, "I don't think I like him, Elena."

"Neither do I."

And I didn't like the absence of surprise on his face when he recognized me.

THIRTY-NINE

Alex leaves us in the hallway with a brief *I know I'm hot* smile and the same suddenness with which he appeared on the weed-choked path outside. It's a warm room the three of us step into, wide and deep but decorated to minimize its size, to make visitors feel cozy. Chintz-upholstered wing chairs and polished wooden tables bring the walls closer, and the bulbs in their sconces are incandescent, yellowish, not that hard blue-white of modern LED lighting that washes out its subjects until they look like week-old corpses. Refinished oak doors lead off the hall, presumably to staff offices. The entire room smells of lemon oil and potpourri.

If I weren't tired as hell and wearing permanently wrinkled clothing from a twenty-eight-hour bus ride, I'd think I was back in the stately women's club–turned–high school just off Dupont Circle. Still, the hall doesn't match the untrimmed hedges or the abandoned playground we passed on our way from the gate.

"Fancy," Mrs. Munson says, taking it all in. Ruby Jo emits a skeptical little hum, same as she did with Alex. It's hard to tell which is the sixty-five-year-old and which is the girl who's a year out of her master's program.

The door closest to us swings open, and a small woman comes out. Her dress is the first clue something is wrong; the mountain of a woman seated behind a credenza inside the office is the second.

Both of them wear the gray skirt-and-jacket combos I've seen on the Fitter Family's child welfare representatives and, only yesterday morning, on Mrs. Flowers and Mrs. Parks. Neither uniform fits the body inside it. The greeter's hangs on her like a sack, turning her dark complexion sallow; the desk woman's strains at her ample breasts and makes her pale face look as if she's a candidate for rosacea meds. They're unhappy outfits for unhappy-looking women.

"I'm Miss Gray," the greeter says, not greeting any of us. *Of course you are,* I think. "You can leave your bags here while you're processed." *Processed. Like tuna.*

One by one, we're called in. Mrs. Munson goes first, and stays inside the office for ten minutes before she emerges with a bundle of gray fabric over one arm and a mask of incredulity on her face. She's told to wait while Ruby Jo takes a turn.

"What's that?" I nod to the dishwater-colored material.

"You wouldn't believe it if I told you," she says softly, and her eyes move toward the diminutive Miss Gray, who is standing watch at the oak door.

So we pass the next ten minutes in silence until Ruby Jo slips out with another armful and a look in her eyes like she's seen this all before, and Miss Gray reads my name off her clipboard.

My turn with the headmistress.

The meeting takes longer than ten minutes, maybe because of the ring on my left fourth finger, maybe because Mrs. Underwood can't conceive how I'll be useful here, maybe because I ask her about my daughter.

"You're married," she says. It isn't a question, but I suspect her voice is as flat as the Kansas plains even when she's excited. And I have serious doubts Martha Underwood, M.Ed., has set any records for excitedness in her career.

She sits back in her chair, which barely helps to narrow the gap between her bosom and the edge of the desk. Her hands stay folded over her stomach, flaccid and unmoving. They're man's hands—thick, ringless, and unmanicured. If she hadn't spoken, I'd think she was a mannequin, a mute statue.

"Yes," I say. Or I was twenty-four hours ago. Who knows what Malcolm might do after discovering I've done a runner?

"Mm-hmm." Her eyes, but not any other part of her, slide to the computer screen that's hidden from me. "And you teach science?"

"That's right."

Mrs. Underwood's eyes slide back to me, narrowed. "Which field?"

"Biology, anatomy, genetics. I can also teach art."

The eyes widen. "You're kidding, right?"

"No. It's what I did before. Like a lot of people."

From the look in her eyes, I can tell she's thinking the same thing Malcolm did while I was working my ass off in college, poring over thick volumes of color plates. She's thinking the student of art history has about as much chance of earning a living as a buggy whip maker in the twenty-first century. Less than that, maybe.

Mrs. Underwood moves her hands and starts typing. "Basic horticulture and language arts," she says, tapping away at the keyboard. "See if you can at least teach them to grow vegetables and write in paragraph-long chunks."

"When can I see my daughter?"

"Excuse me?"

"I said, 'When can I see my daughter?' Frederica Fairchild."

She finishes whatever she's typing and stiffens. "Mrs. Fairchild—"

"Dr. Fairchild," I say, meeting her eyes above the thick lenses that have been creeping down her nose since I walked in.

"Right." She doesn't bother correcting herself. "Let's get a few things straight. You're staff here. I'm the headmistress. I've got dozens of students, twenty teachers who hate that this is the only teaching job they can get, and five former school principals already lined up to take over if I don't run this place like Washington tells me to. I don't know how a parent and child ended up in the same school, but I can't make exceptions. So you do your job and let me do mine." She stands up, signaling the end of the conversation.

At the door, I turn back. "Do you actually like your job?"

"I don't see what that has to do with anything," she says.

I get the whole high school principal persona. Or the state school headmistress persona. When you're dealing with hundreds of hormonal adolescents on a daily basis, you need to put on your hard-ass mask and let the world know you won't take any shit from it. Personally, I've always suspected there's a course in education programs the rest of us don't know about. Something titled How to Be a Bitch and Still Keep Your Job 101.

Martha Underwood, M.Ed., seems to have elected to retake that course ad infinitum.

With nothing else to say to her after a second try at inquiring about Freddie, I leave the office with my own bundle of coarse gray fabric and explicit instructions that uniforms will be washed on Mondays, Wednesdays, and Fridays.

"We're not running a fashion show here. It's a working farm," Mrs. Underwood says as I close the door to her office. *No kidding,* I think, taking a last look at her. I'm not sure what I feel for the woman inside. Maybe hatred, maybe pity. Maybe a bit of both.

FORTY

Outside in the hall, Ruby Jo and Mrs. Munson shake their heads at me.

Yeah. She's a bitch, I say silently to them. But I've missed the point.

"Do you have a mobile phone?" Miss Gray says. "Or a laptop?"

Stupid me takes out my phone, waiting for a Wi-Fi log-in and password.

It takes all of five seconds for me to regret what I've done.

"You won't get reception out here," Miss Gray says, plucking the phone from my hand.

My connection with the outside world takes its place behind another closed door off the hallway, presumably next to Ruby Jo's phone. I don't know whether Mrs. Munson is plugged into the world of portable electronics. She doesn't look the type.

"She took mine, too," Mrs. Munson whispers as we follow Gray through the hall toward the rear door of the admin building. "Brand-new iPhone. One terabyte of storage. My entire Johnny Cash collection, including the live concerts. And *all* my movies. I'm Melissa. Lissa for short," she says, extending her hand and pumping mine with a firm grip. Seeing the look on my face, Lissa adds, "What did you expect? Agnes or Mildred?"

Alex is waiting outside to take Lissa's bag. Once again, he reaches for mine.

"I'm okay," I say. And we start walking as Miss Gray escorts us to, as she puts it, "our quarters."

Even though we've only been inside for half an hour, the open space beyond the building's back door is now shrouded in darkness. I can't pick trees out by looking ahead of me; only moon-silhouetted shadows over my head hint that some form of vegetation grows in the empty space among the state school buildings. Ahead of us, if I'm right about the placement of its corners against the night sky, stands a structure of monstrous proportions, a goliath of stone and mortar if the rest of it matches the granite blocks at its base. In the light of a freestanding lamppost, the cornerstone reads *1895*.

"This is the main education building," Miss Gray tells us. The information, if not her bored drawl, reminds me of my sister's first college tour. I was gobsmacked by the buildings, one for every subject I knew of, and way more than that. An entire city devoted to teaching and learning, with windows lit up even late into the evening and heads bent to serious work, as we saw when we took a stroll through the campus.

Universities are like beehives, I thought at the time.

We pass two smaller buildings, twin brick blocks with light glowing through their windows. Inside, most of the walls are bare white, no posters, no decorations, nothing to say *Hey, kid, this is your room. All yours.*

And the light makes the vertical bars outside each window all the more obvious.

"Jesus," Ruby Jo says. "Granny was right."

"Dormitories." Miss Gray waves an arm toward one building and then the other. In my head, I hear a game show host shouting, *Fail your test, and you can win one of these!* "Boys to your right; girls to your left," she says as we walk between them.

"Look more like cells to my eyes," Lissa whispers.

I turn to squint at the buildings.

They can't be bars, not really. Or if they are, it's only because they were built that way back in 1895. By now, the iron will be rusted through, porous and easily breakable, nothing more than an architectural artifact, a historical remnant that preservationists in some other brick building decided to keep in place.

The things we make ourselves believe.

Our little parade of five plods on for another hundred yards or so. Smaller buildings of the same style as the dormitories wait ahead of us. Miss Gray, still in tour guide mode, points out the dining hall to our left and the faculty residences to our right.

I realize I've just traded my three-thousand-square-foot home for an apartment.

Our escort stops when we reach the door to the faculty residences. "We eat dinner at six. So there's just enough time to check your bags and get keys to your room. You three will be sharing," she says, confirming my suspicion. "Ground floor, to your left through the double doors. Hold on one minute there, girl," she tells Ruby Jo. "Bags on the table."

Before I have a chance to take in the entry hall, two men appear from behind a glass partition. They have no name tags and don't bother introducing themselves before swinging our bags onto a steel table. And opening them.

"Hey!" Ruby Jo says. "What y'all think you're doing with my stuff?"

And my stuff, and Lissa Munson's stuff. One by one, our bags are unzipped and rifled through. My underwear sees more action than it has in years of marriage. Ruby Jo's box of tampons is scrutinized like it's a box of Cuban cigars. Lissa flinches as one of the men inspects three framed photographs, sliding the backing from each one, checking between layers of cardboard stiffener and glass.

"What's this?" the first man says. He's holding up a clear plastic case filled with bottles and tubes.

"My makeup kit," Ruby Jo tells him. "You know, mascara and foundation and things to dye my hair with. Wanna try it out?"

His only response is dropping the case on top of the packing chaos in Ruby Jo's duffel bag and zipping it back up. Compared to these two, the average TSA officer should win a medal for congeniality.

Miss Gray points us in the direction of our room, and Alex follows as far as our door with the suitcase. "I'll see you at dinner." He turns and walks to the far end of the hall, disappearing behind another door.

Ruby Jo rolls her eyes.

I'm the one with the free hand and the key, so I catch the first glimpse of our apartment. It isn't as bad as I expected, but then again, I was expecting a five-by-nine Alcatraz cell, the kind you can stand in the middle of and still reach each side wall. This is more like a scaled-down Motel 6 suite: one large open living area with a kitchenette in one corner, a round table with four chairs, and a crowded sofa–love seat combo arranged at the back wall. There's a window, but no television.

I wheel my bags to an empty space, checking out the bedroom we'll be sharing. It's as scantily decorated as the main room. Three beds—two bunks and a twin—draw the walls in closer. Everything in it is a shade of institutional beige.

"I've seen trailers better decked out than this," Ruby Jo says.

It's Lissa who goes to the window first, pulling back the brown blinds and coughing as a cloud of dust rises from them. She doesn't say a word; she doesn't have to.

There are bars on the windows.

In my experience, bars serve one of two purposes. They either keep people out or they keep people in. I wonder, with an ill feeling building in the pit of my stomach, which purpose these bars serve.

FORTY-ONE

We take turns using the bathroom, a cold and sterile cube on the other side of the kitchenette wall. If State School 46 had a decorating budget, it didn't stretch as far as the faculty residences.

While I wait for Lissa and Ruby Jo to finish up, I read through the information binder left on the round dining table.

Not surprisingly, it's more a list of rules than information.

"There's a lockdown every night at nine," I read aloud so my roommates—soon to be extremely intimate friends—can hear. "'Main door secured. Emergency exits'—and this is underlined—'will sound an alarm if used.' What the fuck?"

If my cursing bothers Lissa's ears, she doesn't say so.

"What the fuck is right," Lissa calls from the bathroom.

"Wait until you hear this next part," I say. "'Faculty must keep to their gender-assigned floors. No exceptions. Rooms are equipped with smoke detectors.'"

"So where can we smoke?" Lissa says.

"We don't, apparently," I tell her, leafing through the binder's five pages. "Nothing in here about a smoking area. Oh, and by the way, alcohol is another no-no. Maybe that's what Tweedledum and Tweedledee were looking for in our bags."

Ruby Jo giggles.

"What?"

"Tell you later," she says. There's mischief in her eyes. "Anything else? They gonna give us them military haircuts next?"

"Just a class schedule," I say. "And we have to wear our uniforms at all times when we're not in our quarters. Quarters. Jesus." I keep reading all the *you wills* and *you musts* and *you will nots*, pages filled with directives and warnings. Nowhere in the binder is the word "please."

Twenty-four hours ago I was on a bus, trading jokes with Ruby Jo and moving forward one seat at a time until the smell of urine and disinfectant was as far behind us as the dimensions of our ride would allow. Twenty-four hours before that, I was eating roasted chicken and drinking Spanish sparkling wine while my husband pretended his brilliant family was still intact.

I feel somewhat less brilliant now as I trade the softness of my blue jersey dress for a skirt and jacket combo that hangs heavily on me, irritating my skin.

"Penny for 'em," Ruby Jo says.

I don't have pennies' worth of thoughts. I have hundred-dollar-bill thoughts, starting with how much Anne must hate me and ending with what brand of temporary insanity made me pack a bag and board a bus and travel halfway across the country without a clue as to what I was getting myself into.

Maybe all mothers are semi-insane. Maybe that's part of the deal we make when we decide to let our bodies become hosts, when we lie with our legs spread and our insides knotted in pain and push and push and push until we think we can't push anymore, when we hold vigil during sleepless nights in rocking chairs and recliners, sweating over the slightest changes in a tiny creature's appetite, body temperature, weight.

183

I was insane to come here. I would have been equally insane to stay at home.

And anyway, the choice doesn't matter, I think, as we pull on our coats and walk back down the empty hall, pass the two Tweedles, and leave the faculty building. Choices don't matter when they've already been made.

We're the last ones to join the crowd in the dining hall, and draw scowls from Mrs. Underwood. I glance at my watch and see that we've arrived five minutes late. A dozen or so men and women in gray uniforms are already seated in groups of four; two middle-aged nurses slide chairs out at the table up front, where Underwood and Miss Gray seem to be keeping an eye on the entire room; and over a hundred children sit cheek by jowl on long, backless benches, plates in front of them.

I've seen tens of thousands of school cafeteria scenes. They run and bleed into one another like a montage of film clips: third-graders peeling slices of bologna from bread, folding it just so, and biting a hole from the middle; varsity basketball players practicing their dribbling skills with one hand while taking monster bites from Red Delicious apples; eggheads sitting alone, poring over algebraic equations. And, of course, the requisite food fights.

I know all the sounds and all the sights and all the smells of school lunchrooms, and one look at the dining hall of State School 46 tells me this one is wrong.

One man, slight and semi-hunched over his plate, shifts his eyes from left to right and back, like he's watching a rapid-fire tennis match. When he lifts his fork, I count three fingers on his left hand. The woman next to him has shocks of gray running through her black hair. She also has a scar on her lip, a souvenir of cleft palate surgery. Otherwise, she's beautiful.

There are fat men and balding women, hook-nosed profiles and recessed chins. In the far corner, four acne-scarred complexions lean into one another, whispering, then draw back when Mrs. Underwood's eyes sweep the room. Tucked under a table closer to me are the wheels of a motorized chair.

It's as diverse as I've seen, except for one thing. Everything about the diversity in this room tilts toward fifty-seven flavors of imperfection.

Lissa sees it, too, because she leans close to my ear and says, "I wish I could say we're not in Kansas anymore."

"No kidding."

The kids range from wide-eyed first-graders to lanky teenage boys who are still growing into their manhood. In the middle of a line of girls is Freddie.

Time stops when I see her, and everything that happens next is in slow motion, a film reel clicking from one frame to the next by the measured crank of an invisible projectionist's arm.

My legs move first, right, then left, then right. Step, step, step. A smile stretches sideways until it seems to reach my ears. Maybe I make a sound, maybe I don't—the soundtrack of this movie is a series of garbled underwater noises. My hand reaches inside my jacket pocket for the package of cookies I've brought. Freddie's favorite, I think.

Step, step, step. Freeze frame.

I see her shoes first, then the fine, downy hair on her calves, then her knees with the small, faded scars of childhood spills. I take her in my arms and inhale her, smells of plain soap and child filling me up. When she says that one word—*Mommy*—it's everything I can do to keep from breaking into tears.

When she tells me she loves me, I break into a million bits. I want to tell her all the things, even if they're lies. *I'm taking you home. Nothing bad is ever going to happen again. We'll go live with Oma and Opa. Everything will be wonderful.*

Freddie takes in these words as if I've said them. For once, she's more than a wall, more than a stiff cardboard cutout of a girl, and she squeezes me back with small arms.

If only we could stay this way.

But.

I feel the pressure of a hand locked tight on my wrist, hear the crunch of a plastic wrapper as something is taken from me, pulled out and away from my grasp.

The scene speeds up around me and in front of me and inside me. Mrs. Underwood stands firm, blocking access to my own daughter, who is, if I'm seeing things right, shivering inside a gray pinafore that's two sizes too large.

"One thing you'll understand while you're working for me," Mrs. Underwood says, leading me away from Freddie and steering me toward the serving counter. Her words are slow and deliberate and horrible as she slides a tray from the stack and sets it down much too firmly on the metal surface. "And you will understand it, Dr. Fairchild. No one is special here. No one." In her hand is the package of cookies meant for Freddie.

But she's taken so much more away from me than that.

FORTY-TWO

I was fourteen when I met Malcolm. I ate lunch alone in my second week of high school, a book in one hand and a cheese sandwich in the other. Every five minutes, I'd have to put one of them down and push my glasses up from the tip of my nose to the bridge where they belonged. It looked as if I were reading and eating, but what I was really doing was counting the eyes of other people watching me and wishing I could vanish, blend into the linoleum floor and plastic chairs.

Malcolm, bucktoothed and skinny, an Adam's apple he wouldn't grow into for another few years bulging at his throat, brought his lunch to my corner. There were whispers, loud enough to make out and sharp enough to hurt, circling in the air between the other tables.

"I don't know about you," Malcolm said, setting his tray down opposite me, "but I deal with them by playing a game."

"Good for you," I said. "I deal with them by wishing I'd disappear."

"That's not a very good game. I've got a better one." He pointed to a table of cheerleaders, their impossibly short skirts flaring out over impossibly tanned thighs. "Stupid. Stupid. Stupid." With each word, his chin moved, like he was counting them out. "If the building erupted in flames, I think we could let those three burn. What do you say?"

"Yeah."

His eyes roamed across the room to the jocks. "Total waste of life," he said, nodding toward one of the basketball stars. "Burn or save?"

"Burn."

"Okay. So you know the rules. Now you pick one."

I scanned the cafeteria, landing on a girl two years older than me who laughed at a dress I wore twice in the same week. "Her. The one with the big earrings. Little Miss Richie-Rich."

"Good call."

And it went on, until we'd burned every single body in the cafeteria except ourselves and one kid from the math club who Malcolm didn't consider completely useless. In fifteen minutes, we got rid of the assholes, the idiots, the "uglies" (as Malcolm called them), and pretty much anyone else we could find an excuse to hate. We even took out the lunch ladies, just on account of them being fat.

"Feel better?" he said when we were, hypothetically, the last ones standing.

"I do. But we can't burn everyone."

"Got a better idea?" His eyes twinkled with mischief.

"Well," I said, thinking I'd like to dive into those eyes and swim in them. "What if we turned it around? I mean, what if we made it so the dumb popular people had to—I don't know—wait in line for lunch? Or pay extra for stuff?"

We grew into ourselves, eventually, got better at blending in. By my junior year, our idea of color-coded identification cards had taken hold. By next spring, every school in Maryland had adopted the scheme. With our gold cards came perks: free tickets to dances, priority cafeteria lines, a separate student lounge. Malcolm used to joke about it being exactly like the classes in air travel.

"If that Margie Miller twit wants a better lunch, she can study harder," he said once as Margie stood at the end of a long line. "Same for the stupid jocks."

Maybe it was the old scars that kept me going, the taunts and jeers about my old dresses or the weird food my mother cooked; maybe it was Malcolm opening them up and rubbing a little salt in the wounds, keeping them red and raw and fresh, reminding me how they treated us before we became they. Maybe I was just a nasty bitch, because I remember smiling when he said that.

It wasn't as if I knew where things were headed. No one could have known.

FORTY-THREE

"Maybe she's got one of them demerit charts in her office," Ruby Jo says, taking two more trays and setting them in a line on the steel counter. "Three strikes and you get walloped with the cook's wooden spoon."

I hear the words and register something like humor in them, but I don't laugh.

Lissa puts an arm around my shoulders. "Oh, honey," she says, pulling my tray along for me.

Dinner is meat loaf, a sludge-like substance the cooks behind the food line call mashed potatoes, and a mountain of corn on the side. When we turn to look for three empty spaces, Mrs. Underwood scowls again and taps her watch.

I smile in her direction, imagining the watch being crammed down her throat. With a little help from me.

Ruby Jo has explained everything to Lissa, so I've got a sympathy contingent on each side as we take our trays across the dining hall toward the only vacant seats.

They would be at Alex's table. A bit of chatter erupts around the room when we sit down, then dies off as suddenly as it began.

Alex's presence bugs the shit out of me, but an ally is an ally, even if his eyes are taking turns studying paperwork and checking out my legs. I make a weak attempt at a friendly smile. He returns it and goes back to multitasking, leaving Lissa, Ruby Jo, and me to talk among ourselves.

I steal several glances at the table where Freddie is sitting, squeezed between two older girls, staring down at an untouched plate of meat and starch. She comes close to disappearing in the oversized pinafore, and now I'm worrying if she's eaten anything at all in the past two days.

At six forty-five, a bell rings, loud and shrill, signaling an end to dinner. As if they've been choreographed, the children push back their benches in unison, stand up, and turn to face the main door leading outside. There's no chatter, no whispered schoolgirl crushes or boyish jokes, only silence as the rows of children assemble into two gender-separated lines. I wonder for a moment what Mrs. Underwood does with the trans kids, the intersexuals, the ones who don't fit into convenient "he" or "she" molds.

Probably nothing.

Freddie files out with the rest of her group, and I notice the purple band around her right sleeve, high up on her arm. It's not something I remember packing on Monday morning, and in any event, I can't recall Freddie ever being a fanatic about purple. That's Anne's color; Freddie prefers greens and blues.

There are yellow bands and red bands and blue bands. An entire rainbow of color decorates the uniforms of the boys and girls following a pair of matronly women out the door. The two girls who were sitting on either side of Freddie wear blue. A small boy, who wouldn't be much taller than Freddie if he were standing instead of sitting in a wheelchair, rolls toward me. His colors are purple and dark blue. The last girl in line, tall and lean with a noticeable baby bump, looks to be about seventeen years old. She's the only one wearing a red band on her arm.

"What are you looking at?" Alex asks when he sees me staring.

Ruby Jo's foot finds my ankle under the table. Hard.

"Nothing. Just the children," I say, pushing my tray away, as far toward the center of the table as physics allows. The corn was edible, but there's still a pile of it left on my plate. Based on what I saw out the bus window, I'm predicting an increase of corn in my diet in the near future.

I'm about to say something to Ruby Jo when I notice an oddness in the dining hall.

It's a strange imbalance I should have registered before, when I first entered the dining hall. Everyone is trying not to look in our direction. They're trying so hard, with such a force of will, that they end up doing exactly that.

And they're all staring at me.

FORTY-FOUR

A million questions are on the tip of my tongue, but the first one I ask when we leave the dining hall and walk back along the path to our apartment building is for Ruby Jo. I've only now realized that this woman, whose cosmetics bag is the size of a small suitcase, doesn't have any makeup on. Not one bit.

"You're not really a makeup kind of a girl, are you?" I say.

"Oh, that," Ruby Jo says. "I'll show you when we get to our place. If you want."

I definitely want. I'm also going to keep wanting a while longer because Alex has been shadowing me since dinner, eyeing me in that way he has. That I'm wearing a gray sack doesn't seem to matter; he's seen me in short dresses and tennis skirts at the club, and I'm sure his memory is just fine. Will he tell Malcolm about the latest faculty addition here? Or—worse—will he hold that information back, thinking it might be to his advantage? I don't know which disturbs me more.

Finally, he leaves us in the common room of the residence building and disappears down the far end of the hall. Several other gray-clad men and women file in, taking seats on the lumpy furniture, raising their voices to above a murmur only when they're sure Alex is out of earshot.

I pick a woman about my age and ask her how long Alex Cartmill is planning on staying.

"I don't know." She shrugs. "He got here yesterday. Something about setting up a clinic. Question is, what are you doing here? You're the one whose husband works for Sinclair, right?"

"That's me. Guilt by association." I say this a little too loudly.

The woman doesn't laugh. "Well, honey, let me give you a piece of advice from all of us." A dozen heads turn toward me as she raises her voice. "We don't want anything to do with you." The woman jerks her head to the door, and the room empties, leaving me alone with Ruby Jo and Lissa and the television. I hear the word "bitch" from the hallway. Along with a few other things.

Ruby Jo takes one of the lumpier chairs and clicks on the television.

"You seem popular," she says as a commercial for laundry detergent comes on. The housewife in it is young and pretty and wholesome, smiling her way through dirt-smudged jeans and collar stains as she touts the magic of colorful pods.

"Being married to a monster does that."

"I'd ditch the bastard," she says.

"Yeah. It's not that easy." I tell her about Anne and about Malcolm's threats.

"Queen Madeleine is on tonight," Lissa says, falling into the sofa next to me. "Our illustrious secretary of education and bedmate of the Fitter Family Campaign."

Ruby Jo groans when Madeleine Sinclair's electric blue suit fills the screen on the wall in front of us. I settle back into sofa cushions that are hard and soft at the same time, and I wonder if she believes it all, or if the Fitter Family Campaign is paying her so much money that Madeleine Sinclair has forgotten what she believes and why. Because I can't imagine anyone—other than Malcolm—buying what this woman is selling. I want to turn it off, put on anything else. Something mind-numbing like *Wheel of Fortune* or reruns of *Lost* would be perfect.

My mother would say it's better we watch. And Oma would say the same. And every last one of my European ancestors who lived through decades of hell.

"And so, to move us forward," Madeleine says, "we've made some bold moves. But boldness is what's required. What's needed now. For all of us." The stress falls on "forward," "required," "now," and "us." I'll give it to her, Madeleine Sinclair knows her rhetoric. She's got that revival preacher thing down pat.

The cheering from the audience isn't canned; it can't be. Thousands of people are packed into the Kennedy Center's concert hall for tonight's speech. As the cameras track up and down the rows and pan from side to side, faces explode into smiles. A youngish couple with perfect teeth clap hard and fast and long. A family of five holds hands. Some high school–aged boys in the back row screech a piercing two-finger whistle.

"Here's a question. When do we finally say 'enough'?" Madeleine is in full form this evening, milking the crowd for everything they've got. "When do we stand up and fight for a better America? A better family? A better human?" Again, the emphasis on "America," "family," and "human" is palpable, audible boldface type.

And there are more cheers. More whistles.

The woman hasn't said anything substantive.

"They love her," Lissa says. "They love her like pagans love a goddess."

"Why?"

"Look." She doesn't take her eyes off the screen when she speaks.

So I look. "What? They're all just regular people." The words aren't out of my mouth when I realize the full meaning of that. *Regular.*

As Madeleine pipes on about families and better humans, the cameras once again scan the crowd. There's an irregularity in the sameness, and I'm just now seeing the problem. Every cheering person is like the next—clean-cut, dressed in that fresh-from-the-ironing-board urban casual look, mostly white, slim, and attractive—the utter antithesis of what populated the cafeteria only an hour ago. Madeleine Sinclair's idea of the new upper class.

And Malcolm's idea. Even my idea, once.

On the television, Madeleine Sinclair looks at me with accusation in her eyes. *You're no different from me, are you, Elena?* she might as well be saying.

"And so I'm proud to share a few key points of the FBP with you," she says. "Working with the experts at the Genics Institute and Woman-Health, we've—"

I look sideways at Lissa. "FBP?"

"Family Betterment Program," she whispers. "Weren't you watching?"

"Sure. Must have blanked out for a second there."

Madeleine continues with the charisma of a preacher on a pulpit. "Number one. English first."

The crowd at the Kennedy Center roars.

"Simple, succinct, and timely," she says, nodding her approval at the audience's reaction. "Number two. Our friends at the Genics Institute have been hard at work, and I'm pleased to announce a new battery of prenatal Q tests is ready for rollout. This is a first major step in the direction of identifying congenital issues before they have the chance to ruin lives."

More applause while Madeleine glances at her notes. "Speaking of Q testing, let's move on to number three. We'll be implementing genetic tests more frequently, beginning with special target populations. Once again, our goal is a better America, and that means better families. Better human beings."

Several hands shoot up in the front rows, where the press is seated. When the camera catches them, I recognize the woman three in from the left as Bonita Hamilton, the rail-thin journalist Malcolm has steadily labeled as "someone who needs to leave her laissez-faire government shit behind and climb aboard the commonsense train."

Madeleine's smile fades. "I'll take questions after I'm finished. Thank you."

Am I imagining things, or did her veneer just crack?

"Number four," Madeleine continues. *Pause for effect.* "This one I think you're really going to like, ladies." *Smile.* "We've approved a major federal grant for WomanHealth." *Another pause.* "All pregnancy management services provided by our new partner are covered by your insurance program, regardless of whether you've been referred by the Genics Institute. Starting tomorrow. That's one hundred percent coverage, no deductible, no co-pay. Not a cent out of your pocket. Now, I'll take a few of your questions."

Bonita's hand is the first up. Madeleine ignores her once, twice, three times while she fields questions with the agility of a circus acrobat, dancing around issues, never really giving a clear answer. Every word out of her mouth rhymes with "better" or "fitter," with "greatness" and "moving forward."

The defining characteristic of Bonita Hamilton is that she doesn't play by anyone else's rules. So when her hand shoots in the air for the seventh time, and when Madeleine points to a prim woman two seats farther down the row, Bonita stands up. All six feet of her.

"I think I love this woman," Ruby Jo says.

"Dr. Sinclair." Bonita talks out of turn, not waiting for approval. "Can you tell us something more about these special populations?"

"I think I've already said enough on that topic, Miss Hamilton."

Miss Hamilton seems to disagree.

"Just a few examples."

Madeleine's lips force a smile. "Like I said—"

"Prisons? Orphanages? Sanctuary cities?" Bonita pauses and smiles back at the camera with false ingenuousness. "Or, maybe, state schools?"

"We're in the process of defining the testing populations. Thank you." Behind her podium, Madeleine Sinclair straightens a moment too late. Her voice has already cracked.

"Thank you, Madam Secretary," Bonita says and takes her seat. "Oh. One more thing. It's really a question for Ms. Peller." She turns toward where Petra Peller sits on the stage. "How did you come up with the name for your company, the Genics Institute? I've always been curious about that."

I'm not curious, not after Oma told us all about Uncle Eugen, not after I looked up his institute and discovered its real name. The Kaiser Wilhelm Institute for Anthropology, Human Heredity, and Eugenics.

Eugenic. Well-born.

All Madeleine Sinclair's talk about a better America and better families and better humans weaves itself into one horrible, sickening concept.

"My granny was in one of them state schools back in the fifties," Ruby Jo says when Lissa clicks the television off. "Looks like we are, too."

FORTY-FIVE

When I think back, when I remember sweating through four years of American history, here's what I recall: dates, presidents' names, more dates, which archduke's assassination started which world war, pages and pages of facts and timelines and annexations of land, and more dates.

What Ruby Jo tells us now was definitely not on the syllabus, but it matches everything I read in Malcolm's books and on the Internet at my parents' house. The difference is she's attaching a real name to the nightmare.

"Granny says the testing vans came around a few times a year. Mostly they were these nasty women who made all the kids answer a bunch of bullshit questions." She looks at Lissa. "Sorry. My momma always said I had a dirty mouth."

Lissa laughs. "Doesn't bother me a fucking bit."

"It was a Supreme Court justice who said three generations of imbeciles are enough," Ruby Jo tells us. "Mr. Oliver Wendell Holmes. That's Holmes, not Hitler. Can you believe it?" Ruby Jo stops, takes a long drink of water, and starts again. "My granny was on a bus to nowhere sooner than you could say Jack Robinson. See, they had a list of undesirables based on the testing and whatnot. And she was no dummy. Or imbecile. Just had some of them mood swings, you know? The kind they treat with pills nowadays. Take a Prozac, the doctors tell you. Back then, there weren't any pills. But institutions, yeah. Hundreds of 'em."

I think of my mother telling me about the school in Massachusetts, of Malcolm dismissing her with a bored "No one's complained so far."

"They came around a lot to our town," Ruby Jo continues. "With their tests and their clipboards and their snooty manners. Well, they weren't snooty at first, my granny said. The women were all smiles and sunshine. They even gave out lollipops to the kids after the testing went on. Funny, though, there weren't any lollipops at the state school they sent her to. And there definitely weren't any smiles."

In the next half hour, we find out Ruby Jo's maternal grandmother spent two years in a state school, all because of a few test-happy non-scientists who thought the world would be better without her. Everything Ruby Jo has told us sounds like bad science fiction, but it isn't.

"But she got out. It all ended," I say.

"Well, I'm here, ain't I? Ruby Jo Pruitt, daughter of Lester Pruitt, who was Betty Anne Pruitt's first son. But I guess I almost wasn't. So yeah, Granny got out just in time."

Lissa and I look a question at her, and Ruby Jo's eyes narrow as if we're supposed to get it.

"Y'all," she says, "I mean this super-nice and everything, but it strikes me you don't have a clue how it was down where I come from. Now, if y'all will pardon me, I'm fixin' to go get myself a little drunk." She slips out of the common room, leaving us alone with the dead television and the sound of a bug scuttling around the far corner, searching for a dark hiding place away from it all.

The bug makes me think of Darwin, of all those little blobs of life crawling out of the muck, changing and adapting to the world around them. Mostly, it makes me wonder whether we're born with bigotry in our blood or if hatred of the strange has to be taught. I think of Malcolm and his supercilious, above-it-all ways. I think of myself as a kid.

I put the question to Lissa. "Is this how we are? Humans? Because if it is, I think I want to be something else." Anything but an over-educated, overconditioned human being. Anything at all.

Lissa doesn't answer my question, not right away. Instead, she flips open a notebook, the old steno kind with the wire loops on the top, and starts writing. When she's done, she leans forward a little, elbows on her knees. "You know what I think? I think I'll take being a human."

"I'm not so sure."

Lissa puts one hand up to stop me. It isn't a harsh gesture, or a domineering one, so I let her go on. "You see that bug? The one in the corner?"

I can't help but see it. "It's a silverfish."

"It is. It's a creature. Conditioned to do what it needs to do to survive." She stands and goes to the far wall where the silverfish's tiny tapered carapace fishtails back and forth, scrambling for purchase on a wall it can't climb. "See how he runs from my shoe? He'll run from other predators. Centipedes, spiders, whatever. But he won't run from another of his kind." Lissa's mouth smiles in a crooked way, one side up and one side down. "Well, unless he's running from a female during a mating ritual, but that's a different kind of running."

This bug is mesmerizing. For a long minute after Lissa comes back to sit next to me on the lumpy couch, we're still in the semidark, watching its iridescent form swish and scuttle, hunting for food, safety, a mate. I know that if I were to get up and walk over to it, the bug would fear me. I wouldn't need to threaten or harm. The bug would run for its life in the opposite direction, seeking out others of its kind.

I was never a bug, but I was a kid once. I guess in the same way there are bug politics, there are kid politics. He's got blue eyes; she has brown. Go with the one most like you. She's fat; he's thin. Go with the one who looks more like a mirror image. He's Irish; she's English. Identify with the known. Humans have been engaged this way for thousands of years: Romans and Greeks, Muslims and Christians, Aryans and Semitics, Brahmins and Dalits.

My question still lingers. Are we born like this? Or are we taught? Either answer is horrible in its own way.

"You want to know my theory?" she asks. There's conspiracy in her voice, like we're a pair of Cold War spies trading state secrets and cash in the back room of an East Berlin bar.

"Sure."

"I think we all have some of the creature in us. Some hardwired instinct that tells us to beware of anything too strange or different from us. That's part of what made us fit to survive. But." She raises a finger before I can agree or disagree. "I know we can turn off the xenophobia switch if we want to. It's one of the aspects of humanity. Does that answer your question?"

It answers one of them. I have more. I want to know what Lissa's writing, why she's continually clicking her pen in that obsessive-compulsive way, what brought her here, and why she didn't flinch at the scene of misfits in the cafeteria tonight at dinner. I want to know what the colored armbands mean and why Alex Cartmill is here. But it's late, and Lissa reminds me we need to be in the dining hall at seven thirty for breakfast, so no more questions for now.

I stay in the common room with only the red LED light from the television for company, and I think about mating rituals, and creatures that run from the strange, and my dreams of dancing Qs whose tails wrap themselves around children, carrying them away.

I think about Freddie and wonder whether she's crying herself to sleep tonight.

Like I know I will.

Tweedledum and Tweedledee are not at their desk when I leave the common room. I check the double doors leading to the faculty building's vestibule, which is more Checkpoint Charlie–type inspection room than lobby. Open.

The main doors, however, are not. A sign on each of them warns again that an alarm will sound if any attempt is made to open them between the hours of nine and seven.

My watch shows eleven forty-five when I let myself into the apartment. One glass with a quarter inch of clear liquid sits on the kitchen table. I pick it up, sniff at it, and recoil. It smells like fire. Corn-flavored fire.

What the hell, I think, and I drain the glass before shedding myself of my heavy gray shell and pulling on pajamas. Cotton never felt so delicious.

Ruby Jo is sprawled diagonally on the lower bunk bed, one leg hanging off the mattress, red curls lying in thick ropes on her pillow. If the mound of blankets weren't rising and falling on top of her, I'd think she was dead. Lissa, on the other hand, already snores softly in the twin bed opposite. She sounds like a content kitten.

And me? I've never been so wide-awake.

I climb the wooden ladder near Ruby Jo's feet, bump my head on the ceiling, and tumble onto a mattress that falls somewhere between rock and iron on the spectrum of uncomfortable. Above me, the plaster is close enough to feel like the lid of a coffin. Terrific.

Wide-awake and buried alive. I can't think of a worse fate.

And I'm still awake.

Sleep eventually comes, and the last thing I remember seeing is the wall directly above my head, white as ignorance and solid as steel.

I need to bust through the damned thing.

And I need to see my daughter. I need to tell her everything is going to be okay.

The problem is, I'm not sure I believe it.

FORTY-SIX

An alarm sounds in a room I don't recognize, and I bump my head on the ceiling. Again. Not an auspicious start to the day.

Lissa is already up and dressed; Ruby Jo is in the kitchen rinsing out the glass of moonshine while I shake off a bad night's sleep and pull on my gray uniform.

On our way to the dining hall, we speculate about the meaning of the colored bands.

"What color did your girl have on?" Lissa asks me.

"Purple. And Freddie hates purple."

The dining hall last night was full of purple bands, some new like Freddie's, others faded and frayed at the edges. I make a mental note to look more closely during breakfast.

What a strange thing, that purple used to be the color of royalty. Now, if I'm right, it's the color of failure. Bomb your test, win a purple band.

"Only one boy had a dark blue one," I say, redrawing the post-dinner exodus scene in my head. "The boy in the wheelchair."

"So maybe that means handicapped," Ruby Jo says. "And the pregnant girl wore red."

Get knocked up, win a red band, I think, *the twentieth-century scarlet A.*

"What about orange? A few of the others are wearing orange," I say, remembering a couple of girls whose backs were to me.

Lissa checks her notepad. "Haven't figured that one out yet."

We walk the rest of the way in silence, our foreheads creased in thought. Really, there's not all that much thinking to do. The colors have meanings. Terrible meanings, like the mark of Cain. Or the scarlet letter.

My grandmother detested things like this, any sort of badge or button that defines a person. As a girl, I only thought she was being mean when she tore off the green shamrock I came home with on St. Patrick's Day, when she tossed the little Mexican flag our Spanish teacher gave us on Cinco de Mayo into the kitchen trash bin.

"Don't wear those, Leni," she said. "Don't ever wear them."

We never had symbols in our house. No crosses or crucifixes, no flags, nothing like that. A few of the girls at school wore pendants—a silver cross, a gold star, a shiny crescent. They seemed cool, but when I pointed to one in a shop window, Oma whisked me away.

"Not for you, Elena. Never for you."

At eight, I didn't understand. Green shamrocks and Mexican flags were what you pinned on for holidays. Sparkling jewelry, what you got to celebrate a first communion or a bat mitzvah or the end of something called Ramadan. For the next three years, I wore what I wanted during school, making sure to hide the forbidden things in my book bag before the bus dropped me off in front of our house.

The fourth year, I stopped wearing them. It was the year Oma sat me down and told me about the colored patches.

Yellow patches. Star-shaped patches. Pink and purple and brown and black patches in the shape of inverted triangles. Bars for repeated offenders.

Lissa snaps me back to the present, to the dining hall now filled with children. "Remind you of anything?" she asks.

Oma's words ring in my ears. *Where do you think my great-uncle Eugen got the idea?*

It doesn't matter anymore whether Oma's stories are her own or someone else's. What matters most are the ideas that take hold, that move through cultures and time, repeating themselves with the help of people like Madeleine Sinclair. And Malcolm. And Sarah Green and everyone else, including me. I feel a sense of disgust when I think about humans turning against humans, one cold shoulder and one "my kid is better than your kid" at a time.

Breakfast displaces my disgust, or at least transfers it. I wait in line for runny eggs (they must be powdered), orange drink from a mix (also powdered), and toast so dry it turns into powder when I try to butter it. The meal is a far cry from the offerings back at my silver school, where faculty and students happily dined on organic greens and free-range chicken.

We take our seats at a free table, and no one joins us. I work on ignoring cold stares from the other teachers and audible whispers designed to reach my ears. *That's her, sure enough. That's the one married to Mr. Education Reform. Serves her right to get demoted to this place.* All the while I'm searching for Freddie at the long table of girls. She's there, and I smile at her because it's all a mother can do. Like the last time, Freddie brightens for a quick moment, and the light disappears from her face as she faces forward, head down, eyes on her plate.

I don't want to see her like this. I can't.

I want to see her in the high chair I took out of the attic. I want to see her smiling through a mask of puréed peaches, reaching out with a tiny hand for the Peter Rabbit spoon I bought before she was born. I want to see her happy and innocent, a baby who hasn't yet been crushed with the weight of our world.

"It's a money thing," Lissa says, bringing me out of the memory.

"It has to be." She takes a pen from her breast pocket, clicks it twice, speaks a few words into it. "Accounting. And document colors."

"What?" I say.

"Never mind." Lissa puts the pen away and pushes some rehydrated egg around her plate, the way Freddie sometimes does until bits of meat and vegetables morph into shapes and symbols.

When Anne was younger, she taught Freddie the alphabet during dinner. Julienned carrots became As and Ls; strands of spaghetti curled into Cs and Qs and Ss. Malcolm, of course, hated the girls playing with their food.

"They all learn differently," I said while Freddie practiced.

"She can learn with a pencil and paper." Malcolm took away the plate and replaced it with a notepad. Freddie asked to be excused.

It's these small things that make me wonder what I ever saw in him, and why I let him tear me away from Joe, who would have let Freddie practice her letters on a rare Hepplewhite credenza if that's what floated her boat.

"Can I borrow your pen?" I ask Lissa.

She does a funny thing. Instead of giving me the pen she's holding, Lissa fishes out a spare from her purse and hands it to me.

Ruby Jo watches while I scribble two simple sentences on a paper napkin. "Whatcha doing?"

"Writing a note to Freddie."

I've barely spoken the words when Lissa's hand clamps around my wrist, blurring the ink on my note. Her grip is strong, and it hurts where the band of my watch digs into flesh. She eases up when I wince, but doesn't let go.

"Don't," she says.

"Why the hell not?"

Lissa checks left and right and, apparently satisfied that Mrs. Underwood is preoccupied with watching over her flock, whispers, "Because I think our headmistress has a sadistic side."

"I can deal with it," I say.

Lissa shakes her head. "No, you don't understand. She might not take it out on you, but you ain't the only one here. Look."

I follow her gaze to a line of girls carrying their breakfast trays from the serving counter toward a table close to where we're sitting. Ruby Jo does the same.

"Do you see? Freddie's right wrist?" Lissa says as the girls walk away from us.

I see. But I don't see my daughter's delicate wrist. I see the ugly purple bruise circling it.

My stomach cartwheels.

For a long moment, all I see is red. The furious, blistering red of an anger I've never experienced and don't know how to handle. A gash of anger; an open wound of absolute rage. Freddie's my daughter. My daughter. Mine. There's no method I have to process the idea of anyone laying hands on her perfect little body for any reason.

"She's so pink," Anne said in the hospital room, moments after a nurse brought baby Freddie back in to me. They do that—take your babies away and, I don't know, clean them or measure them or inject them with genius serum. I missed her in those few moments, and when the nurse laid her against my skin, I felt normal again.

Anne traced a finger down her sister's arm. "So pink and tiny and perfect. It's crazy when you think about it."

"She'll get her scars, like everyone else. A half hour on her first bike and goodbye pink and perfect," I said, still dopey from the drugs. "You can't protect everyone. Not forever."

Anne had grown into big-sister role overnight. "I'll protect her, Mom."

I smiled. Wouldn't that be nice? I'm not even able to protect her myself.

Before I know it, I'm running out of the dining hall, up one flight of stairs, and fifty yards down a hallway to the closest bathroom. Its white tile pattern spins in circles around me, and I fall to my knees. I'm not seeing the perfect pink skin of my baby anymore, only the marks of someone else's angry hand on my daughter's wrist.

My daughter. Mine.

FORTY-SEVEN

All I can think while I take my morning class through two of the three Rs is what I'm going to say to Malcolm when I call him this afternoon. And I will call him, even if it means sucking up to Alex Cartmill to get access to a phone.

I saw my daughter's arm. I saw the bruises. Malcolm might be in the running for Shittiest Father of the Year, but he's still Freddie's father. He'll have something to say about the manhandling.

It's a temporary distraction listening to these kids take turns dissecting the short story we've just read through, a reminder of what I love about teaching. Or what I would love about teaching if I spent more time in front of a classroom actually doing that instead of preparing for monthly tests. My group this morning is a dozen sixth-graders, only a few years older than Freddie, and they've got questions.

"It's like the dog was smarter than the guy," one boy says. "I mean, at least he knew enough to move on to another place and look for something better. And what kind of idiot goes walking alone in fifty degrees below zero anyway? Jeez."

The conversation about Jack London's man and wild dog reminds me of the silverfish in the common room yesterday evening. Humans make choices; animals act on instinct. I wonder which species will survive.

Mostly, I wonder what these kids are doing here. They're too smart, too insightful, to have chances taken away from them. An image of the girl from the Starbucks flashes in my mind.

"Miss?" the boy says. "What do you think?"

I think you shouldn't be here. "Well, I think it's complicated, but you might be onto something." What I want to say is, *What kind of an idiot walks out on one daughter to go find another? Jeez.*

There is no knock on the classroom door, no warning, only the squeak of hinges, and Mrs. Underwood's voice dismissing my students and telling me to come with her.

Immediately.

On goes my coat.

I follow as many paces behind as I dare to as she leads the way back through the grounds, away from the education building and into the admin building. She's muttering about work never being done and if it's not one damn thing, it's another. When we reach her office, two men are waiting in the hall. Underwood nods to them, offering the slightest of frowns.

"I'll be with you in a minute, Doctors," she says. Then her door swings open and she inserts her mountain of a frame into the chair behind the desk. She tells me to take a seat, and I do.

"Are we going to have a problem?" she says, sighing. "I told you I can't make exceptions."

Probably. Most likely. Definitely. I don't say any of this. After Lissa's warning to stay on Underwood's good side—or at least on her less bad side—I only smile and shake my head.

School principals—which is all Martha Underwood is, whether she prefers Headmistress or Queen Bee or She Who Must Be Obeyed—fit neatly in the hard-ass, take-no-prisoners category. I've seen it. No kid wants to be hauled into the dreaded principal's office, and most parents groan at requests to "come in to chat about your child." Age of the audience aside, the school principal is usually not a pal, as the old spelling mnemonic went.

But I do know this: You don't take a head-of-school job because you hate children. Not usually.

While Underwood goes on about rules and enforcement in her little corner of the world, I register her office. It's a cold place, all polished wood and steel file cabinets, twin hard-backed chairs facing the broad desk that separates her from visitors. I stretch up in my chair and have a discreet peek at the area behind that desk, to check if there's a platform or other method of raising her up. The two pieces of art on the walls are not the ubiquitous school-office motivation posters, *Hang in there!* or *If you can dream it, you can do it!*, but dark oil paintings of a fox hunt in progress. In one, the hapless fox is already cornered, baying hounds radiating from him like spectators at a gladiator match.

Comforting.

The only personal touch in this room is a small framed photograph of a younger Martha Underwood sitting on a beach towel with a boy of about ten. She's nearly unrecognizable—thinner, smiling, tan. Nothing like the sour-faced matron sitting across from me.

"Is that you?" I say, nodding toward the photograph.

"Yes." Underwood folds her hands on her desk.

"Your son?"

She nods, and squeezes her hands until the knuckles turn pale.

"Where is he?"

"Somewhere else."

Part of the anger I've felt toward her melts into sympathy; part of it stays intact. I don't press on with questions, but I make up my own story, which may or may not be true. Unfit single mother, kid taken away, downward spiral to demotion and bitterness. It makes more sense to believe this.

I don't know whether she senses my questions, but she answers. "It's a job, Dr. Fairchild. I get paid to do what I'm told. Exactly like your husband gets paid to do his work. There are rules, and I follow them."

Rules. Orders. What's the difference? I think.

She unfolds her hands and wills herself back into administrator mode. Cold, matter-of-fact. "Anyway, I received a call from your husband this morning. He took the early flight from Reagan National." She checks her watch. "He'll be here in an hour, so you might want to get ready."

I expected Malcolm would come to make me return home. I just didn't expect it would be today. Now. In an hour, which is, more or less, my immediate future.

"Thanks," I say, and I stand up.

Before I leave her office, she says, "We all do what we have to, Dr. Fairchild. Best advice I have is to try and get along."

I want to tell her that if getting along means going back to Maryland to live with Malcolm, I'd rather not, but I only nod before shutting the door and running back to the faculty residences, weaving my way between brick buildings and dodging the tree roots that have turned the paths into obstacle courses. The only humans in sight are small, distant figures out in the cornfields. Farm help, I guess.

I need to talk this out before Malcolm arrives so I know how to play it.

Ruby Jo and Lissa aren't in the apartment when I arrive. The note stuck to the fridge says *Gone for a walk before they lock us up again* with a smiley face drawn instead of a signature.

In a normal world, I'd call my mother. A neighbor. Dr. Chen, the chemistry teacher in my old silver school. Anyone with an ear and a mouth. In a normal world, I'd have a phone and a laptop and Wi-Fi at the nearest Starbucks. I'd tweet and Instagram and FaceTime until someone, somewhere, answered. What the hell, I'd grab the closest bike courier on the street and force-feed him my story.

The problem with my current port of call is that I've seen exactly one telephone since I arrived, and it's snugged up between a pencil sharpener and a stapler on Martha Underwood's desk.

Also, I do not look my finest.

The gray shirt-and-skirt combo has more wrinkles in it than a shar-pei, and there's a yellowish blotch of I don't know what on my collar. My breakfast, most likely. After changing back into my blue dress and throwing the rest of my clothes into my suitcase, I twist my hair into a horse's tail, splash my face with icy water from the kitchen tap, and leave the apartment with my bags, taking the outside path around the admin building to give my heart a chance to downgrade to something like a regular beat.

As soon as I see the taxi idling near the front entrance, I paint a smile on, straighten myself out, and rehearse the *now, now, Elena, what in the world am I going to do with you?* scene. I've already decided to make the best of it, to play along, as Mrs. Underwood said, until I can convince my husband to bring Freddie home.

Malcolm is still in the backseat of the car, making no sign of either getting out or opening it for me, so I walk through weeds and puddles to the taxi, reaching out with my free hand to open the rear door. It cracks a few inches, and then Malcolm pulls it closed again.

My smile twitches, straightens, and reverses itself into a confused frown as he shakes his head. Right, left, right, middle.

Then he pulls a legal-sized envelope from his briefcase and passes it to me through the window.

"You're not getting out?" I say, even though I already know the answer.

"My flight leaves Kansas City in three hours." *My* flight. Not our flight. "I came to give you that," he says, nodding at the envelope.

"Long way to come to deliver a letter," I say. The rain has started again. Fat drops fall on the label, smearing my name, blurring me. I tuck the envelope inside my coat before the name on it has a chance to disappear completely.

"It's quicker this way, Elena."

"How's Anne?"

"I need to go."

I say it again. "How's my daughter?"

Smug is the best word I can think of to describe him right now. Smug and superior and severe and every other goddamned S word. When Malcolm shakes his head this time, there's no smile, no parental mock-impatience, nothing.

"Elena," he says, "you're not fit to be Anne's mother. You're not fit to be anyone's mother."

The taxi drives away, throwing back gravel and flecks of mud onto my shoes. I don't see it make the turn toward the main gate, and I can't tell whether the rain has blinded me or whether I'm unable to see through my tears.

FORTY-EIGHT

When I was pregnant with Anne, I'd waddle through the aisles of Safeway, filling my cart with every kind of forbidden food that would fit. I didn't even bother looking at the calorie labels; at seven months, the only thing that mattered was the hungry baby in my belly, what she wanted.

The store wasn't too crowded on Saturday mornings, if I went early enough, and today there were the usual suspects: working moms, working singles, early-morning joggers who had stopped in for protein bars and Gatorade before running home. I was in the olive aisle because today Anne decided she was in an olive kind of mood.

"Mommy," a small voice said behind me.

"Not now, sweetie. Mommy's on the phone." A larger voice, also behind me.

"Mommy."

"I said be quiet, Cheryl."

"MOMMY MOMMY MOMMY MOMMY MOMMY!"

I think I heard the slap before I saw it. When I turned around, the chubby toddler strapped into the grocery cart, little legs kicking air, stared at the back of her hand. I saw now she was in dirty leggings and a dirtier top, both splotched with blobs of dried baby food. Peas on one side, carrots or squash on the other, all held together with a full-body smear of something that might have been oatmeal. I didn't want to think what else it might be.

"Maybe you should dress her in clean clothes instead of slapping her," I said. "What kind of a mother are you?" It was bold, even for me, and I blamed my outburst on late-pregnancy brain. Or I told myself that was my excuse.

The woman looked more girl than woman, a baby-mama, and she had no ring on her left hand. She came back at me there in the middle of olives and pickles and condiments. "Who the hell are you? The kid police?"

I couldn't think of anything to say, so I said the first thing that popped into my mind. "I hope someone makes you get a license before you can have another one." And I walked off, away from baby-mama and her wailing toddler, forgetting the olives.

FORTY-NINE

If I had a list of rain-soaked states, Kansas would not be on it. Maybe they've saved up all their precipitation for today, when I need it the least. Maybe the heavens sense my distress and are crying with me, sharing my pain.

Two pairs of Tweedledum and Tweedledee eyes follow me as I push through the main door of the faculty building and cross the small entry-way toward the double doors. They take in my uniform code violation, start to say something, and then go back to being disinterested when they see the suitcase. It's a short walk, a walk that should take only moments, but time does enjoy playing tricks, turning short walks into long ones. We've all been there: the nervous bride promenading down an aisle, hundreds of faces turned her way; the college girl picking a path back to her dorm, high heels and shame from the previous night making her feet and heart ache; a little girl trudging to school on an icy day, backpack heavy on her shoulders, knowing she will slip and fall, knowing the big kids will laugh at her. These are our walks of excitement and shame and fear, and we do them alone.

I don't know whether I'm relieved or not when I find the apart-ment empty, when I fold back the metal tongues on Malcolm's envelope and slide the contents onto the kitchen table. Maybe some tasks, the most terrible ones, are best done alone, without witness.

Three smaller envelopes stare up at me. I open the fattest one first because the printed name of a law firm in the upper left corner seems matter-of-fact, clinical. That, and I've already guessed what's inside. You don't need a doctorate in anything to know when your husband has served you divorce papers.

I don't bother reading through the pages of complaints and affidavits and notices of service. My signature is required on only a few of them, and my future action limited to appearing in court three weeks from now, an action I can avoid because Malcolm has very generously enabled the hearing to occur in absentia. My absentia.

How kind of him.

The other two envelopes, much thinner, bother me. One says *To my mother* in Anne's handwriting. The other, *Elena*, in Malcolm's pointy scrawl. I open Malcolm's first.

Inside it are two printed forms, nearly identical. Various-sized boxes on each contain my name, social security number, contact information, and medical data. Gestation, gravidity, maternal age—unhappily flagged as "advanced"—all match my own status on the day I went in for the prenatal Q test, which is also the day I walked out of the waiting room, leaving behind two women who thought of babies in terms of numbers on an intelligence quotient scale.

But something's wrong with the second copy.

The first page, the page I created in an afternoon so I would have something to show Malcolm, has a bold *9.3* in the results box and a percentile graph just underneath the number. Of course it does, because I made it that way. On the second page, with all my identifying information, there are three words, even bolder, in place of the number:

And no graph, only Malcolm's pen asking *Did you think I wouldn't find out? Did you think I was stupid?* The "stupid" is double underlined.

I'm okay. The room and everything in it is a blur, but I'm okay. I know this because my mouth is forming each sound in the words, over and over. And over again.

I'mokayI'mokayI'mokay.

I should never have lied to Malcolm, but he left me with no choice. If Freddie's prenatal Q number came in even a millionth of a point below nine, I know what Malcolm would have decided. I know what he would have made me decide.

In the perverse game show I'm currently starring in, envelope number three stares up at me from the small Formica table. Anne's handwriting, a perfect, practiced cursive, is centered on the front. I slit it open with a fingernail, unfold the cream-colored notepaper, and read. It doesn't take long, and it burns.

Anne's letter has no salutation, no closing, and ends with a sentence that I'll never be able to erase from my vision:

I guess you made your choice. I don't ever want to see you again.

The "again" is double underlined.

FIFTY

Minutes have gone by, or possibly hours. I've watched rain streak the window, pause, and start up again. I've listened to the repetitive noise of a distant machine, a generator maybe, and dull, thudding beats in my inner ear. I don't think I've moved from my chair because my feet have begun to prickle with pins and needles.

It's a pleasure to focus on my feet right now. The pain blots out everything else—the paperwork on the table, Anne's note.

Through the open door to my apartment, the two Tweedles at the desk tell each other they deserve a break today. One of them—I don't know which—says he'll drive for the grub. The other comes back with a "Hell no, you won't. Last time you ate half my fries. We both go. No one here to worry about anyway except those new ones down the hall. The doc will watch out for them. He'll call us if they pull anything funny."

There's a whisper and a laugh, a private joke shared between two men with nothing better to do than exchange idiocies. A whir of machinery sounds as the metal grate separating their domain from the rest of the entry closes, then heavy footsteps, then nothing. Silence.

Silence, except for the scream inside me.

The doc will watch out for them.

Of course. Freddie needs to see a doctor.

Quietly, I shut the door and head for the small bathroom, where I comb out the rat's nest on my head, throw on jeans and a blouse, leaving the top buttons of the white cotton shirt undone just enough to look casual without it coming off as an invitation. It's then I realize I'm making noise—the sounds coming out of me are all the sounds a human can make. Crying. Sobbing. Some animalistic guttural sound that can't belong to me. Hissing and whistling and wheezing. But no words, only some primitive form of communication, some ancient way of putting thoughts into sounds.

They work, those ancient ways. They calm me.

I scribble a note to Lissa and Ruby Jo, telling them I'll be back before lunch, and I walk down the hall in the direction Alex went last night.

He's on his sofa writing when I reach the half-open door. His hand freezes, rich-boy Montblanc fountain pen in midair, and he looks up, throwing me that winning smile he's always had for me, even when Malcolm is around.

"Can I talk to you?" I say.

"Come on in."

The apartment is at least double the size of the one I'm sharing with Ruby Jo and Lissa, and there's not a hint of gray anywhere. These are the quarters for the staff who can come and go freely—the only decorations on Alex's windows are curtains.

"Anything wrong, Elena?" he says.

Where do I start?

I could tell him I'm in one of almost fifty state institutions, that I have bars on my windows instead of brocade curtains, that I haven't said more than five words to my daughter since Monday morning, that Malcolm has filed for divorce and Anne wants nothing more to do with me. But I think Alex Cartmill might know most of this already.

"You said you were the doctor here. Just wondering if you could maybe check up on Freddie." I think back to a distant graduate course on blood pathology and make something up. "She looks like she's developing sudden bruises, and I'm worried it might be a blood problem."

Alex puts the Montblanc down and invites me to sit in one of the Eames-like chairs facing him. "Can I get you a drink? I've got water, tea, and bourbon. Your pick."

"Water. Water would be great." The bourbon sounds better.

He's in silk slacks and a white cotton shirt, and he moves from the sofa where he was sitting to the kitchenette in that way people do when they're used to being looked at.

"I know about you and Malcolm. I'm sorry," he says, pouring two glasses of water. "Lemon? I've got lime, too, if you'd prefer that."

I know things, too. I know that when I look toward the coffee table and read the upside-down letterhead on his clipboard it spells *Genics Institute*. Underneath, *Alexander Cartmill, M.D.* "Um, lime. If it's easy."

"No problem. I'll just be a sec."

"I'm cool." But I'm not cool at all. Heat rises inside me in heavy waves, the kind of waves that can pull you under, tumble your body like a rag doll, leaving you disoriented and gasping for air before you realize there's no air to be had. I try to make light conversation—about tennis, of all things—while the rest of me strains to read the document on Alex's clipboard. There's time for only a few words before he hands me a glass of ice water, sits down, and oh-so-casually kicks his feet up onto the coffee table, obscuring the papers.

For the next ten minutes I sip at my water and pretend to listen while he enumerates blood disease symptoms. The room starts to close in on me, all the walls at once. All of a sudden, his cologne is overpowering, sickening. He's moved closer to me and he's leaning in, a breath away from my face. His left hand presses on my knee with such force I can feel each one of his fingers, an independent pressure point boring into my skin. There's a gold band I've never noticed on this hand, and I'm thinking "smarmy" might not be the right word for him.

"So. We should talk more about Freddie," he says. "How about you come back this afternoon. Say, four? We can discuss everything over a drink."

I feel myself smiling and nodding and saying yes, agreeing to whore myself to this mad scientist for my daughter's sake.

"Terrific. It's a date, then," he says. "But right now, I've got some work to do. Deadline in a few hours." He pauses and avoids my eyes. "We're rolling out flu shots before the season hits us." Alex releases my knee and takes my hand, pulling me up with him. "I know things aren't good with you and Malcolm right now, Elena. Maybe we can find a way to fix that, too."

The room suddenly fills with music, a familiar strain of trumpets and other brass I recognize from *Apocalypse Now*. It's Alex's phone.

Of course. He would have his ringtone set to Wagner.

"I have to take this," he says, and I catch a quick flash of the photo on the phone's screen before I let him turn me toward the door.

I steal one final glance at the coffee table. The papers are gone.

FIFTY-ONE

When I leave Alex's apartment, it's nearly noon. I'm high on adrenaline and low on morale as I jog back along the beige hallway to my own quarters with three phrases from Madeleine Sinclair's speech last night echoing through me.

Better America.

Better families.

Better humans.

I think of the Genics Institute, really the Eugenics Institute, and break into a run, hoping Lissa or Ruby Jo will be in. There's so much to tell them.

I should be shocked, but I'm not. Appalled, maybe, and all the other words I can think of that go with it, but not shocked. We've always done this, we humans in our little societies. We categorize and compare and devise ways to separate ourselves into teams, not so differently from the rituals of a grade school gym class. *I pick her,* we say. *But not him.*

Someone is always last; someone is always at the bottom of the barrel, the last to be chosen.

You'd think we'd grow out of that nonsense.

Ruby Jo listens while I give the digested version of Malcolm's visit, the guards' conversation, and the papers in Alex's apartment. Lissa, curled up on the sofa and alert, scribbles notes on a pad of paper, only stopping to mutter something about a twenty-first-century Jim Crow state, only the dividing line of segregation isn't skin color but Q scores.

"Fucking Progressives," Lissa says.

I have no idea what she's talking about.

"It's a Progressive thing. Progressive with a capital P, that is. They were a big deal in the early 1900s with their Get-Rid-of-the-Idiots programs."

Ruby Jo shifts in her chair. "I hate that word."

"Progressive? Or idiot?" Lissa says.

No one laughs.

"There were two doctors hanging about near Underwood's office today," I say.

Lissa's head jerks up from her notepad. "M or PH?"

"I don't know." The men outside Underwood's office weren't wearing white coats and stethoscopes, but they didn't have the tweed-and-Birkenstock mien of career academics. "Medical doctors, maybe." Of course they'd have more doctors here. With over a hundred kids crammed together in dormitories, colds and flu would spread, well, like a virus. And the chill air today is a harsh reminder that we're about to start another round of flu season, just as Alex said. The entire school will need shots, especially the younger ones.

"You okay, Elena?" Ruby Jo says.

No. Yes. I have no idea. "Sure. Fine."

Click. Click. Click.

"Lissa? What is it with you and that pen?" I say finally.

She grins at me, and the grin takes twenty-five years off her face. "It's a camera, honey. I used to be a teacher until I retired," she says. "History. Now I work as a reporter. Freelance, but it keeps me busy. The only question is how I'm going to get enough credible information to expose these assholes. Well, make that two questions. I don't know how I'll get that information out of here without a phone. Tricky. What else did you see in his apartment?" Her tone is sharp, and she softens it. "Sorry, I can't help being brusque when I'm in reporter mode."

I shrug and think back to the sights and smells. "Coffee. Good Scotch. A pipe on one of the shelves, tucked back behind something else."

"That's all?"

"Oh—when I was leaving, his phone rang. The lock screen had a shot of him with a woman and two boys. She seemed familiar. I don't know—the way she stood or something." I try like hell to conjure it up in the space before my eyes, but I can't; it happened too quickly. "She was wearing a hat. That's all I saw before I got the hell out of there. He's married, but he was coming on strong."

Lissa's eyebrows waggle up and down and up once, and stay high on her forehead.

"Told you I didn't like him," Ruby Jo says.

What matters, according to Lissa, isn't that any of us like or don't like Alex. What matters is that he seems to like me.

Two sets of eyes are on mine now, reminding me of a childhood playground game. In Ruby Jo's and Lissa's stares, I hear three words.

Tag. You're it.

FIFTY-TWO

We leave for lunch, filing in past the lines of children walking into the dining hall. I stay close enough to them to brush my hand against Freddie and whisper, "It's going to be all right, baby girl. Trust me." Freddie looks up with wide, frightened eyes, and I wonder if she can hear the uncertainty in my voice.

The next-to-last girl in line turns hard, accusing eyes at me. I recognize her as Sabrina Fox, the girl whose mother was practically dragging her into a car, insisting they go home at the same time Sabrina insisted the opposite. She nudges the girl next to her. They're close enough that I can hear Judy Green's words spoken so softly they sound like sighs.

"It's her fault. She's a monster. And you know I should have crushed that test last week."

Judy and Sabrina continue to whisper. I get every poisonous syllable they say.

Only a week ago, I watched Judy's mother, Sarah, pull yellow flowers from the beds in front of their house. I don't want to revisit that place, but not wanting to isn't enough to prevent me from going there, from hearing Sarah scream at me while a yellow bus took her daughter away.

Every single report we got said her Q was almost perfect.

Did you know something? Did you hold anything back from me?

How did she lose the Q points? Tell me that, El.

I guess you'll have more time for your top two percent now, El. Good luck with them.

And a few days after that, Jolene Fox blowing smoke in my face, calling Malcolm an asshole, wondering why her girl dropped from a silver school to here in the blink of an eye.

Now I'm back in the dining hall listening to the girls, wishing I could stop my ears. Did I know something? No, I didn't.

When I pass close to Judy, she stares hard into my eyes. "You should have studied history, you bitch. Don't you know it repeats itself?"

"What did you say?"

"You heard me."

Sabrina mumbles something about Judy not being herself. "She's sorry. Really." Judy doesn't seem to agree, but lets Sabrina lead her by the arm and pull her gently along to one of the long tables, out of earshot.

The same woman who gave me an earful in the common room last night is here. She calls after Judy, "You tell her, honey." When she turns to me, she smiles innocently. "Don't even think about reporting that. We'll all swear we didn't hear a thing. Enjoy your meal."

Over lunch, while I'm worrying over Freddie and wondering if everyone in the world sees me as a bitch, Ruby Jo talks about the Fitter Family Campaign.

She shrugs. "They don't like us mountain folk none too much. It's funny, 'cause before my mom had me, the FF—that's what we called them—was pretty strong down in our parts. I mean, they weren't Q testing back then. It was more like making sure the town didn't get taken over by Italians. Or gays. Or anyone who wasn't purebred, homophobic white trash." She pushes food around her plate as she talks.

"Still is, I guess. Some of them don't give two shits about how smart you are."

"Some of who?" I say.

"Some of the FF people. You know."

"No. I don't." Since it started, the Fitter Family crap has always been about smarts. Measurable smarts in the form of Q scores. Although when I think back to this morning's class, I wonder if that's all they're about.

Ruby Jo looks me over and decides I need to be educated. "See, I think lots of 'em are like that, all wanting to be smarter than the next guy, make sure they got little Einstein babies and Einstein boyfriends and Einstein wives. That's a good one. Einstein babies." She laughs. "But that ain't all of it, Elena. You think I left that piece-of-shit town because I wanted life in the big city? No way. I hate the city. If it were up to me, I'd hang out in my little piece-of-shit town, ride my bike, go apple picking, stuff like that."

"But you left anyway?" I say.

"Well, where I come from, people like me don't fit in so good. I mean, well."

It's not the first time Ruby Jo's corrected herself. I want to tell her not to worry about it so much, but I don't. Right now, I'm trying to imagine a place where someone as clever as Ruby Jo Pruitt wouldn't fit in. Hell, maybe?

She leans in close, a schoolgirl ready to confess a secret crush on the captain of the football team. "See, the thing is, I don't like boys so much."

"So what? You like girls," I say. "There's nothing new about that."

Ruby Jo cracks a crooked smile and shakes her head. "Maybe in Washington, but you haven't spent much time in the sticks." She nods her red curls toward Judy Green and Sabrina Fox. "You see those two over there? The tall ones who are always sitting together and whispering?"

"Sure. I saw them. The one with the darker hair lived on my street." *Used to live on my street.* Now, Judy Green lives in the girls' dormitory at State School 46.

"You see the way they look at each other? The way their hands touch when they think no one's watching?" She doesn't wait for an answer. "Those chicks are in love, Elena. Like with a capital L."

Once again, I hear Sarah Green's voice screaming at me on the street. *How did she lose the Q points? Tell me that, El.*

The only answer I have is this: Judy Green didn't fail anything. No fucking way. And if she didn't fail, maybe Freddie didn't, either.

When lunch is over, I make sure to pass close to Freddie again. This time, there's less fear and more pleading in her eyes.

"I want to go home, Mommy. Can't you take me home?"

I die a little on the inside.

FIFTY-THREE

I was in the kind of pain I knew from experience I would soon forget, but right now, the pain was an all-over pain, a leviathan of misery that squeezed and worked its way around every part of my body. Malcolm, gowned and gloved in hospital green, told me to push. Again. He'd been telling me to push for hours, it seemed, while a nurse fed me ice chips and patted the sweat from my forehead.

"Almost there, sweetie," the nurse said. "Just one more little push and we'll be done."

She said this the last time. And the time before that. Inside me, Freddie was twisting and turning and contorting into position.

It was hell.

And then it was over, the fiery torture behind me and forgotten. I was in the now, in a place where the only thing I knew was Freddie's warm body on mine. I wondered at her size, how eight pounds of human could have grown in my belly, how there could possibly have been room for all this complicated biological material to thrive and live, how any part of me could possibly have opened a door wide enough to let her out into the world.

At the same time, she was tiny, miniature. I examined each long finger, yet to fatten with baby pudge, unable to fathom how anything could ever be so small and so helpless. So utterly dependent on me for survival.

An invisible hand reached out and tagged me while I lay in the delivery room. *You're it, El.* And I was. I was the bringer of life and the protector of that life, the only thing an eight-pound newborn could depend on, the wielder of those thin marionette strings that had the power to lift my baby up or let her fall. I was everything, all-powerful and all-knowing. If my baby cried, I would soothe her. If she got sick, I would stay up all night and pour cough medicine into her. If she scraped a knee, I would kiss it and make it better. I'd done all of that with Anne, and I would do it all over again, helping her through colic and crushes on boys, making sure no one would ever do her harm.

To Malcolm, I was still me, still Elena Fischer Fairchild. There was no way to explain to him that I wasn't, and that I hadn't been since the day Anne was born. These babies of mine took something when they left me, thin slices of myself, leaving empty spots. Dead spots. I think I died a little when Anne was born, and I think I died a little more this time around.

With Freddie sleeping on my bare breast, I whispered to her.

"I'll do anything for you, baby girl. That's a promise."

When she stirred and stared up at me with those big eyes, those eyes that would be the same size at three and at sixteen and at eighty, that would see all of her life through the same physical lens, I cried.

They say it's postpartum depression. Or hormones. Or who knows what. But I knew then what the deal was—a simple matter of trading myself for my baby, should it ever come to that.

FIFTY-FOUR

When Martha Underwood marches toward me, I know I'm in trouble. Which means Freddie's in trouble, and that can only mean I'll die a little more. But Underwood's voice surprises me this time.

"Dr. Fairchild, there's a call for you. I've asked them to ring back so you can take it in my office." She sighs. "And you can bring your daughter along."

My first thought is that Malcolm has changed his mind, that he's worked something out to keep his family together after all; my second is that Alex actually took some pity on me and made a call to Maryland. But then those two words on the state school letter from last weekend come back to me. *Family emergency.*

Oma.

We follow Underwood out of the dining hall and down the weedy path toward the administration building, Freddie's hand small in my own.

"Are we going home?" she says. Her eyes are premeltdown wide.

I don't think so, but all I say to her is, "Sh. Just hold on," and I squeeze her hand in a steady rhythm to soothe her.

The rain has left a mosaic of puddles and muddy patches for us to dodge as we make our way through the grounds. Freddie trips on a ragged tree root, nearly falling flat on her face. A hand that isn't mine reaches out and catches her by the upper arm. The ring I saw earlier today winks at me.

"Whoopsie-daisies," Alex says. Then, hurriedly to Underwood: "That's for FedEx to pick up. I rang them just now, and they should be here within the hour. Monday-morning delivery, okay?" He gives her a large-format envelope before announcing—a little too loudly—that he'll be in his apartment all afternoon. That was for my benefit, I suppose.

When he's gone, Freddie whispers, "I don't like Daddy's friend."

Neither do I, but I may need to pretend I do, at least for a few hours.

We wait in Underwood's office until two, when my parents are due to call back. She's brightened up the room for us, turning lights on and even pulling over an extra chair with a few pillows on it for Freddie to sit on. All this sudden kindness should reassure me, but it has the opposite effect.

"I'll leave you alone here," Underwood says when the clock chimes the hour.

Freddie and I wait, but not for long.

I pick up the phone on the first ring, dreading what I'm about to hear, hating my husband and every single one of the people who have denied me a final goodbye, hating that Freddie won't see her great-grandmother again.

Mom's voice comes on, and I know something is wrong.

FIFTY-FIVE

I've known for a long time my grandmother would die. I imagined a tearful phone call from one of my parents, secondhand news from an oncologist being passed along, Oma's body weakening over months and weeks and days until it gave up. But I also imagined there would be time to adjust, to say goodbye.

My mother sounds as if she hasn't slept for a week. "Elena? Are you there?"

"I'm here, Mom. Is Oma—"

She changes to a tone that's less tired and more at wit's end. "I don't know. She's okay, but she's not okay. Your father called Dr. Mendez, and there's nothing wrong." There's a dry laugh. "Nothing wrong. He had to give her a sedative to stop her ranting, and even then she wouldn't stop. Kept screaming that I had to call you. I told her we couldn't, and she screamed some more. Oh, Elena, the woman's been in her room all day banging that cane of hers on the bed frame. They don't want to give her anything stronger because of her heart, but I think she'll kill herself if she keeps up like this." She pauses, says something to my father, and comes back on the line. "I'm going crazy here. One hundred percent batshit crazy. Oh, Gerhard, will you please make her stop that?"

Freddie stiffens next to me at the noise, and I mouth an "It's okay" to her. "Calm down, Mom. I'm sorry I'm not there."

"I'm not. You don't want to be here. She's been going on and on and on about Miriam's sister. Since last night, El. It's driving your father mad. Oh, hell. Here comes your father. Hang on, okay?" As if it's an afterthought, she adds, "How are you? How's Freddie?"

I want to tell her everything, but I bite my tongue. "I'm okay, Mom."

"Your father says she wants to talk to you. Just humor her, all right?"

I follow the sound of my mother's footsteps as she leaves wherever she is and walks toward the back room. Oma's voice is thin, but piercing, and grows louder with each step. When Freddie hears her, she reaches for the phone in my right hand. "In a minute," I say, although I'm not sure I want Freddie to hear her great-grandmother in this state.

"Are you okay, Oma?" I say.

"I don't like to be old. No one listens to old women."

I start doing my best to humor her. "I'm listening, Oma."

"Your mother had to call Malcolm and lie to him about my heart before he would give us a telephone number for you. You see? I told them it was possible. But no one listened."

"Sure they did. And I'm here now. Freddie wants to say hello."

"Not now, Leni. After. Now you listen to me. You remember I told you about my friend Miriam," she says. There's the slightest of pauses before she says "friend"—almost imperceptible, but it's there. Without waiting for me to reply, Oma continues. "I've been thinking. About my great-uncle." Another pause. "And about what happened to Miriam's sister."

I'm only half listening. The rest of me is trying to work some patience into Freddie and looking around Martha Underwood's office, more brightly lit than the last time I was here. It's because of the desk light, a Tiffany knockoff that shines a kaleidoscope of color onto the wall. "Look at that, Freddie," I whisper. "Look at those colors, and you can talk to your Oma in a minute, okay?"

Oma says something to my father in German, then comes back to me. "Miriam's sister had the epilepsy. You know, those fits."

"I know what epilepsy is, Oma."

"Yes. Of course you do. A year after I joined the Girls' League, Miriam came to my house. That was in September, I think. Maybe early October. Not too cold, and I think it was raining."

In the background, my father coughs. "Just tell her, Mutti. She doesn't need the weather report."

"I still think it was raining," Oma says. "Miriam and I weren't talking then, but she came anyway, alone, and asked my father if she could see me. Yes, Gerhard, it *was* raining. I remember because Miriam had on her shiny coat and she didn't come all the way into the house because her boots were muddy."

She's rambling, and now I'm also staring at the colored lights, at the pieces of glass in the fake lamp, at its brass base and the polished wood underneath it. Martha Underwood's desk is so neat, not a paper out of place. Pencils are lined up like little wooden soldiers, ruled notepads stacked in paper mesas, everything squared off. Which is why my eyes draw automatically to the envelope lying at a casual angle next to the phone. It's that one thing that isn't like the others.

It's the packet Underwood set down when she went to bring over an extra chair for Freddie.

The envelope is closed with one of those metal butterfly clasps, the gum underneath the flap dry as a bone, forgotten in Alex's haste. I know this because, while Oma talks about Miriam's epileptic sister and how the cellar flooded because of the rain and how Oma herself had to clean up the muck in the foyer after Miriam left, I've reached over and picked it up, turned it over, hefted it. I've read the address twice, and the *EYES ONLY* stamp on the front and back.

And, before I register what I'm doing, I've tucked the phone between my ear and my shoulder, pried the metal wings of the clasp
open, and slid out the contents. Words fly at me from the first page:

Petra,

*Per our discussion, here's the plan. You'll understand why I
didn't want to send an electronic copy. Too many eyes on us.*

Love,
Alex

Oma says something about a doctor and Miriam's sister, and then
something else about how the carrots and potatoes in the root cellar
went rotten because of the damp. I don't know. I'm on the second of
several pages.

GENERATION: zero (between thirteen and fifty-five years); female
students and faculty at selected state schools

TARGET POPULATION: substandard Q, ethnic groups (TBD),
congenital or social anomalies, evidence-supported anomalous
progeny

METHOD: quinacrine? (see previous reports on hormone therapy
complications)

RISK TO SUBJECT: light to severe; potential for fatalities

LIKELY OUTCOME: considered positive; untestable

COST-BENEFIT RATIO: good to excellent

". . . and Miriam stood there, accusing me, as if I'd done it myself."
Another pause. "Did you hear me, *Liebchen*?"

"Yes, Oma," I say automatically. "I'm listening." On to page three.

GENERATION: one (under twelve years); mixed-gender students

TARGET POPULATION: SEE ABOVE (with exception of progeny)

METHOD: inheritable mutation via targeted gene drive; insertion method TBD

RISK TO SUBJECT: negligible

LIKELY OUTCOME: 80–90% in generation one with geometrical increase over subsequent generations

COST-BENEFIT RATIO: dependent on insertion method; initial outlook positive

The clock chimes its quarter-hour bells. Underwood pokes her head in. "Everything okay? Do you need more time?"

"Just five minutes, please. It's serious." I hear myself saying the words.

And then, Oma. In German. Screaming at me to listen. "I said they sterilized her, Leni. They took her away and they cut something out of her and then they brought her back. Do you hear me? They did all that to Miriam's sister and then they brought her back!"

She's yelling at me in two languages, calling out numbers and years, talking about quotas and doctors competing with one another to meet them. The only numbers I remember are fifty thousand, and one.

Fifty thousand operations in one short year.

Somehow, and I don't think I'll ever know how, my hands work the papers back into the envelope. Then I drop it on the desk into the pool of colored light, as if holding on to the paper for even one second longer might burn me. I'm already burning with shame for doubting my own grandmother.

"I hear you, Oma. I hear you."

"You need to come home, *Liebchen*. You and Freddie. You both need to come home before something terrible happens."

"Sure, Oma. I know." *I'll just click my magic shoes,* I think, feeling the room start to spin around me. I hand the phone over to Freddie. "Go on," I say in a dry voice. "Say hello to your Oma."

While they talk, it's all I can do to sit up straight in this chair inside this bright and formal office where a few sheets of paper wait to be mailed.

My left hand reaches forward. I could take it, I think, this envelope with its evil, bloodcurdling message. I could hide it away and hope no one catches me, and then destroy the hateful thing. But another envelope would take its place, reach its destination, be opened by hands and read by eyes. I could take one page, though. One would be enough if I could deliver it to the right people.

Freddie watches me open the envelope a second time and slide out the most damning page, folding it into thirds, and then into thirds again before tucking it up my sleeve. "Don't say anything about this," I whisper to her. "Not to anyone."

She nods.

And the door creaks open.

I'm going to be caught.

Freddie starts crying, putting the waterworks into full gear. I can hear Oma through the phone, telling her everything's going to be fine.

"Sorry," Underwood says and slips out again.

She's smart, my daughter.

In the seconds before Martha Underwood comes back into her office for the final time, I lick the gummed strip on the envelope, press it shut, and arrange it cockeyed on the desk. Freddie tells her great-grandmother a tearful goodbye.

"I'm sorry," Underwood says, standing next to me. "It's always hard to hear bad news."

Yes. It is.

On the way back to my apartment, after hugging Freddie and feeding her another set of reassurances that I won't be able to fulfill, I study the barred windows on the dormitory building. If what I've read is right, soon there won't be a need for bars. Or state schools or yellow buses or Q scores. Within a few generations, everyone will be perfect.

The unanswerable question I ask myself when I enter the faculty building is whether I would have believed Oma if I hadn't seen the contents of that envelope.

FIFTY-SIX

Everything about the puzzle that's been slowly piecing itself together is wrong: the shape of its parts, the ugly picture beginning to form, the sinister sounds of its individual words, the numbers of Q scores, test grades, colored armbands on children.

The apartment is empty when I return. Only a note from Lissa and a heavy book with generic brown library binding are on the kitchen table. *Read p. 460*, the note says. *Back soon.*

I open the book to the page Lissa marked and start to read. The section header is long and rambling, but its message is simple.

Preliminary Report of the Committee of the Eugenic Section of the American Breeders' Association to Study and to Report on the Best Practical Means for Cutting Off the Defective Germ-Plasm in the Human Population.

There's an audible gasp, and I realize the sound is coming from me. I reread the second part of the title: *Cutting off the defective germplasm in the human population.*

Defective.

Germ.

Human.

Cutting off.

I'm expecting to see a list of names with "Grand Dragon" or "Imperial Goblin" next to them, those ridiculous ranks of America's premier racist club, the Ku Klux Klan. That, maybe, I could swallow. It would taste like shit, but I could handle it. I'm not expecting three out of the five committee members of the American Breeders' Association's eugenic section to be medical doctors.

"Jesus," I say to the walls, and I let my eyes roam over the page, reading aloud. "Doctor. Professor. Judge. Johns Hopkins, Harvard, Cornell, Princeton. Columbia." All men, of course, except for the single female listed next to *Woman's Viewpoint*. She was Mrs. So-and-So from Hoboken.

I turn to the front pages of the book. Lissa's copy is old, yellowed with time, and frayed at the edges. The article on page 460 is relatively short, only one of thirty-some papers delivered at the First International Eugenics Congress held in the summer of 1912. Not in the backwoods of some underpopulated town in the middle of nowhere. In London. I scan the table of contents, my mouth dropping at every fresh theme: education before procreation, new social consciousness, healthy sane families, the influence of race on history. It reads like something from the Third Reich, but it isn't. The authors are French, English, Italian, Belgian.

Eight of them are American.

My fingers fly through the brittle pages, hurrying back to the chapter where I began. There's another list, ten lines of blurred, black ink headed by a single word:

Remedies

Number eight, unlucky and unhappy and foul-smelling number eight, stands out.

I'm not a sociologist. I don't know shit about economics or labor forces or how to manage population dynamics. I know, though, about animal shelters. Any mother with a pair of young girls dying for a puppy does.

Euthanasia.

Like an unwanted dog. I think I say it out loud—I don't know.

The world begins a slow spin, gaining momentum. It's the feeling of being drunk and high and sick all at the same time. I fall back, but I don't sink deeper into the chair. I go straight to the hard tile floor of the kitchen, breaking the fall with my head.

FIFTY-SEVEN

Malcolm wouldn't have any of it. Between the threat of fleas and the inconvenience of twice-daily walks, he had zero enthusiasm in us getting a dog. I took Anne and Freddie to the local SPCA anyway, behind their father's back.

This was a major life mistake.

Inside the barn-sized building were rows and rows of kennels, each one the temporary—and, in some cases, extremely temporary—home of an animal no one wanted. While Anne and Freddie ran up and down the corridor in search of fluffy little beasts with big eyes and paws they hadn't yet grown into, I counted the pit bulls, the thin hunting hounds that had been turned in (or—more often—discovered starving in the woods) when they lost their scent or their sight, the street dogs with ribs rippling underneath flesh. There were scabrous old Labs, once-handsome German shepherds with eyes that said, *Don't kick me. Please don't kick me,* when my shoes clicked on the concrete floor. There were barks and yelps and whines. One sign said *Queenie. Twelve years. No further information available.*

Queenie. Someone had named this dog Queenie once.

Queenie had been deposed.

"There aren't any puppies, Mom," Anne said. "How come there aren't any puppies?" She had gone from gung ho to bored in the space of a few minutes, finally stomping out to the entry room, where she sat with her arms crossed and a frown as long as a rainy Saturday afternoon plastered on her face. "Not one single good dog."

She was right. There weren't any good dogs, not the kinds of dogs people wanted. I took Freddie's hand and led her away from the world-weary—and, apparently, kick-weary—shepherd.

I should have left sooner.

A young woman came in through a door at the end of the corridor, a door marked *Staff Only*. She flipped the latch on Queenie's kennel and clicked a lead onto the dog's collar. "Ready for a walk, girl?"

Queenie, despite her tired legs, looked ready. You could see it in her eyes.

"Sometimes," the woman said, "I hate my job."

So get another one, I thought. What I said was, "You don't like dogs?"

"You kidding? I love dogs. What I don't like is that we just got ten more in this morning. Ain't no room; ain't no money. Ain't never enough money. And Queenie's been here the longest."

I watched them leave, and I saw Queenie's whole life in a flash. She was a newly whelped pup, suckling at her mother's teat, nestled together with brothers and sisters. She was rolling in grass as high as her little legs, warming herself in the sun. She was playing with a ball, with a squeak toy, with one of those hard rubber things you stick peanut butter in. Her head out the car window, she was tasting air as it whistled by. She was curled in a corner, head down, knowing she shouldn't have peed on her master's rug, knowing she couldn't help it. She was being walked into the sterile, bleach-scented SPCA, sitting obediently while forms were filled out, signed. She was watching out the window as the young man who once named her Queenie drove away.

I couldn't cry on the drive home. And I was harsh with Anne, telling her to shut up after she'd complained about all the sucky dogs I took her to see. Roads and trees blurred together as I steered through late-afternoon traffic. All I really wanted to do was howl and scream at the humans around me. But I didn't do that, not with the girls in the backseat. I waited until we pulled into our driveway, and I made some excuse before running to my bathroom, turning the tap on full, and bawling until I didn't have any tears left.

FIFTY-EIGHT

"Slight concussion, but I think you'll be all right," a voice says. I can't tell where it's coming from, only that it's soft, and that it rounds off the edges of the pain on the left side of my head. For an amount of time I can't measure, all I know is the voice.

New sensations come in, slowly, one following the other. Something like ice close to my temple. The pressure of fingers opening my eye wide. Another eye, only an inch from mine. Girlish sounds, thick with the strains of Appalachian English, worrying, ordering me to lie still and hush.

Concussion or not, I need to move, and I need to speak. Ruby Jo's right hand disagrees, keeping me down on the sofa while Lissa talks, telling me what she believes. "Yeah, we've been tracking the Fitter Family assholes for a while now. Trying to find out where the money comes from, who they're backing for seats in the legislature, what their plans are. Bonita Hamilton's been on them like flies on shit, and all we come up with is a fistful of nothing. But she's got a theory."

"Eugenics," I say.

"Bingo."

"Most people don't know about it," Lissa says. "I taught history for almost thirty years and never saw a textbook mentioning the Human

Betterment Foundation or the Eugenics Research Association. Not a single one. Like it's our dirty little secret, an embarrassment we think we can get away with not talking about by sweeping it all under a rug."

She boils water on the small stove and pours a double dose of coffee grounds into the filter-lined funnel, while I listen to facts, numbers, the movement of oodles of money from Progressives like Rockefeller and Carnegie and Harriman, the Ivy League scientists who mangled data.

"It was huge," Lissa says. "And really got rolling in 1912 with that paper." She nods toward the kitchen table.

"It says—" I begin, my voice shaking. "It says euthanasia."

"We don't think the FF will go as far as a lethal solution," Lissa says. "They didn't try it a century ago. Not here, anyway."

"That's reassuring," I say.

Ruby Jo frowns. "They did so. My granny said they did all kinds of things. Most of it was passive. You know, not feeding a baby, accidentally forgetting some old man's antibiotics if he came down with an infection. She had a million stories from working in the town hospital. But, yeah, Lissa's right. They had other ways. I think if the institution my granny was in hadn't closed down, I probably wouldn't be here."

We all look at her. Even me, although it hurts to move my head.

"What?" I say.

Ruby Jo puts on a sour face. "Don't you get it? I just said I almost wasn't. Like, at all."

I do get it, and I don't want to. I don't want to get it in the same way I don't want to get leprosy or syphilis or cancer.

Ruby Jo looks us over and shakes her mop of red hair. "Remember how I told you about Oliver Wendell Holmes? There's something else he said. He said that if we had laws to cover mandatory vaccinations, we could have laws to tie up your Fallopian tubes. And that's what they near about did to my granny back in 1957. Someone figured out they didn't need to kill anyone. They just needed to stop them from breeding."

Lissa pipes up. "And it went on for decades, right up until 1979."

I fight my way to my feet, taking the folded paper from my sleeve. "No. You're wrong. It's still going on."

If there's a thin strand of light in this room where Ruby Jo sits lost in thought and Lissa presses a cool cloth to my head, it's the documents I found earlier this afternoon. None of them points to a solution as final as the eugenics committee's proposal of elimination. This is when I push the women away and go back to the kitchen table; I page through the appendix of Lissa's book. My eyes float down to number nine on the list and I will them to focus, concussion or no concussion.

What I read in Martha Underwood's office fits perfectly with the ninth remedy proposed by the Committee of the Eugenic Section of the American Breeders' Association:

Neo-Malthusian doctrine, artificial interference to prevent conception.

Ruby Jo has been quiet, staring out of our barred window toward the larger building across the grounds, and this time I'm the one asking if she's all right.

"Sure. Just thinking there ain't enough room for all of them," Ruby Jo says without turning. "The dormitories are large enough to handle a few hundred boys and girls each, but not much more. And I haven't seen any signs of construction on the grounds of State School 46. Then again, it's a big country. They could always build new schools. Or—"

"Or not. They could stifle population growth," I say, smoothing out the page I stole, closing my eyes and trying to picture the other sheets of paper, recalling the salient terms. "But everything I saw smacks of sterilization—permanent contraception."

Lissa nods, expressionless, waiting for me to go on. The hardness in her eyes tells me she can handle it.

I hope I can. I take a deep breath, slide a sheet of notepaper toward me on the table, and draw a line vertically from top to bottom. In the first column I write the heading *Fertile Stage*; in the second, *Pre-Fertile Stage*. "Premenstrual girls are in the second category," I explain. "Everyone else is in the first."

Again, a nod. Lissa gets it.

The second part is trickier to explain, so I simplify. "If you want to prevent conception in fertile women, you have two main choices: surgical or chemical. Surgical is riskier—not that I think anyone gives a shit, but they might care about the cost and logistics of opening up millions of abdomens just to tamper with a pair of tubes. Chemical sterilization is easier. Less risk, less time, less cost. And it's just as effective."

Lissa wants to know how it works. I'm not sure I want to tell her. The thought of someone pushing a bunch of quinacrine hydrochloride through my cervix with the intention of burning my insides is too gruesome to articulate. But I tell her anyway. "The idea is to initiate sclerosis in the uterus." I draw her a quick sketch of an isosceles triangle with the acute angle pointing down and circle the upper two angles. "Here and here," I say, tapping the right and left sides with my pencil. "So you end up with scar tissue forming—"

"At the juncture where the Fallopian tubes enter," Ruby Jo interrupts from the window. "It's basically a barrier method. But a permanent one."

Lissa is still all business. "Side effects?"

I blow out a massive puff of air. "Cancer. Ectopic pregnancy. Uterine damage. Central nervous system fuckups. Burning in your vagina.

The stuff was banned after a few test subjects suffered uterine perforations and went into septic shock." The thought makes me shiver. "Not a nice way to die."

"Reversible?" Lissa says. She's gone a shade paler now.

"Not without invasive surgery." I tap the left and right edges again. "And you'd have to undo the scarring on both sides because you can't predict which ovary is going to produce the egg that ends up fertilized. But yeah, it's technically reversible. So is messing around with gene drives, I guess, but that's newer research." I explain, as simply as I can, the technology behind altering trait transmission from parent to offspring through genetic engineering. I don't add that there's plenty of room for screwing it up, especially when I remember Alex's paperwork noted the insertion method as "TBD." It might as well have said "No fucking clue yet."

By the time I'm done walking Lissa and Ruby Jo through selective gene propagation and DNA tampering, through the manipulation of genetic patterns that can be passed down from one generation to the next, it's four o'clock.

Time to go see Alex. Time to find out what I have to trade for a ticket out of State School 46.

"You have to find a way, Elena," Lissa says. "I'd do it myself"—she looks down at the flat front of her uniform—"but something tells me you've got better odds. I'll stay here and write up something for you to take with you."

When I leave, she's at the table drafting notes, her mouth moving and vocalizing as she works through our talk.

FIFTY-NINE

I reach Alex's apartment door feeling more like Mata Hari than a demoted biology teacher in her early forties. Ruby Jo straightened out my hair, unleashing it from a ponytail holder and arranging waves of blond over my shoulders, fixing them so they lay in long curls above my breasts. One look in the mirror and all I could see were those horrible Q tails waiting to trap some unsuspecting failure and whisk it into state school hell.

I'm hoping the curls and the breasts and the makeup will be enough.

A girl in my fourth-grade class was the first person to tell me about sex. She had a big sister who had filled her in on everything.

"And the boy gets all hard and then he sticks it in you," she said, as we nestled into sleeping bags in her parents' den. I went wide-eyed at this revelation. "And then he shoots this stuff out and it's all over. No big deal. Except you don't want to get pregnant."

To me, it sounded like an enormous deal. It sounded disgusting and terrifying at the same time. "Has your sister done it?" I said, not really wanting to know, but this seemed like the grown-up thing to ask, something she would like.

"Not yet. But two of her friends almost did. They're fifteen."

That night I lay in my sleeping bag, unable to stop thinking about this new, unexplored territory called sex. My friend told me where they put it, and I let my hands find that place, careful to not rustle the sheets in case she woke up and caught me. Certain things, like teaching yourself about sex for the first time, are better done without interruptions.

None of what I discovered that night sounded appealing, let alone possible. Years later, when Joe and I went at it in the backseat of his Mustang, I discovered it was possible, and more than appealing, if I was with the right man. But the idea of Alex's hands and mouth on me, the thought of him pushing into my body, takes me back to that age of sexual latency and fills me with dread.

He offers me a drink when I step inside, a small crystal glass of neat Scotch. I'm thinking I might need a few of them.

"So," he says. "What shall we talk about?" Alex takes a seat on the sofa after inviting me to sit across from him in one of the Eames chairs.

I take a sip of my drink and let it fill me with warmth. Direct is probably best now. "I want you to help me get home. With my daughter," I say, crossing my legs, letting some skin show.

His lips curl into a smile, but the smile doesn't reach the other parts of his face. Cold, calculating eyes stare back at me, leveling themselves with mine. Not even a glance down to my legs.

Forty is a strange age, a milestone. A time to sit down and think about life. Growing older never bothered me, and I always thought the few wisps of gray at my temples lent a scholarly sort of air. I dyed them, of course, at Malcolm's suggestion. "It'll take years off your life," he said. About a thousand times.

I still run and do the weights routine at my gym, I haven't yet acquired that dreaded middle-aged band of fat around my waist, and whatever skin-care nonregimen I've been on for the past decade seems to be working. But forty hit me hard. It just didn't hit me as hard as the realization that Alex doesn't seem to give a shit about the only thing I have to offer him.

"There's a way out of here, Elena. If you want to take it."

"Tell me."

He leans back, letting the sofa receive him, folding his hands behind his head as if we were two people having a chat over drinks. Casual and carefree. "I need volunteers. For some tests I want to run. Tell me, and tell me the truth, because I can find out. Are you still menstruating?"

I feel naked, exposed, the way I felt the first time I went in for a Pap smear, feet up in stirrups, the entirety of me opened up for a doctor to prod at. My voice is a hoarse whisper when I answer yes.

"Regular?"

"Yes." I am, but I know one day I won't be. I won't bleed to the tune of a clock anymore. We tell our girls when they start their periods that they're women. We say trite things like *You're a woman now*. Does the converse also hold? At the other end, when nature stops us, do we become unwomen? Do we dry up when we cease being capable of breeding? I've always put this question off, and now I can't put it off any longer. I know what Alex is asking, and what he is about to propose.

"Good." He reaches forward for a small book and leafs through it. "I can schedule this for later. Seven o'clock this evening." It isn't a question, only an order.

"You're one of them," I say. "Aren't you?"

"Yes."

The air in his apartment goes stale and cold.

"We're doing good work at the institute. Great work. Another twenty years and we won't need the state schools anymore. Think about it, Elena. Think about a world where everyone is at the top. No

257

more disease, no more social inequality, no more competition. We'll be rid of the bad apples."

Bullshit, I think. "It's the fish barrel problem again. Take out the old ones, and you still have the problem. Sameness is an illusion, Alex."

He waves a dismissive hand at me. "Malcolm was right about you."

"You talk to my husband about me?"

"I talk to him about quite a few things. But yes. You've come up." He stands, smooths out his trousers, and pours himself another drink. There's no offer of a second for me. "I'd love to sit here and discuss your marital problems, Elena, but I have to call my wife." He opens the door, waiting for me to go through it. "Seven tonight. Sharp. Meet me in the lobby. And I'll arrange to fly you home immediately after."

He hasn't mentioned Freddie. Not once.

"What about my daughter? I'm not leaving here without her."

"You're the first trial subject," he says. "After a week, we'll know more. And then we can make arrangements for your daughter."

Make arrangements for my daughter.

I hesitate at the door.

"Anything else?"

"Only that you're a monster." And with that, I go.

When I leave the way I came in, I think about how I came to Alex's apartment expecting him to put something into me. I didn't expect he would be taking something out.

SIXTY

My flight is only hours from now, a direct hop from Kansas City to Washington Reagan. There will be two passengers: Alex Cartmill and me. The fare? Nothing.

Well, that's not true. This flight is going to cost me.

Alex even arranged a surprise. I got to have an early dinner with Freddie. Just us, no one else, unless you count Alex himself, who made sure I kept the conversation to banalities. Dinner was easy. The goodbyes were not.

"I'll see you soon, baby girl," I say, stroking her back, lulling her into a quiet place. "Very soon." I didn't know whether it was true, but I made it seem so, saying it over and over again until Freddie's grip finally relaxed and we let each other go.

The monster watched us with icy indifference.

At six thirty, Lissa walks me through the workings of her pen. "Camera's at the butt end. Click once to snap a picture, click twice to record. I've captured an image of the page we went over this afternoon. No sense trying to take a hard copy of anything with you," she says. "And I recorded my article. It's all on the drive. Micro-USB."

I'm half listening.

"Elena." Her voice is hard. "You need to get this to my contacts at the *Washington Post*. Bonita Hamilton, if you can. If not, ask for Jay Jackson. That's it, get it? Those two and no one else. One or the other of them is always there. And, for chrissake, don't lose this. It's got everything on it." She hugs me briskly and turns me over to Ruby Jo.

"You sure you wanna do this?"

"No," I say, my cheek pressed against Ruby Jo's. "But I have to."

She doesn't ask me again.

SIXTY-ONE

When the time comes, I walk through the doors of a building on the far side of the school grounds, accompanied by Alex. He smells of antiseptic instead of Scotch and expensive cologne, and he avoids looking directly at me.

Inside a room that brings back uncomfortable gynecological visits, there's another man waiting, a diminutive man in a white coat who instructs me to strip from the waist down and lie on the examining table.

"There's a paper sheet for you, ma'am," he says, pointing to the table. "Just give us a shout when you're ready."

I'm dumbstruck when they leave me. My limbs don't want to work, refuse to perform the simple tasks of removing my shoes and slipping off my underwear. For several moments, I stand still in the center of this cold and bright room, wanting to run back out into the night. I don't know where I would go, or how far I would get, but my feet want to run.

A knock at the door startles me. "All set in there, Dr. Fairchild?"

No, I'm not all set in here. I'm not all set anywhere. It takes me a moment to find my voice.

"Just a minute," I say. The words come out in a hoarse whisper, and

I search the room for another door, a window, an air-conditioning vent. Any escape that will carry me out of this and back to the apartment with Lissa and Ruby Jo.

How strangely one hell becomes a sort of heaven.

Another knock, but this time the voice isn't the pleasant little man in the white coat. It's Alex informing me I have exactly one minute. One minute to decide whether to let this monster have his way with me.

My hands move on their own, working one leg at a time out of jeans and a pair of silk panties I bought to tempt Malcolm once, back when tempting him was still a thing I wanted to do. I clamber up on the examination table and unfold the sheet that will hide my lower half, both protecting me from being seen and protecting me from seeing. Every motion is automatic, dictated by some part of my brain that can only think in future images: Freddie on a table, Anne on a table. The woman I am tells me to run, but the mother inside me makes a different choice. The only choice, really.

Maybe I say "I'm ready." It's possible I don't, but the door opens all the same, and Alex walks in, followed by the much shorter, much less handsome man. They're a striking contrast, one perfect silver school poster child and the other not.

"You may feel some pressure," the short man says as his hands disappear under the sheet and he begins prodding me with latex-covered hands. "Here's the fundus," he says. "Anteverted seventy to eighty percent. Ovaries appear normal."

While he fingers my flesh from inside and out, I get a close-up of the embroidered name on his lab coat. It reads *Mender* in light blue script. Nurse Mender. How fucking ironic can you get?

A steel tray is on the table next to my elbow. On it is a pouch, one of those sterile tear-apart envelopes I've seen during doctor's visits, the kind that hold specula and swab sticks, single-use paraphernalia. Alex snaps on a pair of latex gloves, tears the pouch with a practiced gesture he must have done a thousand times, and slides a foil packet of poison from it.

The label says *mepacrine hydrochloride.* I know this is the International Nonproprietary Name for the same drug I found in Alex's paperwork. What I don't know is how I snap a picture of it on Lissa's pen camera without being seen.

I cough. "Could I have a glass of water before we start? Please?"

Nurse Mender smiles at me. "Of course, dear." And he leaves the room as Alex turns to his phone and I wiggle my right hand free of the paper sheet, holding my breath.

Click.

Alex's head snaps up and the smile fades from his lips. "Problem?"

"No. Just felt my arm falling asleep," I say.

Then his hand is on me, under the sheet, working its way up along the inside of my thigh.

My eyes widen. "Stop."

He stops, but only to lock the door. When he comes back, he leans in, close, and I can smell the aftershave and pipe tobacco underneath a heavy layer of soap as he takes off his gloves. "Are you as cold a fish as Malcolm says you are?" One hand is back on my leg now, skin to skin, the other pushing me down into the examination table. "I'll bet you aren't."

The paper sheet crumples as I jerk myself to one side and swing my left hand out. Alex catches it in midair, as if my fist were a foam ball, not flesh and bone and nerve. It hurts. It hurts like hell. "Let me go." Again, my voice is small, weak, thin. I try again, and Alex laughs.

"I'll let you go. All the way to Washington." He releases my hand, goes to unlock the door, and turns to the sink to scrub. The water runs and runs and runs, and it seems like he's trying to scrub me off of him. Then, with dry hands, he pulls on a fresh pair of latex gloves. "I could hurt you, you know," he whispers in my ear at the same time he tears the wrapper off a plastic speculum. "I could puncture you or make your insides burn. I could do all kinds of things, and you wouldn't even realize it until it was too late. I could make you disappear."

Disappear.

It's the right word. The word for what I'd like to do now if I had the power. All I can do is think about Rosaria Delgado and Joe's baby and all the other ones I made disappear. And someone else. A memory I suppressed long ago.

Nurse Mender is back and holds a paper cup of water to my lips. "There you go, dear," he says. "Nice and slow. Small sips." His hand is cool against my forehead, soothing. He takes it away after I drink and presses me back against the exam table, then tells me to scoot down a bit. My feet move into the stirrups without my help.

"This should take less than a minute," Alex says, pushing the speculum in, opening me up artificially.

I lie still, and for the first time in my life, I allow my body to be violated. In a way, I deserve it.

SIXTY-TWO

THEN:

I started hating Mary Ripley when I was in the twelfth grade, a few months after Mary transferred into the new private high school where I now found myself running with the in crowd of lipsticked and hair-sprayed girls I'd always thought I wanted to be a part of. Every day, I had to sit behind her in Mrs. Hill's AP English class; every day, I had to watch flakes of dandruff fall from her scalp onto the same black pullover she wore.

She was a thin, redheaded girl from the other side of town, not stupid, but not like the rest of us, just one of the half-dozen charity cases Rockville Academy took on each year. Mary brought her lunch in a crumpled paper bag, worn soft from folding and unfolding and refolding. Her shoes were scuffed and a size too small, so Mary would slip her heels out of them sometimes during class, revealing thread-bare socks whose heels had been rubbed to translucency. But I didn't hate her for being poor, or for being one of ten siblings.

I hated Mary Ripley because she was going to drag me right back to the bottom of the barrel I'd tried so hard to climb out of.

The girls I hung out with called her Scary Mary. They flinched away from her in crowded hallways, worried they might catch something; they huddled at cafeteria tables over bags of chips and hoagie sandwiches they bought with their allowances; they whispered epithets about her overbreeding Irish parents when they thought she couldn't hear.

"She's not that bad," I said that early November Tuesday at lunch. Three pairs of mascaraed eyes flashed at me.

"Maybe you should take her to the homecoming dance instead of Malcolm if you like her so much, El," Susan joked. She slid down into her chair. "Oh, God. Here she comes."

Mary was on her way over to us.

"Hi, El," she said, ignoring the rolling eyes of the other girls. "Maybe we could hang out on Saturday if you're not doing anything." Mary had a soft voice, the kind I associated with a dog that had been kicked one time too many.

"Sorry," I said. "It's homecoming."

Susan tittered, elbowing first Becky to her right, then Nicole to her left. When Mary was gone, she said, "You *have* to get rid of her, El. I mean, people are staring at us."

On Wednesday, Mary bumped into me after gym class.

One minute I was up, forcing a comb through a still-wet mass of hair, yelling to—I don't know—Becky or Susan or Nicole across the room. Homecoming was this Saturday, and we were in full *what are you wearing?* mode, worrying over shoes (strappy or closed toe) and lipsticks (matte or gloss) and what color polish to put on our nails (French mani or classic vixen red).

"I'm going for a Midnight Mauve lipstick this time," Susan called out from under a towel.

Nicole reached over and snapped the waistband of Susan's panties. "Like that's a surprise. They might as well call it Midnight Missionary Position. Or Midnight Billy Baxter's Cock, since that's where it'll end up."

Susan came back with something equally catty, Nicole howled a laugh, and I started across the locker room to show off my latest makeup acquisition. That's when Scary Mary, head bent in avoidance or supplication or self-loathing, walked into me.

Give it up, Elena. You walked into her. You didn't see her because she was invisible and you walked right into her.

And we both went down in a tumble of towels and gym shorts.

Nicole howled again. "Watch it, Len, or you'll get those Catholic cooties on you."

I could have said something. Well, I could have said something other than what I said. I could have said anything besides what I said. I could have said something different from the last words I ever said to Scary Mary, words I haven't dared let myself remember.

Because, after all, Mary wasn't as important as whether I'd be back at the bottom of the fish barrel.

I think we all have a built-in defense mechanism, a protective shield that kicks in when we make stupid mistakes. Mine kicked in that morning like some fucking force field out of a bad science fiction movie, a gravitational pull that sucked me in and wouldn't let go. I stood, leaving Mary bewildered and probably shattered forever on the tile floor, as if she had been some delicate crystal ornament teetering on the edge of a mantelpiece while spoiled children played around her, never caring what devastation a wild hand or a quick turn of the head might bring about. I stood and I walked away and I said to myself that I'd rather die than be her.

All of this is true. Except I said something far worse. And I didn't say it to myself.

After that, Mary turned into a ghost of a girl, so none of us was surprised when Mary turned into exactly that.

I don't mean a real ghost—I don't believe in that shit. But one day in early December, Mary stopped coming to school. The next week during assembly, we found out why.

Someone said it was pneumonia. Someone else, cancer. Someone from the football team, coarse as always, spread around a story that Mary looked in the mirror one morning and died of fright. It being high school, all the someones went to her funeral—the principal handed out free passes.

This is what I remember about that day:

I sat in the back pew, all the way to the left, not really wanting to see Mary's parents when they entered, definitely not wanting to approach the plain wooden coffin, slathered with varnish to make it look more expensive than it was. I studied my hands, the hymnal in the little rack, the kneeling bench that creaked when my foot absently rocked it up and down, up and down. I did everything I could to keep my mind off Mary's body in that box as her five brothers carried it down the aisle, weeping like children.

Word made its way around our town, speculations about how she did it, whether it happened quickly or slowly, who found the body and where they found it. Bathtub? Garage? Basement?

By the spring term, when college acceptances began rolling in and the first daffodils replaced slush and snow, everyone had forgotten about the girl who wore the same moth-eaten sweater and the hand-me-down Thom McAns with soles as thin as early winter ice.

Almost everyone had forgotten.

SIXTY-THREE

When he's finished, Alex removes the speculum with a swift pull, hurting me intentionally, leaving me open and slick with lubricant. I don't have words for what I feel like.

"Get her cleaned up and get her out of here," he says to the nurse. And then he leaves, not looking back at the broken woman on the table. He's gotten in and gotten out, and the worst part is that this perfunctory business is his job.

Nurse Mender turns his attention to me. "All done, dear," he says, wiping me clean with a gentle hand. He's the good cop in this moment, tidying up the mess made by his bad-cop colleague.

While I lie here with chemicals inside me, already working to re-form my insides, Nurse Mender tells me what I can expect over the next few hours, days, weeks. My right hand clicks the pen twice.

"You may experience some cramps. Hopefully, it won't be much worse than typical menstrual cramping. If it becomes debilitating, take one of these. Motrin." He takes two prewritten prescriptions from his pocket and places the first on the table next to me while continuing with his list of side effects.

"Loss of appetite is normal."

"I'll live," I say.

"This is important, though." His eyes are calm and serious. "If you experience fever or elevated heartbeat at any time—even if it seems normal to you—you must seek immediate medical attention. Understand? The risk is low, but the sooner you report to an urgent care facility, the better."

One word plays on my lips, and I find myself saying it out loud. "Sepsis."

Mender sighs. "Like I said, the risk is infinitesimally low. But it isn't zero." I'd like to tell him what Alex said. He might rework his risk calculations. "That's what this one is for." He taps the other slip of paper, already typed out and signed. "You can have it filled when you get home and start the course tonight."

"What is it?"

"Just Augmentin. High dose, strong antibiotic. Should zap anything."

Doctors and nurses are not politicians. They don't have time to watch their words. As Mender tidies up the remnants of my treatment, disposing of the speculum and insertion device in a lined container marked *Biohazard*, he talks. I suppose he thinks he's being soothing.

"You won't be alone, dear," he says, patting my hand. "A lot of women will be making the same choice as you before long."

"Doing what?"

He shrugs. "Going in for an appointment at WomanHealth. If the trials work and the risk assessment is as low as we think it will be, hell, my wife'll be thirty-five in December. Christmas baby, actually. She'll go to her local clinic and take care of things. All for the good, if you ask me. I mean, the prevention's easier than the cure, right?"

"So it's on a volunteer basis, then?"

Mender continues. I hope to hell this contraption of Lissa's has storage capacity larger than it looks like it does.

"Oh, I think so. In most cases. Everyone wants to keep the breeding with the young and fit. Thirty-five's too old, they say. Too many things can go wrong."

In most cases. "What about the other cases?"

He clears the rest of the debris from the stainless steel countertop and washes up. "Don't you worry about that, dear. There'll be plenty of incentives."

I really hope Lissa's pen is getting all of this.

Because as soon as I get back to Washington, I'm going to make sure it's blasted over the airwaves so loud they'll hear it on the fucking moon.

SIXTY-FOUR

I sleep through most of the three-hour flight from Kansas City to Washington. When I'm not sleeping, I'm pretending to, so I don't have to look at Alex. We step off the plane near the general aviation building into a field of tarmac and concrete. I wrap my coat around me, tight against the windchill, as Malcolm emerges from one of the doors and begins a slow walk toward us. I don't remember DC ever being so cold in early November.

Inside the building, Malcolm and Alex leave me for a moment. I can't hear them, but I watch my phone exchange hands. I'd forgotten about it, sitting in that little storage room next to Martha Underwood's office, keeping company with others of its kind. There's a bit of backslapping and laughter before they part.

Malcolm's mood matches the weather when he takes me by the arm and leads me out to the hourly parking lot. Without a word of greeting, he opens the passenger-side door and watches me climb in before rounding the front of the BMW and taking his own seat. When he starts the engine, I've got so many words I want to scream at him I don't know where to start.

He seems to read my mind. "Just don't say a word, Elena. Not a goddamned word."

I turn up the heat on my side and stay quiet, counting the cars we pass as he navigates us out of the airport and onto the parkway, thinking about what I'll say to Anne when we get home. Really I'm thinking about what she'll say to me, if she says anything at all.

Malcolm cracks the driver's window; I turn up the heat to eighty. He lowers the window a further two inches; I twist the dial again until the digital readout glows eighty-five. We argue in this way for the half-hour drive to the house, a wordless battle of wills, and the cold air curling around the back of the car and hitting my right side tells me I'm losing.

"Can you please shut that window?" I say.

He responds by pressing a button to his left, and the window slides all the way open.

Our house—I suppose it's Malcolm's house now, or soon will be—is as cold and dark as the night. Not even the back porch light is on. At after midnight on a Friday, Anne might still be up, if not studying then watching a movie. But if Malcolm's told her I'm arriving, maybe she decided to stay in her room. Still, the house seems wrong.

I unbuckle my seat belt and think of running. Up the street to Sarah Green's house. In the opposite direction toward the Delacroix's or the Morrises' or the Callahans'. Through the empty playground. Hiding inside my Acura that's parked in its usual space in the driveway. Anywhere, really. Anywhere that isn't this dark house with only my husband for company.

Malcolm kills the engine and comes around to my side, opening the door for me and taking my arm, squeezing it. He holds me like this until we reach the back door. His key slides into the lock, the door swings open, and I'm pushed inside.

"Go to bed, Elena," he says.

"There are some prescriptions I need to fill." I take the slips from my pocket, feeling Lissa's pen nestled in the folds of material, and Malcolm takes the papers from me.

"I told you to go to bed." Then, only slightly more civilly, "I'll take care of it in the morning."

"I need them now. There's an all-night pharmacy down by—"

"Elena, I said Go. To. Bed."

I expect Anne to poke her head into the hall at the sound of his voice, but there's no opening of a door or feet running down a hall. We're alone in this darkened house, with the shades pulled and the lights on their dimmest setting.

"Where's Anne?" I say.

"Staying with some friends."

"Which friends? When is she coming home?" I don't know why I ask this; the answer seems pretty clear to me.

"Soon."

What follows is five full minutes of a standoff until I finally leave him and go toward the hall to my room. A part of me expects him to stop me, to tell me I'm no longer welcome in his bed, to sleep in Freddie's. But he doesn't say a word.

My finger finds the wall switch and flicks it to the up position. This room is mine, and it isn't. The dresser has been wiped clean, bare wood where photos of my family once sat in their frames, where a round silver tray used to hold my perfumes. I open the bottom drawer, where I keep pajamas and nightgowns. It's empty. Every single one of my dresser drawers is empty, only the floral shelf paper liners covering the bottoms. One hand automatically goes to my mouth and stifles a scream.

Breathe, El. Just breathe. But I can't.

In the mirror's reflection, my walk-in closet beckons me to open it, to check inside, to see that all of my stuff is hanging on rods or folded on wire organizer shelves and that shoes are lined up in neat rows the way they always have been. I answer the door's call, crossing the room, one hand still over my mouth, the other reaching out for the door lever. A hideous *Let's Make a Deal* scenario plays through my mind: *What's behind Door Number One, Elena? Want to take a guess and win the big prize?*

No. No, I don't.

I do.

The white wire frames are there, in the same place they've been since I paid some consultant from a bed and bath store to design and install them. They line the side and back walls of the closet, virgin territory waiting to be piled with wool and denim and cotton. The carpeting is freshly vacuumed, stripes of beige pile shimmering under the light.

It's like I've disappeared.

I spin away from the closet, reaching the window on Malcolm's side of the bed in three steps, pushing the curtains aside and rolling up the roman blind, hearing it snap and spin. The shade pull taps a monotonous rhythm against the glass, then loses momentum and goes silent. I don't bother sliding the latches and lifting the window before letting the curtains fall back into place. The lock on the casement, and the keyhole on that lock, tell me not to bother.

I am a prisoner in my own house.

It's impossible to know how long I've been standing here with my hand to my lips, how long I've been staring at the geometric print of the comforter and the blue of my pajamas neatly folded on my pillow. Minutes? Hours? Somewhere in between? And I don't know how long Malcolm has been standing in the doorway, leaning casually against the frame, watching my desperation.

"The windows and doors are alarmed, Elena," he says. "And the glass. You should go to bed now."

"You fucking monster," I say.

"Well, you should know, I guess. See you in the morning." He turns and closes the door, and the key in the lock clicks.

SIXTY-FIVE

I was on fire when I woke up a few moments ago. Now a wintery chill runs through my bones, and I roll to one side, burying my head under the comforter to block out the sun. Someone opened the curtains. Malcolm, I suppose.

Malcolm.

My hand reaches over to his side of the bed. It's cold and dry, and any fantasies about the past few days being no more than a nightmare fade away. I think they do. I'm not sure. The same invisible hands that drew the curtains and rolled up the shades may have been at work filling my head with cotton while I slept. Every part of my body tells me to stay here under the covers. Except one part—one part tells me I need a bathroom and I need it now.

Afterward, I collapse on the floor with the bath mat my only barrier between skin and cold tile. The room spins around me, beige and blue and white forming whorled patterns like an Escher drawing of an impossible staircase. I can no longer make sense of up and down, or of cold and hot.

I sleep.

When I wake, my pajamas are stuck to me, translucent in places where I've sweat the most, and damp curls cling to my face. It's all I can do to pull my weight up, and then I fall to my elbows on the sink's edge after catching a glimpse of my reflection. The woman in the mirror did not look like me.

One by one, I fling drawers open in the vanity. There are pills somewhere. Aspirin, Tylenol, leftover prescriptions from bouts with strep throat and muscle aches. Or there were. Now there are empty drawers, cleaned-out medicine cabinets. Only a toothbrush and a new tube of Crest are on the little shelf next to the sink. Even my makeup is gone. All of it.

"Malcolm!" I cry weakly. "Malcolm!" And then, "Anne!"

The only response is utter silence.

I shouldn't think the worst, but it's all I can think about. That one word, the bane of humans for thousands of years. A word that doesn't matter in the twenty-first century.

Infection.

And then all the words that go with it: *Untreated. Bacterial. Toxic.*

I scream Malcolm's name once more with all the force I have left and stagger back to bed, sick and defeated. So this is what the end of hope sounds like.

There's no knock to announce him, only the clean click of a key in a lock.

"You don't look well, Elena."

No shit.

He tidies up the room, tucking in bedclothes and fluffing pillowcases, making this prison with its thousand-count sheets and Persian carpets comfortable. "Here's something to eat," he says. On the tray are two slices of toast, scrambled eggs, and a glass of juice, none of which I want. Right now, my body wants antibiotics. All of the antibiotics there are in the world.

"What about my prescriptions?" I say. "I don't care about the Motrin, but I need the other stuff."

"Yeah. Sure. I'll get them when I go out."

Liar. Malcolm has no intention of getting the meds for me.

He holds up his phone. "There's an app on here, Elena. It's connected to the house security system. I'll likely be around most of the time, but I might go out." He shrugs. "I don't know. For groceries. Whatever. Maybe I'll be gone an hour; maybe ten minutes. Maybe I'll park down the street and get some paperwork done. I'm going to stay close to you. Just in case you need me."

In other words, I shouldn't try anything. Like the windows.

"Malcolm," I say, pleading.

"Don't beg, Elena. It isn't your style."

When he leaves, the lock clicks again, sealing me in this room. But my pillows are fluffed, so there is that.

Outside, his car starts up and the engine fades to a hum as he backs out of the driveway.

Along with my breakfast, there's a book. It's one of my favorites, spine broken from repeated readings, held together with a thick rubber band. Right now I have zero interest in reading tragic love stories; the title reminds me too much of Anne's note—*I guess you made your choice*—and I can't help but think Malcolm is trying to send me a message. Underneath the book is a torn-out crossword puzzle from today's paper, as if I needed any more puzzles. Also a napkin and a bottle of sparkling water. There's no phone because Malcolm hasn't given my phone back yet.

And I know he isn't going to.

SIXTY-SIX

I must have slept through the morning and early afternoon. When I wake, my untouched breakfast is replaced by a slice of quiche and a salad, another bottle of water, and a bottle of cranberry juice. I drink the last of these down greedily, get up, and go into the bathroom to do the necessary.

Nothing happens, even though I finished off the liter of water before I crashed, so I go back to bed, sweat-sticky and shivering. There's also a note on the tray from Malcolm reminding me that he's not far from home. The words disguised as reassurance are, in fact, threatening. I prop myself up in a half-sitting, half-lying position and stare at my lunch.

There are no pills. No Motrin, no Augmentin.

I can understand his wanting a divorce—I never climbed aboard his commonsense train, or if I did, I stepped off long ago, maybe before Freddie was born, maybe years before that. What I can't understand is why my husband is going to let me die in my own bedroom.

This is when I start feeling like the worst mother in the world. I should be wondering about Freddie, asking myself if Anne is really at a friend's house or somewhere else. I should be crying for both of them. Instead, all I can do is cry for me.

I know more about septicemia than I want to right now. Undiagnosed and untreated, it can kill inside of a week, poisoning the blood, shutting down organs, twisting the insides of its victims to the point where they want nothing more than the quiet of death. I know the only thing that will help me is massive, gargantuan doses of antibiotics, right the hell now. So I pardon myself for the self-pity. If twenty-four hours has brought me to this state, I'm not sure I want tomorrow to come.

I'll try the lock on the door soon. Very soon. Just after I rest for a bit.

Get the fuck up, you.

I will. In a few minutes. First, I'll shut my eyes and will the nausea away.

Get. Up. Now.

Two sides of me are fighting, the woman and the mother, the part of me who is me, and the part of me I gave away when I delivered my daughters. I think the woman may be winning, but the mother is putting up a good fight. She doesn't seem to want to let go.

Okay. I'll try.

Good girl.

Malcolm cleaned out the bathroom, taking everything. But I know things most men don't. I know that you can always find bobby pins in the corners of drawers, hiding in crevices, invisible in the shadows. I used to count them as I found them. One pin, two pin.

Red pin, blue pin.

Mine aren't red or blue but blond, a perfect match for the light wood cabinetry in the bathroom. On my knees, I run my hands over the smooth bottoms of the drawers, searching for any irregularity. I don't need to count the pins I find. I need one.

Keep looking.

I keep looking, but only after I throw up the thin mix of water and juice I've managed to keep down until now. And then I look again until I find it. The lone bobby pin is there, in the second drawer down, wedged into the joinery. I pry it out and hold it up like the goddamned Olympic torch.

Ten minutes later, I'm a sweaty mess, lying on hardwood by the door to my room with a racing heartbeat for company. I can't breathe. *Breathe. Think of Freddie and Anne. And breathe.*

I can't. Oxygen comes to me in shallow, bird-like bursts as I hear the purr of an engine, far away, then closer, telling me Malcolm is back. In a way, I'm thankful for the excuse to crawl back into bed and hide myself in the sheets.

SIXTY-SEVEN

I have dreams tonight.

I'm in a small room that smells of burnt coffee and medicine while men in white coats pull at my limbs, stretching and contorting me until my muscles scream high notes. On my right and left, girls in pleated blue skirts dance together, arm in arm. One of them is Oma. The others are my daughters, Judy Green, Rosaria Delgado, Mary Ripley. Everyone has the face of a human and the body of a fox. Or maybe it's the other way around.

There's a door at the far end of the room, half-open and half-closed. *Is the glass half-empty or half-full?* the old question goes. I think "full," and the other part of me says "empty." I think "closed," and the other part, the mother part, says "open." Freddie begins to cry, while Judy Green holds something to my throat, something shiny and sharp.

Lissa and Ruby Jo walk into this room, one on each side. They take turns leaning down to me, whispering.

It wasn't all coercion.

There was consent, too.

Most people don't know.

And the ones who know don't care.

Now, Judy leaves the parade of girls and steps forward, accusation in her eyes. *You knew about the tests being swapped out, didn't you?*

No. No, I did not. My lips and tongue form the words, but no sound comes out. Someone has taken out the piece of me that makes sound.

They hurt us in there. They hurt me, and they'll hurt your daughter soon, too.

I see ugly pictures forming in my mind. I see the fat guard at the state school. I see a key in a lock, and bolts tumbling out of their chambers. I see boots, heavy and black, moving across a wooden floor. I see dirty hands fumbling with zippers, buttons.

And I hear things, too: guttural sounds, feral grunts; the whimper of a *no* silenced by a cupped palm; rustling sheets and the sharp crack of a slap that turns everything still.

I hear *no* and *No* and *NO!* And then, nothing. Only pillow-stifled cries and that single word everyone says when things get too black to bear. *Mommy.* Not God, not Jesus, not any spirit from above, but *Mommy.* And then my own voice, stronger now, saying, *Don't you dare touch my little girl.*

Everything hurts when I wake up, squeezing my eyes to a bright November sun. The tray on the side table is still there with its book and crossword puzzle and fresh bottle of water. Instead of quiche, there's a cold grilled cheese sandwich. Somewhere outside, church bells ring. Sunday morning is here.

I've been asleep—or unconscious—for sixteen hours.

I could do the crossword puzzle, I guess. No. Too much mental effort. I pick up the Styron book from the tray and decide to read a few pages. At least the beginning isn't depressing, and it may take my mind off the fact that I'm closed inside this room while the rest of the world dresses for Sunday services and goes to all-you-can-drink champagne brunches.

Styron rests in my lap for a few minutes while I let my body rest and recover. Who knew it would require so much effort for such a trivial task as picking up a book? Reach, pick up object, retract arm. Each action saps my strength, and I have so little left.

I think I might be dying. No. Dying is a passive experience. Someone is killing me.

The rubber band, dry and brittle, snaps when I try to slide it off. No wonder, it's been holding these pages between their covers for too many years now. I really should have replaced it and given Anne a fresh copy of her own when she told me she wanted to read it. I really should go back to sleep.

Oh no, you shouldn't. It's Mother Voice again. I've begun to hate her.

My book is not a book anymore. When the spine shifts at its weakest point, dividing it into two separate volumes, its guts are missing, sliced out clean to form a cavity in the middle, as if someone has carved out the heart of this story and replaced it with a new one.

Mother Voice speaks to me, urging me on.

Stay awake, El.

I read Anne's note five times, and each time it brings fresh tears.

Mom,

Dad made me write that stuff. I'm sorry. I saw something on his computer. Hope you find this and bring Freddie back. I love you.

Anne

"Bastard" isn't a good enough word for what my husband is.

Underneath her note is a slip of paper with a string of letters and numbers. That's one key. My problem right now is that I need a different one, a metal key that will unlock my door and get me out of here. Also, I need a new body, a body that doesn't hurt and vomit and sweat, but I'm stuck with a password to Malcolm's laptop and a fucking bobby pin. So I start to work, hoping Malcolm's car doesn't come purring up the driveway.

This time, I last more than five minutes with the bobby pin, my ears straining for any foreign sound, anything other than the distant bark of a dog or the pealing of Sunday-morning bells. When I'm tired, that other voice, that Mother Voice, tells me to get up and start all over again. She's like some sick cheering squad. One more try, one more wiggle of the straightened bobby pin and desperate turn of the door now. If it doesn't open, I'll rest. To hell with Mother Voice.

But the knob turns in one glorious, hallelujah-worthy twist. Expecting the resistance, I turn with it, slamming my shoulder into the wall as the door swings open.

I'm out of this room.

My house has none of me in it anymore. No wedding photographs, no pictures of me with the girls, no piles of mail or notepads or shopping lists, nothing that says Elena Fischer Fairchild. It's an odd thing to realize I don't exist. When I manage to climb the stairs and reach the office, everything of mine is gone. This is okay. I don't want anything of mine; I want something of Malcolm's.

I yank the power cord from his laptop and dash downstairs, tearing past Anne's and Freddie's rooms at the slow speed my limbs allow, stumbling back into my bedroom for the book and Lissa's pen, which I stuffed into the downy insides of my pillow on Friday night. I wish the next stop could be this bed, this soft down pillow, but I ignore their temptation and race back to the kitchen, to the junk drawer in the corner where we keep spare keys.

Please let the Acura key be here. I'll trade my soul if it's here. I try not to think about the fact that I may have already traded said soul, that I have nothing left to bargain with.

The key is here.

There's a thirty-second delay when I leave the house through the back door, the November cold hitting me like a punishing slap on my cheeks and bare arms and shoeless feet. I throw everything into the front seat of the car before falling into it myself and making another trade with fate in exchange for the Acura starting up. When it finally rumbles to life, I reverse out of the driveway, just as the alarms begin their screaming.

SIXTY-EIGHT

If I turn to the right, I can reach Sarah Green's house in a matter of seconds. If I turn left, I'll reach Chain Bridge Road and face another choice. Right, hospital. Left, city. House, hospital, city. My brain weighs the probabilities.

Sarah Green may be home or she may not be. A drive-by won't tell me which is true; her car is religiously garaged. If home, then no problem. If not home, then I'm wasting time I don't have.

Because I don't know where Malcolm is.

Maybe I'll be gone an hour; maybe ten minutes. Maybe I'll park down the street and get some paperwork done. I'm going to stay close to you. Just in case you need me.

So I turn left toward Chain Bridge Road, and I start the process all over again. If right, hospital. Drugs, bed, sleep. If left, city. Newspaper, scandal, daughter.

In my mind lurks a single question: Which do I want more?

A computer would calculate the input, the output, and the consequences. It would do this coldly, in the same way a bank of computers measures each of my daughters' test scores and birth weight and the combined income of her parents. A computer would work in a series of zeros and ones, and it would spit out a new number, a different number, a quotient. Its product would be invariable.

I'm also calculating. I'm counting the numbers of phone calls to nearby hospitals, and how many transfers will be necessary before the right nurse answers with a cheery, "Oh, yes. She's here. Are you the next of kin?" I'm counting the ways Malcolm will find to corrupt my story, and the lies he will tell to doctors before assuring them he'll keep my belongings safe. I'm counting on him to use everything he has to discredit me.

So I turn left. Toward the city. Toward Bonita Hamilton and Jay Jackson and an end to all of this.

Thirty minutes later, I'm at the intersection of Thirteenth and K Streets, in time to watch a crowd of people pour out from the Methodist church a half block away from where I've parked. They're pouring out because they aren't working. Today is Sunday, Washington's day of rest. Time to pray up and eat pastries.

The District of Columbia doesn't have the landmass or the population of New York, so I count on anonymity while I wait. That, and the probability that Malcolm will be checking out neighbors and hospitals instead of newspaper offices. With the Acura still running and the heat at full throttle, I wait, watching for signs of life at the entrance to 1301 K Street.

There isn't any. Not for the first half hour, and not for the second. Or the third.

But I've kept busy. I've been playing inside Malcolm's computer.

SIXTY-NINE

I turned off the Acura's engine at eleven, and an old blanket from the trunk is the only thing between me and the chilly air that's seeped into the car. But this isn't what turns my blood cold. I've just read the first line of Malcolm's email from the end of September.

> Maddie,
>
> Happy to hear the project is a go. Am waiting for complete list of undesirables to be compiled. Will send over when ready. So you know, I have five teams working on the decoy tests for history, math, physics, chemistry, and life sciences. We should be ready to roll by the late October exam date.
>
> Malc

Monster.

His file system has more layers than the goddamned Pentagon, and the first dozen documents I open are nothing more than bureaucrat-speak, memos, and dry reports. Until I get to the folder labeled *Tests*. These are new. I open three of them, their cover pages familiar because I've been handing them out on a monthly basis for a few years now, right before I read my students the rules.

You have one hour.

You may not speak to any student.

You may not leave the room for any reason.

When time is called, put down any and all writing implements. If you do not, ten points will be automatically deducted from your score.

Further along, when I get to the meat of the monthly exams, everything is different. The math essay questions demand knowledge of at least five instances of false proofs of Fermat's last theorem; the chemistry tests want in-depth information on Nobel Prize–winning research from a century ago. And the anatomy and bio I couldn't ace if I had a year to study. It's doctoral-level subject matter, and it was given to kids.

No one could pass this, I think. *No one.*

I keep the Word documents up and start moving through spreadsheets. My fingers are icy, not always registering on the trackpad. In a folder within a folder within a folder, I find an Excel sheet called *SpecPop*, very un-Malcolm-like in its snappiness, but then I remember a phrase Bonita Hamilton used. *Special Populations.*

A list of names and addresses and Q scores fills the small screen. They're all off the charts, these numbers, all Qs anyone would be thrilled to have.

Each one is color coded, including Freddie's.

From the spreadsheets, Malcolm's preferences are clear. He hates immigrants and minorities; Catholics, Muslims, and Jews; anyone with a middle-class income or lower; the entire LGBTQIA crowd; and about thirty-seven flavors of differently abled human beings.

He doesn't seem to have any negative feelings where Madeleine Sinclair is concerned, though.

I scan another batch of emails. Madeleine became "Maddie" sometime last year. And, this past summer, "Maddie" became "Darling."

Motherfucker.

It isn't hard to see why. Madeleine is six feet tall in heels, blond, and gorgeous. And, according to the Wikipedia bio I read a few weeks ago, she's thirty-six years old. Not what I'd call a spring chicken, but the woman has eight years on me—eight years of better skin and better ovaries. A hot flash of fever rolls through me, a reminder that as of yesterday, Madeleine Sinclair has more than better plumbing. She's still functional. She's still cool and smooth. I feel a furnace starting up inside me and go back to Malcolm's emails, looking for hard evidence of what I know he's done.

I stop cold when I see the email from acartmill@genics.com.

It's probably nothing. Just some Fitter Family–Genics Institute–Department of Education bureaucratic bullshit. I run the back of my hand over my forehead, wiping away a trickle of sweat, and I click the email open.

Very little of it is bureaucratic.

Malc,

She's in Kansas. Showed up yesterday. I'll see what I can do, and you shouldn't have any problems with the divorce.

Cheers,
A

Bastard. I don't know which of them I mean, and I don't care. But I get it. I can wrap my head around a man who doesn't want me for

292

a wife. I can understand Malcolm ditching me for Madeleine Sinclair. The numbers, though. The numbers I read in the SpecPop table and in all the other files, these are the workings of a sick mind, a monster.

You should know, Elena.

SEVENTY

Two weeks after the new ID card system went through, I was sitting in the cafeteria with the same old group—Malcolm, Roy, Candice, and the others. We were still pariahs, but we were pariahs who got first dibs on lunch, discounts at the bookstore, and free tickets to football games. Not that any of us gave a shit about football, but we went anyway, piling into whichever car could be borrowed from a parent, flashing our gold cards at the gate on Friday afternoons. It was worth the boredom just to see the looks on the faces of kids who had to stand in the white card line and fork over their allowance money.

I'd stopped buying up the last salads. Margie Miller never got her first choice anyway, and that was good enough for me.

"There she is," Malcolm said. "Little Miss Brainless."

He said it in a stage whisper, loud enough for most of the tables near ours to hear. Margie flushed, shook herself out of it, and pushed her chair back. She was on her way over to us.

I felt sorry for Margie just then; I don't know why. Maybe being the odd girl out for most of my school career did it; maybe I just thought Malcolm didn't need to be so obviously nasty. Aside from acting as if I didn't exist, Margie Miller hadn't ever been truly mean to me.

"Saw your name in the paper, Elena," she said.

I went cold. The newspaper article had been Malcolm's idea. He'd said something about credit where credit was due, and I let the reporter interview me, answering her questions with simple one-word responses, not really wanting the word to get out about my spontaneous brainchild of merit-based cards and separate lunch lines and free tickets to Friday games. I nearly blurted out an apology to Margie right there and then, in front of a hundred pairs of eyes and ears.

She beat me to the punch. "Here's what I think of your stupid idea."

Now I really did go cold, even though my face was hot with embarrassment. Margie had been taking delicate little sips of juice from a bottle. She wasn't drinking anymore; she was pouring it on me. My hair absorbed most of it, but didn't stop the sticky liquid from streaking my white blouse, from staining me from head to toe.

"There. Now you look like a Creamsicle, you stinking Kraut." She marched off, back to her table, and the cafeteria exploded around me with laughter.

I'd been called names before. Four-Eyes in grade school. Miss Know-It-All later on. Foul-Ball Fischer in gym class. All of them were at least based on something. But Kraut? I'd never heard that one, and it stung, mostly because it wasn't true. My parents were Americans, as was I.

In the hall bathroom, I changed my yellow-stained blouse for a T-shirt from my gym bag, and I thought of how much I hated Margie Miller and the rest of her stupid, snooty friends. I didn't want to be like them, I decided. I would never be like them.

Margie Miller ended up with a three-day suspension, during which she sat in a library carrel polishing her nails. I ended up with a new nickname that I didn't shake until my senior year, when my parents transferred me to a private school an hour's drive away. It reached a point where I stopped buying anything in the cafeteria, if only to avoid the notoriety of the gold-and-green-card line. I made excuses to avoid football games and dances, anything that set me apart.

None of my actions did one bit of good. Margie seemed to be ever present in locker rooms and hallways. If I took a shower after gym, eyes squeezed shut against soap, someone would turn off the hot water, giggling as I scrambled to find the tap or ran out from the stall covered in suds. The frogs and worms and crawfish from biology lab would mysteriously make their way into my lunch bag. One Monday morning, I opened my locker to find a spray-painted swastika on the inside of the door.

"They're stupid pranks," Malcolm said after each occasion. "Ignore them."

I tried, and I couldn't. "They're stupid people," I said. Margie waggled her manicured nails at me from her table with the pretty/rich/jock people.

And then, I said something without thinking, something I'd one day regret.

"Wouldn't it be great if all the people we hated could carry their crappy GPAs around for life?"

Malcolm agreed. And he smiled.

SEVENTY-ONE

After another early-afternoon crowd crosses from the Methodist church to Patisserie Paul, it dawns on me that I haven't eaten since Friday. I've been living on sparkling water since Malcolm brought me home. The fact is, even the thought of water brings a fresh wave of nausea, but Patisserie Paul will have Wi-Fi. And happy, pastry-munching churchgoers with cell phones, the kind of people who read stories about good Samaritans.

If I were dressed in anything but sweat-stained pajamas, I might venture it. But I'm not. One glance in the side mirror tells me I look like hell. Also, I don't have shoes and I don't have money. I don't have anything I need, and there are so few good Samaritans to count on. The jogger to my right, ponytail swinging like a pendulum, is listening to music, puffing her way through another mile. A couple passing me does a double take before herding their children quickly away, the wife checking twice over her shoulder. Families cycle by lazily, trailing babies in covered Burleys, and the morning dog-park crowd congregates on a corner, engrossed in observing their pets' antics and picking up their pets' leavings, hurrying on after they get a good look at me.

They aren't used to seeing the imperfect, not here, not anymore.

What I want most right now is a number. I've learned to hate numbers, but I want three digits plus three digits plus four digits. The public hot spot where I'm parked must be weak, not even one bar, so I drive the Acura up several blocks, stay long enough to find the *Post*'s confidential tips page, download the Signal app, and send a hopeless message asking for Bonita Hamilton or Jay Jackson. Then I cut off the Wi-Fi on Malcolm's computer before he can track me, and I return to K Street.

And I wait, curled up in the backseat, with the blanket that's protected the trunk from plants and mulch and topsoil wrapped around me like a shroud.

I dream about all the things. Freddie as a baby and a girl and a woman. Girls in blue skirts and white blouses, not knowing what they hate or why. Qs with their long, curly tentacles, reaching out for a new victim. I dream in the present and the future and the past, jumbled images of love and hate and peace and war. I dream of my body going quiet, resting. I am an object at rest.

I don't know how long I've waited. I don't know whether I've slept or whether I've dreamed of sleep, and when the sound of an angry fist on the window over my head bangs again, I shrink, trying to become smaller, trying to become invisible.

A voice, filtered and fuzzy, calls my name once, then speaks slowly.

"I am Bonita Hamilton. You called me."

Go away.

Mother Voice drowns me out. Even she sounds defeated right now, but she answers. Her fingers find the edges of the shroud and she unveils me. When I open my eyes, a face, framed by two hands to shield the sun, is pressed against the window.

SEVENTY-TWO

Hospital.

I hear the word "hospital." It sounds like a place I'd like to go.

But I have work to do first.

Bonita has her phone in one hand, and my wrist in the other, the pressure of two fingers hard against my veins. I hear words, questions, a female voice counting. And another voice, maybe my own, saying *laptop, password, pen*, calling for Freddie. Someone asks me who the president is. I think I say Malcolm. Right now, I can't think of anyone else who has that much power.

I'm on a bed, or a sofa, a softness that I want to sink into and let absorb me. My limbs are so heavy, so tired, and there's pain. Each move, even the smallest twist of my neck or the flex of my fingers as I point to the stolen laptop, requires superhuman force. I close my eyes to the lights above me, and even that hurts. It should not hurt to close my eyes.

Someone says, "Four hundred photos. Jesus."

Someone says, "I can't believe this shit."

Someone says, "Call the Kansas City office."

A hand rests on my cheek, cool and dry until it absorbs some of the heat I seem to be putting out. "Honey? You still with me? Elena?

If you can hear me, I'm Bonita Hamilton, and that's Jay Jackson over at the desk. I've called for help, and you're going to be fine. Everything's going to be fine."

"Thank you," I say, slurring the two syllables.

"No, honey. Thank you."

And then all the someones, in a chorus, say, "Where's the goddamned ambulance?"

Mother Voice tells me it's okay to go to sleep.

SEVENTY-THREE

My mother is here. And other shapes. A bright light, blinding in its whiteness, shines into my right eye and then my left. I sense it without seeing it, that whiteness. It's no more a thing than the needle under the skin of my right hand, or the bag of clear liquid hanging at the side of my bed. Light and steel and liquid have all melted together into a series of textures, all these objects trying to keep me alive.

"Happy birthday, sweetie." This is my mother. She can only be my mother, that much I know. Mothers seem to be there, always. The first and the last people you call for, from the beginning until the end. She lowers her voice, thinking I won't be able to tell. "How much time do we have?"

Another voice. "All you want."

And then a door shuts.

Happy birthday. I've had forty-four of them, but these are the ones I remember.

Oma, spry and sixty, holding me on her lap, helping me blow out the four candles on a chocolate cake.

My father lifting me high, putting me on a horse twice as tall as I was at eight years old.

Joe, sending me a box of carnations in my first year at college. The note said, *Sorry I can't afford roses.*

And, more recently, Anne and Freddie and Malcolm storming into my room the morning of my fortieth birthday with a tray of coffee, fruit chopped in chunks that looked like the pieces in a game of Tetris, and a single rose from the garden in a bud vase. Three voices, two high and one low, sang me awake. A good start to the day. Good starts set you up for a fall, though.

Later that day, in class, I watched a few of the girls giggling over pictures on their phones. It hadn't been that many years ago I was one of them, stealing Mom's lipstick when I thought she wouldn't notice, passing notes about the new boy in school—*Do you like him? Do you think he likes me?* The technology changed, but girls are girls, new women, life stretching out before them, futures unplanned and uncertain. What killed my birthday buzz was that old sonofabitch called time.

I know I'm running out of it.

The Mother Voice whispers one word.

Wait.

SEVENTY-FOUR

From the *Washington Post*, Monday, November 11

SILVER SCHOOL TEACHER BLOWS WHISTLE ON COVERT DEPARTMENT OF EDUCATION PROGRAM

by Bonita Hamilton

In what may soon unravel as the scandal of the decade, Dr. Elena Fischer Fairchild, a life sciences teacher from the Davenport Silver School, has supplied heretofore unobtainable evidence concerning the DoE's current practices. Photographs, voice recordings, and other documents point to a . . .

Dr. Fairchild, the wife of Deputy Secretary Malcolm Fairchild, was taken to Sibley Hospital early yesterday afternoon and remains in critical condition. No comments have been made by her family or by the attending doctors, but . . .

From CNN, Monday, November 11, 1:04 PM EST

BREAKING: SECRETARY OF EDUCATION MADELEINE SINCLAIR RESPONDS TO OUTRAGE

"I had no idea," Secretary Sinclair said as she emerged from her offices earlier today. "This is a faction that has regretfully gone unnoticed, and on behalf of this department, I want to extend my gratitude to Dr. Fairchild for bringing it to light." Sinclair, in her signature blue suit, has denied any knowledge of . . .

From Twitter, Monday, November 11, 2:53 PM EST

@Sec_Ed_Sinclair You stole my children and I hope you go to hell. #BringThemBack #NoMoreYellow

From the *New York Times*, Tuesday, November 12

LAST OF 46 YELLOW SCHOOLS RAIDED

As the hashtag #BringThemBack, started by an actress-turned-activist, continues to trend in the social media sphere, an emergency team of federal authorities has announced the removal of over one hundred minors from a state boarding school in Winfield, Kansas. The late-nineteenth-century building and its grounds were once used as the site of the Kansas State Asylum for the Education of Idiotic and Imbecile Youth prior to changing its name to the State Training School in 1930. From 1998, the facility was used as a correctional facility before being condemned. Roy Tolliver, who led the operation in

Winfield, has released a statement attesting to the substandard conditions at the institution. Judith (Judy) Green and high school classmate Sabrina Fox both gave interviews. "It wasn't a school," Green says. "Maybe we got an hour or two of actual class time in the mornings. The rest of the day, we were in the cornfields." Fox, who has been taking care of nine-year-old Frederica Fairchild (daughter of Deputy Secretary of Education Malcolm Fairchild) since her arrival last week, adds, "This little girl was picking corn. Can you believe it? Picking corn. Like we don't have machines for that." Fox holds up the girl's wrist. "You don't pick fast enough, they make you. They have guards, see, and . . ."

From *Forbes* Online, Tuesday, November 12, 10:00 AM EST

Spokespeople for the federal wonder-contractors Genics Institute, Inc., and its subsidiary WomanHealth, Inc., confirm that the companies will seek refuge under Chapter 11 bankruptcy rules. Earlier this year, Genics acquired the prenatal services company in what now appears to be a calculated effort to consolidate genetic testing and abortion services in accordance with the Fitter Family Campaign, a grassroots movement that many experts are now analogizing to the eugenics craze of the early twentieth century. Petra Peller, chairwoman and CEO of the Genics Institute, could not be reached for comment, but a source close to her says . . .

I've had death threats and hate mail. I want them to stop. I am no longer associated in any way with the Fitter Family Campaign. This will be my last post. Thank you for bringing my daughter home.

From the *Washington Post*, Wednesday, November 13

FAMILIES REUNITED—BUT AT WHAT COST?

by Bonita Hamilton

Sixteen-year-old Anne Fairchild should be planning for a homecoming dance this Saturday. Instead, she holds vigil in a hospital room while her mother lies in a critical state. "I knew something was wrong," Fairchild says, wiping a tear from her eye. "So I installed a key tracker on my father's laptop. When he found out, he sent me to Petra Peller's house. All I wanted was to bring my mom and my sister back." Also in the room is Anne's great-grandmother, Maria Fischer. "I hope nothing like this happens again," Fischer says. "But, of course, that is what we said the last time." During this bittersweet family reunion, Fischer, who emigrated from Germany in her twenties and still works as an artist, explains . . .

From CNN, Wednesday, November 13, 8:22 AM EST

BREAKING: SECRETARY OF EDUCATION RESIGNS

From Twitter, Wednesday, November 13, 8:23 AM EST

Ding, dong, the bitch resigned! #BringThemBack
#NoMoreYellow #NeverAgain

SEVENTY-FIVE

I've had my fifteen minutes of fame, and I've slept through all of them. Dad reads me the headlines from three days, hitting all the high points, while Mom tries to get micro sips of water into my body. I don't know what withering sounds like, but it's how I feel—dry, weakened, cracking into parts.

Oma's got Freddie on her lap in the love seat near the window. She's rocking her back and forth, singing lullabies in German. Freddie has tried to wriggle away a dozen times, but Oma holds her back. It's been like this since my parents came in with both girls early this morning.

"Let her come if she wants to," I say.

Freddie nearly flings herself on me, like she used to do as a toddler. Anne tries, and fails, to keep her off the bed. I used to push them away when they got too clingy, too needy, when I had paperwork sprawled over my lap and my patience had run out after a day of mothering. It wasn't that I didn't love them, but I could only love so much and for so long. Now, I wish I could love forever.

I don't push Freddie off the way I used to do. I hold her and rock her and smooth her hair with unsteady hands. "I'm sorry, sweetie," I tell her, but it doesn't seem like enough to make up for any of the past week, or for any of the past years.

"You have the flu, Mommy?" she says.

"Maybe just a little fever," I lie. My body is a furnace. When it gets tired of being a furnace, it becomes an icebox.

I wish for more time. I wish for a body that could hug back and walk out of this room. I wish I'd run screaming from Malcolm Fairchild twenty years ago and married a regular guy named Joe. I wish all these things, but the genie in the bottle is fresh out of wishes.

Besides, without Malcolm there would be no Anne and no Freddie, and I don't wish that.

Freddie smooths my hair back with her small hand. "You're going to get better soon, right?"

"Sure, baby girl. Sure I am."

"I'm going to be a doctor when I grow up," she whispers in my ear. "And I'll make everyone perfect."

I smile at this, but it's a thin line of a smile, forced and dry. "You can be anything you want."

"Promise?" Freddie says, still close.

"Cross my heart."

"And?"

"And that's all, Frederica. Cross my heart." I'm not interested in the second half of the promise.

My mother locks eyes with me, then turns to the nurse who has just walked in to sponge me off and dab my lips with some oily substance that keeps them from cracking. She mouths a silent question to the woman. The woman mouths something back. It looks like "Soon."

"I want to go home," I say.

The nurse nods, understanding. "I'll see what I can do." Then, to Freddie: "How about we go get some hot cocoa? I've got the good kind, lots of marshmallows." Freddie follows her out, one tiny hand holding on. I think this woman in white must be some kind of genius.

I've never thought much about what my girls would do without me, where they would live, who would take the parent baton if I had to pass it along. Malcolm's and my wills name my parents as guardians, but only in the far-fetched case of both of us dying at the same time. Malcolm, as far as I know, isn't going to die, but I imagine the place he is going won't be somewhere he can take his children. So, my parents. *Tag. You're it, Mom.*

Still, this reality is fresh. My mother's eyes tell me so.

Dad signs the papers while two orderlies work on shifting my body to a gurney, my temporary bed until I reach the one in my parents' house, and then, later, a more permanent bed. My body feels light in their arms, ghost-like. The gown falls away, revealing skin stretched over bones. I think I hear my mother let out a horrified gasp.

While I continue to be in this lucid state, various people visit. My doctor. A social worker. The representative from our local hospice. Papers get signed, and instructions are recited while another nurse disconnects me from the monitors. I feel naked without all that plastic. There's no arguing about who rides in which car; Dad announces he'll drive Oma and Freddie home while my mother and Anne ride along in the ambulance. No sirens this time, no need for them. Sirens are for situations that can be fixed.

One final document needs my signature, and I scratch it out as if I'm signing a check, or the receipt for a delivery of groceries.

This, I suppose, is the dull and dry business of dying.

SEVENTY-SIX

SOON:

Bright hospital lights and the constant bleep of the machinery that has been keeping me alive are gone. In their place, a white ceiling and the rustle of leaves outside my window keep me company while I dream.

I can't know what will happen in these next days and weeks and months, but I can speculate. My mind is still very much at work, even if my body has started to power down.

Madeleine Sinclair, convicted of multiple charges of misappropriation of funds, perjury, fraud, and every other type of political death sentence, will trade her tailored blue suit for a new look: institutional gray, which is a perfect match for the one Malcolm will be wearing when my father takes the girls to see him on visiting days. The Genics Institute's stockholders will be left with worthless paper, and Petra Peller—according to the rumors—will attempt to leave the country with whatever remains in the coffers. I think she'll get caught at the border.

Handsome Alex Cartmill, convicted of the kinds of crimes for which there is no excuse, will take the most sensible way out. A suicide befitting a war criminal—likely a steel barrel in the mouth. No one will care when the note he leaves claims he was only following orders. He actually calls my parents to say he's sorry before he eats the gun. I hear Dad swearing in German at him.

Martha Underwood, and others like her, will be reunited with her boy, forgiven when she says she was only doing what she was told. The forgiveness will be official only. Martha will find this out on trips to Safeway when she feels the stares of fathers and when she hears mothers whisper. She'll move to a new state before long.

I think it will be a good Thanksgiving, and the weeks before Christmas promise to be even better. My parents will have a full house again, both the old and the young to take care of. By the time Thanksgiving rolls around, they'll have a ton to be thankful for. On her tenth birthday, which happens to fall on the same date as the demolition of five buildings formerly known as Kansas State School 46, Freddie will celebrate by wearing her Wonder Woman costume for a solid week. She'll stop taking her anti-anxiety meds at the same time, and nothing horrible will happen. Anne will meet a boy, a nice boy, who will take her to the winter dance. She won't get as far as asking him what his Q was, but she'll probably let him get to first base. The papers will report a rash of divorces, of which I would have been a happy statistic. Everything will be different, and I love it this way.

I love that Lissa and Ruby Jo will both return to teaching and found a different kind of school, the one I'll insist shouldn't be called Fairchild Academy but the New School. Simple is better, I'll tell them, even if I have to make the funding conditional and tell them that in legalese.

The hashtags #NeverAgain and #NoMoreYellow will do what all hashtags do. They will trend, and then not trend, and then be replaced by other, more timely hashtags. Anne will keep them pinned on her social pages, though. She's set on taking a journalism course next year, and Bonita Hamilton is going to offer her an internship. I think maybe Columbia University is where Anne will end up. Unless she turns to hacking and cryptography. Who knows?

And Oma, my lovely Oma, will still paint. She might switch from fences to doors, but they will still be strange, abstract things that ask more questions than they give answers.

SEVENTY-SEVEN

My parents run in a constant upstairs and downstairs routine, checking on me with blood pressure cuffs and thermometers, bringing me blankets or ice water, depending on my state. One afternoon, Oma comes in.

"You haven't been sleeping." She fixes the covers I've thrown off, pulling them up to my chin and tucking them in between the mattress and the box spring. "Were you cold again, Leni?"

I nod. Dad brought up the portable oil heaters and put one on either side of the bed. He's fit for a sixty-five-year-old man, but his shoulders don't square themselves on their own. If he's not thinking about it, they curve down in two sad arcs. He doesn't realize I notice, but I do.

Oma sits beside me on the bed and reads the cards that arrived in today's mail. "I didn't know there were this many people in the world, Leni." When she gets to one from Ruby Jo, I ask her to read it again. The words say something about the most amazing woman ever. Funny, I don't feel so amazing right now.

Then Oma gets to the point.

"Do you remember the time I struck you? When you were in high school?"

"Barely," I lie.

"I have never forgiven myself for that," she says, choking back the words. "It was a cruel thing."

I reach out to take her free hand, and she squeezes mine gently.

She continues, "It was cruel, but that is not the point. I struck you because that day when you came home and told me about your school friend, that Irish girl from the poor family, I did not see you. I saw me."

"I really don't remember, Oma."

But I do.

She pats my hand now and holds the cup of water to my lips. After two sips, I lie back, exhausted from the effort. I think she stays with me while I sleep; I don't know, but I hear myself saying I forgive her. Oma's slap might have been cruel, but what I did and said that day was worse.

While I'm out, I'm seventeen again. I've showered the sweat of three volleyball matches off me, combed through my hair, and taken my usual place on the locker room benches. I'm thinking of Malcolm and homecoming, of what color I'll paint my nails, of whether I'll wear strappy silver sandals or black patent pumps next Saturday night. Becky and Nicole are mercilessly teasing Susan about her date, about whether she'll go all the way, whether Billy Baxter or whoever is Susan's flavor of the month will finally score a home run.

Another Wednesday afternoon, another post-gym-class chin-wag among us girls before we head off to biology, English, trig.

It's the Wednesday when Mary Ripley bumps into me.

And I don't want to be here, but I am. I need to be.

We teased Mary differently than we teased Susan. Susan was a friend; our words made her laugh, and we laughed along with her. Mary, though, Mary we ripped into, digging for the bone and sinew and nerve, finding the tender spots that would sing with pain when we touched them with our stupid adolescent tongues. We did it because we could, because it was funny as hell, because Mary wasn't worth a second thought. Or a first thought.

Nothing happens when Mary walks into me (*you walked into her, El*), nothing more catastrophic than a few wrinkled pages of geometry notes when I knock them off the bench, a tube of Soft Sienna lipstick tumbling to the floor and rolling until inertia forces it to stop somewhere in the middle of the room. It's a bump. An accident. It isn't North Korea deciding to go nuclear on its southern neighbor.

And still, I open my mouth.

Language plays little tricks on you. Our words don't mean what we think they mean. An "I love you" is an all-purpose response to the friend who lends you her scarlet sandals; an "I hate you" works just as well when she aces her physics final without studying. We go to extremes to make a point.

I'm on the floor of the locker room, picking myself up, collecting spilled purse contents, and rubbing my elbow where it hit the edge of the bench. And I look up at Mary Ripley while she blubs a weak apology and offers a hand to help me up. I swat her hand away. And I speak.

"You're too stupid to live," I say.

There. I've remembered.

SEVENTY-EIGHT

It might be night. Or it might be day. I might be awake or asleep. Opening my eyes is the hardest work I've ever done; they want to stay closed. They demand darkness.

Freddie is here; I can smell her soap, and her bubble gum–mint toothpaste, and the No More Tears stuff I've put in her hair—although not lately. So maybe this is morning. I want to tell her to draw me a picture, to make my old studio her own, but my mouth seems to be stuck together. I can feel my tongue moving, forming the sounds of words, but the sounds hit a barrier and stay locked inside. Trapped.

A quiet, familiar voice takes the place of hers, one I haven't heard in twenty years. "I saw the papers and flew in late last night," the familiar voice says. His words are far away at first, then closer as a chair scrapes over the floor and a hand wraps itself around my own. "Got my own plane and license now, El. How about we go for a ride?"

Sure, I think. *Up, up, and away.* So Joe traded cars for airplanes. He always was good with machines, but I don't think he'll be able to fix the one lying in this bed. This one's what we call totaled.

Mom comes in next, followed by Dad and Oma. Anne, who has been with me all night, squeezes over to make room, and my mother perches on the edge of the narrow bed. She takes my other hand, and she turns her back to me, as if this were enough to fool me into thinking she isn't crying.

"Elena," she says.

The hand holding mine is cool, but the contrast lasts no more than a moment. Soon, my heat transfers to her. There's a law about this, about energy not dissipating, only being transferable from one entity to another. In the darkness of this hellish sweat I imagine some part of myself leaving, moving along, changing form.

Voices talk around me and over me.

Is she . . . ?

Can they . . . ?

Did the doctor . . . ?

How long will . . . ?

I close my eyes.

A door swings open. Two doors, actually. One of them is in my room. The other, the one I see but don't hear, leads somewhere else. Beyond it, there are pictures.

In my dreams beyond that open door, I'm teaching high school art instead of biology. I'm married to a man who loves when I wear red lace to bed as much as he loves everything else about me. I'm pushing swings in playgrounds and taking the kids out of school on sunny days—to hell with rules. Someone like Ruby Jo would call me happier than a pig in shit.

The hospice nurse puts something on my arm, a balloon that inflates. I think of the Child Catcher from that old movie, the one with the pretty balloons and the too-sweet smile.

My nurse says words that sound like "shock" and "immeasurable." And there is another sound, a chorus of weeping.

But I don't weep. When my eyes flick open again, there's that door, yawning its welcome. In five steps, I'm there. My pulse stops racing and I'm out of the heat, into a place of cool and calm. I look back once before the door closes, and I see all their faces. I see my parents bringing the girls to visit me on Sundays, Oma teaching Freddie how to mix colors, and Joe speaking quietly to my daughters, telling them he'll take them up in the plane as soon as he can—if Freddie's okay with that. She says she isn't nervous at all. Freddie and Joe's twins act like siblings, even though they're not. Anne has decided to change tracks, to go into teaching instead of journalism, but she'll change her mind again at least five times.

There are other faces, too, clear at first, then quickly dissolving and fading. One by one, the ghosts of Mary Ripley and Rosaria Delgado and that old trickster the Child Catcher drift away until they're all gone.

My last thought is about the letter Q. It doesn't stand for quotient or question.

It stands for quiet, and that brings a smile to my face.

AUTHOR'S NOTES

This book is a work of fiction. The characters are wholly a product of my imagination. The historical events mentioned in the preceding pages, however, are very real.

I haven't sat in a history class for several decades, but I remember the material. I can tell you about who invented barbed wire and the cotton gin, the assassination that catalyzed World War I, and the details of the first televised presidential debate. None of my textbooks included a word on the American eugenics movement, on the practice of forcibly sterilizing men and women, or on the harsh realities of state institutions for the so-called feebleminded (many of whose inmates were children).

If the references in this novel disturb you, then I have done my job. Because these events *are* disturbing. For a deeper understanding of how we, as a nation, came to sanction the labeling and mistreatment of tens of thousands of individuals, I encourage you to look at various eugenics archives, which are widely available on the Internet. For an enlightening account of the state school system, I highly recommend Michael D'Antonio's excellent *The State Boys Rebellion*.

Patriotism does not require turning a blind eye to the darker chapters of our country's history; if anything, the opposite.

Christina Dalcher
October 2019

ACKNOWLEDGMENTS

Of the hundreds of pages in this book, this is the most important. It's also the hardest to write because finding the right words to thank the legions of people who took this project from concept to shelf-ready isn't easy. That's a hell of a place for a writer to be, so I'll invite you to insert as many superlatives and qualifiers as you can conjure in front of my expressions of gratitude.

Thanks to:

Literary agent extraordinaire Laura Bradford for her constant support, hand-holding, and words of reassurance. Laura, you're the best.

My US editor, Cindy Hwang, who gently told me the book could be better—and helped me make it so.

Charlotte Mursell, my editor across the pond, for her unlimited enthusiasm.

First readers and critique partners and sob sisters Stephanie Hutton, Sophie van Llewyn, and Kayla Pongrac. It's a privilege to count these ladies as friends. Also, they rock the hell out of the writing world.

#TeamDarkness in the Twittersphere (including a certain doughnut-eating rat bastard named Aeryn Rudel) for setting the bar high and then raising it higher.

The publicists and the graphic designers and the copy editors and everyone else who works hard to make a book happen.

Michael D'Antonio for his helpful correspondence and sharing of data. The book you are about to read would not exist if I hadn't come across Michael's excellent *The State Boys Rebellion*. You can thank him yourself by picking up a copy.

And my husband, Bruce Dalcher, who reads everything with a sharp eye and responds with an honest tongue. Everyone deserves a partner like him. I hope I do.

ONE PLACE. MANY STORIES

Bold, innovative and
empowering publishing.

FOLLOW US ON:

@HQStories

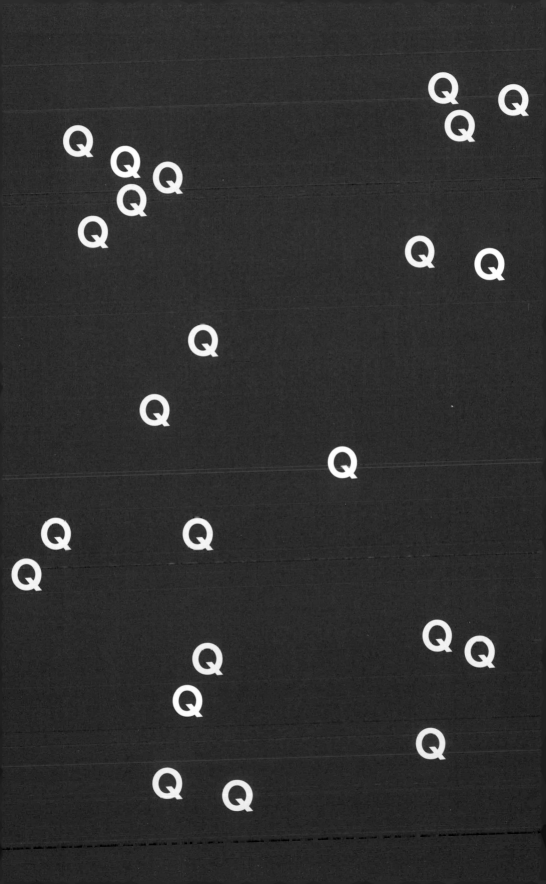

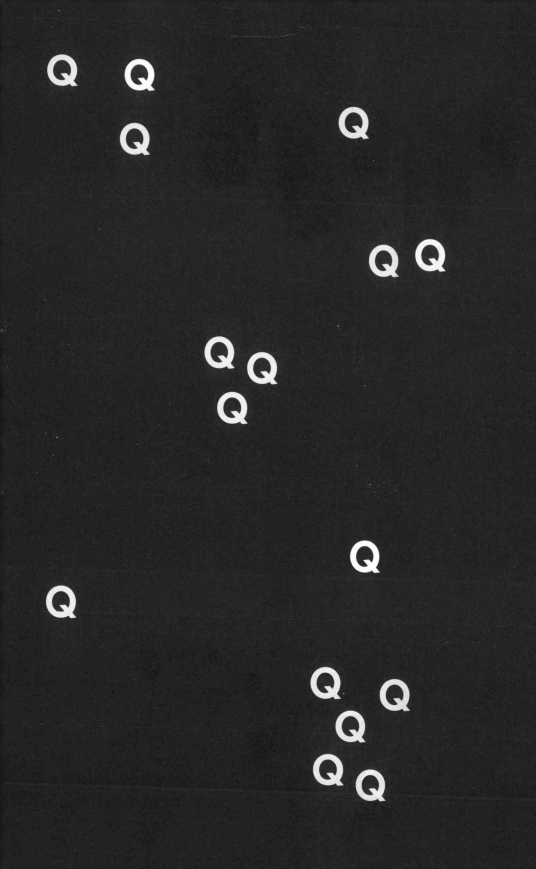